Sleepless Nights

ISBN: 978-1-932926-36-1
Copyright 2014, 2019 by Pierre C. Arseneault
Cover design: Pierre C. Arseneault

Printed in the United States of America.

Names, characters and incidents depicted in this book are products of the author's imagination or are used fictitiously. Any resemblance to actual events, locales, organizations, or persons, living or dead, is entirely coincidental and beyond the intent of the author or the publisher.

Shadow Dragon Press
9 Mockingbird Hill Rd
Tijeras, New Mexico 87059
info@shadowdragonpress.com
www.shadowdragonpress.com

Visit the author at his websites:
Mysterious Ink - www.mysteriousink.ca
PCA Toons - www.pcatoons.com

You can also follow Mysterious Ink on Facebook at:
https://www.facebook.com/pages/Mysterious-Ink-Pierre-C-Arseneault-Angella-Jacob/167392516657647

or email:
pierre@mysteriousink.ca

Also available from Pierre C Arseneault, written in collaboration with Angella (Jacob) Cormier is *Dark Tales for Dark Nights* and *Oakwood Island*.

Sleepless Nights

By

Pierre C. Arseneault

Shadow Dragon Press
Albuquerque, New Mexico

This book is dedicated to my good friend Angella Jacob. Without really knowing it, she inspired me to write, reawakening my desire to tell stories.

Table of Contents

Subliminal

1

"*I can't believe how much blood there was,*" Jason Donavan thought as he walked at a brisk pace. He was looking down at the sidewalk, marching toward the campus on the way to his dorm room. He struggled with his heavy backpack, his heart still pounding from the adrenaline; it felt as if his feet barely touched the ground as he hurried along, focused on his destination.

2

About forty minutes ago, without knowing the following events would be leading to this moment, Jason was sitting down to lunch at one of his regular spots, Pickadeli's Sub Shop.

The taste of the lettuce was overwhelming his taste buds as he crammed a large portion of the cold cut sub into his mouth. A pickle fell onto the table before him as he wrestled with what was left of the fat, foot long sub that was the Tuesday special. Chewing, he heard nothing of his surroundings, drowned out by his own personal music choices from his iPod. This current playlist featured a local Indi group with an original song he loved.

He looked up and scanned the room, trying not to be obvious about it, but Jason couldn't help himself. He stole another glance her way. The girl in the slim fitting, black jeans was sitting across the sub shop from him with an older lady, who had to be her grandmother. Her long, raven-colored hair hid her pale face a little when she looked down at her iPhone. She would occasionally glance away from it and look his way. When she would catch him looking at her, she would smile coyly at him, sipping at her Cherry Cola in the giant, frozen glass mug Pickadeli's was known for. Her grandmother tugged at her arm to get her attention and showed her an older model flip phone. The girl grinned at Jason, adjusted the ear buds of her own iPod and took the phone from her grandmother's hand. After a few fast motions of adept thumbs, she handed it back to her. With his ears still full of the music his iPod was spewing, Jason watched as the older woman's frown turned into a smile when she took hold of her phone. He could see her mouth the words "*thank you,*" and she put the phone to her ear, listening intently.

When Jason looked down again, he saw that a glob of ranch sauce had fallen onto his iPod when he was looking away. Quickly he dabbed at it with a napkin that was already dirty and made it worse. Frustrated, he reached over to the table next to him and picked up some clean looking napkins the previous customers had left behind. He rubbed one of these against his glass Cherry Cola filled mug, using the condensation to dampen it, and proceeded to clean off his iPod.

As he shot a glace around the room, he noticed the older couple, a bald man and a woman with an old-fashioned perm, get up and make their way out of the place. A familiar looking man in his early forties wearing a brown tweed jacket with old fashioned elbow patches proceeded to get his soft drink in his frozen glass mug from the self-serve counter. The pimple-faced teenager behind the cash register put his sub into his tray and said something that Jason didn't understand because of the beats of the Indi group in his ears. With a nod and a smile, the man gathered his tray with his drink and sat at the table near the young girl and her grandmother.

Just then Jason felt his iPhone vibrating on the table as he reached for his Cherry Cola. With his attention on the text message from his fiend Tony, and a quickly sent reply, Jason never noticed when the raven-haired girl stood up. What did catch his attention was when he saw Cherry Cola splash all over the table behind the girl, spraying her grandmother as she hoisted the heavy glass mug above her head. She stood behind the man with the tweed jacket, and before anyone could react to what was happening, the girl brought down the glass mug as hard as she could with a loud crunch that echoed through the room. Jason could see that she was stone-faced, almost without emotion. The seated man was clearly stunned by the blow and unable of stopping the young, emotionless girl as she raised her now bloody mug to strike him again, and again, and again. The man in the tweed jacket stumbles as if to get up, but his legs buckle under him as all the strength is drained from his body. Blood trickles down his face as he struggles to grasp what has just happened.

Leaving a trail of blood mixed with droplets of Cherry Cola on the ceiling the girl strikes him again. This last blow sends him sprawling forward onto the table, tipping it over. Falling to the floor he drags along everything that was on it, spreading his food and drink onto the ceramic tiles. He lay on the floor amidst the food and spilled Cherry Cola for a brief moment before the convulsions start and the blood pools around his head. The girl, standing over him, watches numbly as he spreads the blood with his body and head while twitching and gasping for what would be his last breath. He stiffened and then lay very still, his tweed jacket now covered in blotches of dark crimson consisting of the cola and his own blood.

The girl lifts her blood covered hand letting the slick, bloody glass mug fall and shatter loudly on the floor as she begins to shake uncontrollably. She looks over her blood-speckled arms and then touches her face, looking at her fingers in amazement. It was as if she had just come to realize that her face was speckled with the stranger's blood. She let out a very loud shriek as she began shaking violently. Her eyes rolled back into her head and she crumpled to the floor, unconscious. The stunned onlookers, including her grandmother, only now reacted to the horrific scene they had just witnessed.

"OH MY GOD!" cried her grandmother.

A man's voice called from the back. From somewhere behind

the counter he could be heard shouting "Somebody call 9-1-1," which came out sounding like nine whon whon.

Across the room sits a small piece of a cold cut sub with napkins covered in ranch dressing, a heavy glass mug still containing some Cherry Cola, but the young man who had sat there was gone.

3

"I can't believe what I just witnessed right there in Pickadeli's," Jason said to Tony, who had arrived just in time to witness the event. They were walking quickly away from the restaurant.

"What the hell did the guy do?" asked Tony.

"I didn't really see what happened," panted an out of breath Jason.

"I was at the door, just about to go in when I saw the guy fall on the floor and she started screaming. I mean it happened so fast. And then I saw you coming at me before I ever made it through the fuckin' door."

"Dude, I had to get out of there before I tossed my lunch," Jason uttered as he struggled with his heavy backpack hanging over his left shoulder. He felt his stomach churn as he fought back the urge to vomit as he replayed the scene in his mind.

"Do you think it's like that guy last week from across town?" asked Tony. "You know; the guy who beat the old lady to death with his skateboard and then said he didn't know why he did it."

"Maybe," replied Jason.

"And that fourteen-year-old kid who beat his stepmom to death with her own groceries. With a fuckin' canvas bag of canned goods for fuck sakes."

"How the fuck should I know!" exclaimed Jason as he walks across a busy street, cutting through traffic. A car swerved to miss him and honked his horn, screaming something they didn't understand. But neither of them acknowledged it as they marched on.

"It happened again last night in a pool hall downtown. This guy beat his best friend to death with a number nine pool ball." Tony looked over his shoulder nervously and added "people are fuckin' going crazy man."

"Tell me about it."

"Well I guess a greasy burger it is then. I've got a sudden craving for red meat. I'll see ya at class, dude," said Tony as he jaywalked across the street and headed for a place called Greasy Al's Burger Joint. (A place where the burgers aren't greasy, Al is.)

4

Having made his way back to his dorm room and kicking off his smelly sneakers, Jason booted up his custom-built desktop computer and locked his door. He sat at the machine he had put together himself out of discarded parts he had collected from friends and had built the best computer on the campus. Opening his backpack, he removed his laptop and his new books on psychology that he had just bought for his second year in university. Jason looked at his cluttered desk, and then tossed aside a pizza box that still contained a few bits of crust, and several empty cans of Monster Energy Drink, placing them into the trash to clean off a small space on the desk. He then collected some scattered books on music into a stack and neatly placed the new psychology books on top. He removed his iPod and placed it on top of the stack of books.

For a moment he sat there with mouse in hand staring blankly at the screen. He couldn't get the image of the girl out of his head. He could still see her holding the mug over her head just before she brought it down hard, smashing in the stranger's skull. A stranger he now was starting to remember as Mr. Baker. A substitute teacher he had had last year for a couple of classes. Shaking off the thought, he unlocked his computer and opened a browser, clicked on *Bookmarks*, scrolled down and clicked on *Ramstunes*.

The web site's home page showed the latest song picks by the site's owner, who was a big fan of music. The same man who Jason got to know very well since he was also his music teacher, Harold Ramsey. The professor encouraged his students to record original music and put it on his web site for people to download for free. He told them that it could make for great lessons in many schools of life. Teaching you humility when you failed, he also emphasised the value of being humble when you succeeded. Jason found the thought of all this to be very interesting as he, like a few others also, was studying both psychology and music. But it also inspired him to use this idea for his own studies and perhaps research into psychology by using his talents in music.

Harold had said that if your song didn't get many downloads and people didn't like it, then it would teach you valuable lessons about failing. He loved to use phrases like "if at first you don't succeed, try again."

This inspired Jason and so he recorded and mixed a couple of instrumentals, which he posted under the fake name he still uses. They had a slight peak at first as people checked them out for the first time, but eventually they failed to attract an audience. They had been strictly rock-style grooves. His latest effort was different, a blend of a rhythmic techno beat, with a rock flavour.

Checking the download stats, he saw that his latest song was getting a great number of downloads considering the small population of kids using this site. It had been downloaded a total of 1,106 times over the last week.

Jason pulled a red notebook from a drawer and noted the date and the download stats in a list on a well-worn page. He went to the site's general list and saw that he was sixteenth in a list of top one hundred downloads from the site's Indi chart.

He looked up the song's downloader's comments and saw thirteen new comments since his last visit to the website.

"This song rocks, dude," posted a guy called "RockStar Phil."

Another comment from a girl named Debbie, who said. "Best workout song EVER!!"

He scrolled through all the comments and stopped to re-read his favourite on his previous instrumental piece called Slumber, which read "Truly a hypnotic masterpiece." This was the comment that had inspired him to create his latest work and had surpassed his previous efforts.

Logging out, Jason then logged in under his own name. He went to see the anonymous account he had created tagged under the name "The Sublime Rocker." Once logged in as a user, he clicked on "download" for the song listed as *Subliminal* only to get a message reading "File not found." He smiled in satisfaction that the program he had embedded in his music file was working. With a quick logging out and back in as "The Sublime Rocker" he proceeded to upload the song to the site again. Another fact he wrote in his notebook in a list of dates and times. A list that was keeping track of the cycle of times his file became corrupt and the times he had to upload it again. This he did to prevent people from being able to share the music without his approval. This was important if he was to keep control of his experiment.

He got a great deal of satisfaction from having this control over the file. Satisfied the song was in the process of being uploaded again he sat back, plugged his iPod headphones into his computer and hit play on his song. Listening intently to the music's hypnotic techno beat and heavy rock sounds that were filled with the repetitiveness he had worked hard to achieve. The lyrics he had recorded himself more as spoken word than actual singing. Then using a few computer programs, he turned the spoken words into a guttural tone that was barely understandable to most and layered this on top of the music track thus creating his latest masterpiece called *Subliminal*.

He clicked play, mouthed the words and sort of sang along to it. While listening, he clicked on his browser and typed in "random murders in Stonevalley," as the lyrics echoed in his mind.

7

Subliminal
Subliminal
Subliminal
Subliminal
You're getting sleepy
Subliminal
You're getting sleepy
Subliminal
You're getting sleepy
Subliminal
You only hear the sound of my voice
Subliminal
One the count of three you will do as I say
Subliminal
You will pick up the nearest thing to you that will make a good
weapon
Subliminal
You will beat someone near you
Subliminal
You will not stop until they are dead
Subliminal
Once you awake from the trance
Subliminal
You will remember nothing
Subliminal
One
Subliminal
Two
Subliminal
Three
Subliminal
Subliminal
Subliminal
Subliminal

The song had been downloaded a total of 1106 times and had been effective to prove the power of hypnosis over the subconscious a total of seventeen times. He wrote more notes in his red notebook as he read about the latest news on the recent outbreak of violent murders. Later that night he would visit the news site again and write notes on the witness accounts from Pickadeli's Sub Shop and the girl named Clara who killed a stranger named Franklyn Baker and claims to not know why she did it.

5

Jason found himself sitting at his regular table at Pickadeli's, unsure how he had got there. He looked around the room and everybody in the place was looking at him. Before him was a foot long, cold cut sub and an ice-cold frozen mug, empty except for a single red-stripped white straw. The blood-speckled, pale-faced, raven-haired girl was standing over a man who lay on his back, propped up on the leather patched elbows of his blood-spattered brown tweed jacket. He was turned towards Jason, blood on his pale face, his hair matted and dripping while staring directly at him.

Before his eyes he saw the frost-covered frozen mug begin to fill with a dark liquid. It rose up from the bottom and filled the mug. When he peered in it he saw that it wasn't Cherry Cola but rather a thick, red liquid that he knew was blood.

Jason glanced around the room; everybody was staring at him. The girl's grandmother was smiling at him as she sat at her table behind the girl.

"Why are you staring at me?" he shouted in frustration, looking around the room.

The mug began to overflow, covering the table with blood. It spilled off the table and onto him. He felt it flow onto the front of his pants as it soaked in, warm and wet. He reached for a napkin to clean himself, but the napkin was soaked and dripping blood. He looked up at the girl and the man on the floor,

9

both of whom were covered in blood and staring at him. That's when he suddenly awoke; sitting up in his sweat-soaked bed and came to the realisation that he had pissed himself in his sleep.

"Fuck me!" he exclaimed as he pulled the wet boxer shorts away from his body with the tips of his forefingers and thumbs. His mind raced through the memories of his childhood and stopped when he was thirteen. The last time he had wet himself in his sleep which was also the first time he had smoked weed and then binged on ice cream afterwards.

"Fuck," he said as got up and pulled the sheets off his bed and placed them into a blue plastic laundry basket.

6

Early that morning he had the Laundromat all to himself. The sound of the three washing machines all running at the same time would have made his mother proud. A load of light colors, a load of dark colors, and a load of bedding that needed washing after last night's incident. The smell of urine now being overpowered by fabric softener was a relief to the young man. It would save him from a potentially embarrassing situation if other customers would arrive, especially if it was someone from campus that might recognize him.

With the washers set and beginning to fill up, he sat at the long folding table in the middle of the room and pulled out the battered laptop from his backpack. Being so close to campus they had Wi-Fi available for the students, who were their best customers. Quickly he opened a web browser and typed in "random murders in Stonevalley". His search quickly found the latest incident, which had happened off campus. A young, fifteen-year-old girl beat her younger, thirteen-year-old brother to death with a cast iron skillet in their own kitchen. A picture of the crime scene was leaked online, and the media had posted it on their website. The picture had been taken from outside the house through the glass of the patio door. It showed

10

a blood-spattered girl curled into a ball against the door of her parent's house. She was obviously in hysterics and a female paramedic knelt before her trying to calm her down. The one fact that might escape the detectives on scene, but that Jason noticed right away was the iPod that was in her pocket with the ear buds now draped on the floor. Jason knew that not long ago they were in her ears and she had heard his song one too many times.

Seeing this made his heart race and beads of sweat appear on his forehead. The look of shock on her face and the bloody handprint smeared on the glass. That's when he noticed the foot of the victim behind the paramedic. The sight of all this brought on feelings of guilt as he noticed that in the background. This boy was dead because of his experiment, and he knew it. Was what he was doing wrong in some way he wondered to himself as he zoomed in the picture and could see blood on the boy's dirty white sock?

He read the headline again. "Police baffled by series of random killings."

Logging into the "Ramstunes" website he checked his stats and the song now had been downloaded 1,412 times. That's when he noticed a few more comments on the song. One of which read "Awesome song dude!! Ya gotta post some more stuff."

Another girl, whose profile picture was of a Japanese animation character wrote "Simply awesome, dude!"

The sense of pride he got from these comments made him forget the guilt. He reminded himself that this was a scientific experiment in psychology that had never been done before. He would be a pioneer in the field before even ever graduating. Reaching into his backpack he pulled out his red notebook and his energy drink and started working on his paper titled "Subliminal, a journey into the subconscious by Jason Donavan, also known as The Sublime Rocker."

7

The squealing of a few chairs being slid back, and the shuffling of feet could be heard from all over the room as a few people got up to leave. Then silence fell again across the campus library, just as it should be. All the usual people filled the place to cram for the next day's test. The place was silent to most, but not to all, as many sat with their earbuds crammed into their ears; their own soundtracks playing. Jason looked around the room and couldn't help but wonder how many of them might have his song on their personal Playlists.

Smiling to himself, he pulled out his red notebook and the largest can of his favourite energy drink he could buy. It was going to be a long night and he had lots of work to do. He tried to stifle the sound, but it opened with a loud crack that echoed and made a few heads turn in his direction. A female sounding "shhhh" was heard from behind him and then silence dominated the room again. He put in his earbuds and turned up his iPod slightly. He took a large gulp of the energy drink and then started compiling the stats from his notebook into charts and graphs. He set his iPod onto the table next to his laptop and tuned everybody out. Jason was lost to the world around him as he began typing up the introduction to his term paper.

Completely engrossed in his work as he glanced at his notebook, typing away, he never noticed as someone walked up behind him. He noticed a slight reflection in the screen of his laptop and when he turned, he saw Christina Bellford; the barefoot young blond from his psychology class holding a huge, heavy book over her head with a completely blank expression on her face.

"Fuck!" He barely had time to say a single word as she quickly slammed the book down on his head as hard as she could. Stunned he leaned forward over the table knocking over his large energy drink with his left forearm. She hoisted the book again and struck him for a second time. The second blow completely dazed him and made him very aware of the sudden taste of blood in his mouth as he bit his tongue hard. The third blow made the blood flow from his nose and his legs turn to mush from under him. Bewildered, and trying to get away from Christina, he started to stand and fell forward and with one more blow of the now bloody hardcover book he fell sideways sweeping his laptop to the floor with him. The already battered laptop smashed and broke in two, scattering bits of electronics and keys from the keyboard. The screen part skidded under the table while the other half smashed open like a cooked clam's shell and settle next to Jason's twitching body. Energy drink pooled on the table engulfing his red notebook in the dark, thick syrupy goo, causing the ink from his gel pen to run, before it started dripping off the table and onto the floor. Jason twitched a few times before Christina brought down the book one last time as the room echoed with the sound of his head rebounding off the hard-tiled floor. She stood, hoisting the book again and stopped when she saw that he lay perfectly still. Blood pooled around his head and engulfed the half of his laptop the lay next to him.

Christina lowered the book in her white knuckled hands as she watched the body, as if waiting for it to move. It didn't. Her hands relaxed and the blood-stained book fell to the floor with a loud thump. She watched the blood cover the floor around his head, the crimson liquid swallowing bits of electronics and keys from the keyboard and the dead computer. As if just realizing what she was staring at, she held up shaking arms and screamed.

8

In the days that followed, there were three more of the mysterious random killings. A freshman named Darrol was killed by his girlfriend Chloe when she beat him to death with the handle of his own sword he had hanging on his wall. She had grasped it by the dull blade and beat him with the brass handle using it as a club.

A young friend of Jason's named Tony killed an old lady named Mimi while riding the bus on his way to Pickadeli's. He beat her to death with her own cane and then threw up on her when he came out of his trance and saw the bloody body before him.

A student named Caleb killed his teacher, Harold Ramsey, beating him to death with a large basketball-sized steel globe. A gift he had gotten from his wife that the teacher had proudly displayed on his desk. Even if the globe was so old that Zaire had yet to change its name to Democratic Republic of the Congo. And what baffled the detectives the most was that after a few days, there were no more killings. The mysterious beatings stopped as suddenly as they had begun.

9

A purple and black spandex clad Debbie Carson from the cheerleading squad stood next to a treadmill. She was looking down at her iPod with her usual not so bright confused look that always pissed off her exceptionally bright best friend Anna McPhee.

Anna had to ask, "What's wrong?"

"I don't know why but my favourite work out song won't play anymore."

"What song?" inquired Anna.

"*Subliminal,*" said Debbie. "It's the best work out music. I tried to download it again last night but can't even do that either."

"I love that song too. But pick another song, Deb and get cracking. We got classes later," said Anna as she started her treadmill and got on.

The Statues of Pine Glen Forest

The rising sun shone through the trees, casting dancing shadows everywhere. The breeze stirred about the tall canopy of multiple shades of green that was ever-present overhead. If one stood still at this very spot, and made no noise, you could hear nothing but the swaying of branches full of new leaves freshly grown in the early spring. They flowed gently in the wind with a hypnotic sound that was very soothing. If you were quiet long enough you could also hear the occasional chirping of birds. This was the entire reason that Gary Chapman found himself out here wandering in Pine Glen Forest. The doctor's advice finally sinking in after all these years, a lesson he had learned the hard way, having been repeatedly told to slow down. Learn to relax before he found himself having a real heart attack instead of angina.

A month ago, he had found himself lying in a hospital bed struggling to breathe, making the same promises to himself that countless others have done before him. *"If I get through this I am going to start exercising and eating better. I will take better care of myself"*. He vowed this out loud, as if trying to convince himself more than anyone else. This was just the scare he needed to make what Doctor McCormick had been telling him for years finally make sense. He was not indestructible as he had previously thought, especially not at his age of fifty-two.

He had wanted to take more time to himself and enjoy life's simple pleasures. But sadly, golf had always been more stressful than relaxing to him. The constant competition between himself, his friend Jack, and the other members of Bear Lake Golf Club had gotten out of hand many times before. That would not likely change anytime soon, so better to find another hobby that could help him relax instead of adding to his anxiety.

A few days after his ordeal, while sitting in Doctor McCormick's waiting room, he came across a book on the perfect subject. He had heard much on the subject in the past but today, in this very waiting room, Chapman decided he would take up bird watching. He could jump into his soft beige Lexus at any time and just drive out to the beautiful, serene countryside and find the tranquility he suddenly found himself craving. After all these years of owning his own company in the fast-paced, deadline-oriented shipping business he needed to find time for himself. *"Find ways to relax or die,"* the good doctor had so bluntly said to him not so long ago. It would be hard for him to do but it was time to ease up and leave the worries to Dwight, whom he had been grooming for this very reason. He knew someday he would pass the torch to his only son and now would be as good a time as any.

"Why yes, sir. We have some great books on bird watching," said the nice young lady at the local bookstore. She leaned in, softly touching his arm with her hand and whispered. *"The fanatics call it birding, just so you know."* Smiling, the clerk stepped on a stool reaching up on a shelf to grab a copy of the best bird book in the store. His thinning and greying hair that was often covered by his beige, wool packer hat and the worry lines often got him this kind of "respect your elders" treatment from the younger people. Something he had not gotten used to since he started going grey in his early forties. He had grown to accept that he looked a bit older than he really was a little bit at a time. He was often being offered a senior's discount, which he found himself taking advantage of on a few occasions.

Chapman soon realised that he had much to learn about relaxing as he snapped out of his daydream and found himself lost in thought about the last week's events. While standing under a tall oak tree with his mini atlas of birds almost falling out of the back pocket of his tan cargo pants, he had all but forgotten the binoculars hanging almost at his waist by the band that looped around the back of his neck. He could barely feel them through the light jacket he had been wearing all week. The new medications that thinned his blood also left him constantly feeling chilled without it. He had his hands in his pockets while unconsciously fingering the pocket lint as he often did when he was deep in thought. He was so focused on his thoughts that he never realised that right above him was a sight that would have many a bird watcher frozen in their tracks. It wasn't often one would see a Blue Warbler in this area, and he was standing under not one but a pair of them. That was a fact that would go completely unnoticed to this novice bird watcher on his first venture out.

I wonder if the shipment of sheet metal coils made it to Quebec, he thought to himself. Frustrated at his failed attempt to leave work behind he aimlessly wandered off again, blissfully unaware that he had no idea where he was heading as his shoes sunk slightly in the softness of the forest floor.

He had told everyone at the office he was going golfing to save himself the ridicule he thought he would get if he told them he was going to take up bird watching. Instead of going to Bear Lake Golf Course like he had told his secretary he ended up in Pine Glen Forest, which stretched out for a great many unfamiliar miles. The entire area was filled with a healthy mix of coniferous and deciduous trees broken up only by streams, rivers and was full of many types of bird species. But Chapman, wandering without a care in the world, hadn't even removed the lens caps from his binoculars yet and had not seen a single bird. Even though they were all around him at times, his mind was clearly not focused on this task on his very first outing. He was more enthralled by the wondrous amount of nature and its contrast to the city life he was so accustomed to.

But something eventually caught his eye though, in a small clearing deep in the woods in the tall grass stood an animal near a tree. From the shape of what he could see of its body and head it looked to be a deer. Crouching down in a small patch of tall grass he watched it for a while, waiting for it to hear him and bolt.

After a good few minutes Chapman stood up abruptly, his old stiff knees making loud popping noises that almost echoed as he straightened up, but the deer still never moved. Perplexed at this he began to slowly walk, trying hard not to make sounds that might scare it away. Finally, as he felt them sway like a pendulum, he remembered he had binoculars hanging around his neck. He quickly put them to his eyes only to see complete darkness. Cursing under his breath he fumbled to remove the lens caps and for a second time put them to his contact lens enhanced eyes.

Without realising that it was out loud he muttered "What the hell?"

He looked through the binoculars at what he thought to have been a deer. To any onlookers, if there had been any, it would have looked as if suddenly without a care he began to walk toward the animal. No longer worried about making noise he crunched though the debris on the forest floor without trying to avoid it like before.

The first thing he did in his haze of confusion when he was a mere few feet from the deer was to reach out and touch it, out of disbelief. He had never seen a statue of a deer before and one of such amazing quality at that. The detailing was simply amazing that it was no wonder that from a distance he thought it to be a living deer. It looked to be made of some sort of grey plastic at first but up close it became apparent it was granite or something. Really, he couldn't tell what it was as he knew nothing of such materials. Giving it a nudge he realised that the deer was not hollowed out either and would not be easy to move or ship. The thought of how somebody got this out here crossed his mind from too many years in the shipping business. Why would such an amazing statue be here in the middle of the woods, he wondered? He ran his hand over its head, which was turned a bit looking away, and he felt the small stubs of antlers. Female he thought to himself as he marveled at the attention to detail.

While examining it he noticed that he was not the only one to ever mistake it for a living deer. There were two marks on its hindquarter on the opposite side from where he had come from, which could only be where a hunter had mistaken it for his next kill. The deep gouges were the only imperfections on this otherwise flawless work of art. For the first time he regretted not having brought his digital camera. The same one he had gotten as a Christmas gift from his son three years ago but had never used for anything other than business. He remembered now that it sat in the drawer of his office desk with dead batteries inside it. Something he had never even though about until this very moment since he realised that nobody would believe any of this without seeing pictures and even then.

For the first time since he carelessly wandered off Chapman took a moment to notice the area looking for landmarks of any kind that would help him find this location again. With a natural ability to walk around in circles without any effort he figured he would make his way back to whence he came. But finding this exact location where this amazing find was again would be hard. He would use the tall pine tree that seemed to tower over the rest by a good twenty feet. That would serve as his landmark as it was only about fifty feet away, more or less.

Looking back at the statue as he walked off, he couldn't help but wonder why it was out here in the middle of the forest. He wouldn't have the time to ponder this question for very long as a short walk away revealed another masterpiece. This one even more amazing and stunning than the first. On a branch that was out of reach, sat a grey statue of a squirrel. It was impeccably wrapped around the bark, coiled as if ready to pounce.

Chapman lost track of how long he spent looking at this marvellous creation and how it almost perfectly fit on its perch. *Truly amazing,* he thought as he looked back to note the location of the tall pine tree and the deer. He simply had to come back and bring his son to see this. The only thing he couldn't decide on was if he would tell him first or just bring him out here and show him.

Still reeling from the amazing craftsmanship, he was certainly not ready for his next find. Walking past a small cluster of young pine trees Chapman froze in his tracks as he saw another statue made from the same concrete-like grey granite. But this statue was of a hunter who had his rifle aimed in the direction he had come from. His head was cocked to the side a bit as if he was looking towards his prey with his rifle still pointing the way. The details of the buttons and zippers to the life-like stone fingers were simply incredible.

Standing next to the statue he looked down the barrel of the gun and sure enough, it pointed straight to a small clearing amidst the bushes and trees where he could see the deer. That's when he realized that the markings on the deer were most likely done on purpose. Through his binoculars he could see the deer in the distance. His only thought now – how was he going to get his son to come out so he could show him all this. And he needed to remember to bring a camera instead of binoculars.

Shortly afterwards Chapman came across a small granite statue of a rabbit, which he thought about taking with him as proof, but he remembered how far he would have to carry it. After recent events he felt that carrying a heavy granite statue on the long hike back might not be a good idea. Not far away, emerging through a thick ridge of trees he came upon a clearing. Gary stopped, suddenly transfixed by the sight that took his breath away. He had heard that expression many a time but had now experienced it for the first time in his life. In the clearing stood about a dozen or so statues all made from this grey granite stone. They were scattered with no discernable pattern all over the small clearing amidst the knee-high yellow grass. Some looked to have been there for a while as they were more weathered and had discoloration and spots of moss on them.

There was one of a bear standing on three legs as it was carved as if in mid stride. A pair of statues stood near the bear, a modestly dressed middle-aged woman with a small boy next to her. Both statues positioned such that their hands were mere inches from each other's, as if about to grasp them together. Each statue in the clearing was more marvellous than the last he thought to himself. Close by stood a statue of a cowboy wearing a cowboy hat, a vest with a pocket watch tucked away and barely showing and he even had a pistol on his hip. Next to the cowboy was a smaller statue of a dog with his head cocked to the side, its ear lifted as if listening intently. What made Chapman laugh was the fact that the statue had one leg lifted as it was about to pee on the cowboy. The one statue that stood out the most of the all was the one of the shirtless native warrior poised in a slight crouch. He was holding a tomahawk in one hand and the intricate details on the fringes on the sides of his pants were simply incredible and must have taken months to make. Near him stood a statue of a coyote with his mouth in a snarl and another statue of a deer in a very upright position gazing into the distance. He found himself wondering if there were any more statues and if the owner would be willing to part with a few.

Until now this part of the forest had almost an eerie quiet to it that at first, he hadn't noticed. Only when he entered this clearing did that eerie silence get broken. But being completely absorbed by the amazing workmanship in each piece of art he had failed to hear the unmistakable sounds that could only be a river flowing close by. It took a good while before the sound caught his attention and he tore himself away from marvelling at the statues. It was coming from the opposite end of the clearing, which was the same direction he had been heading. That's when he heard something else, it sounded like a melodic voice as if someone was humming nearby.

Without hesitation he walked into a small patch of forest

at the edge of the clearing. He entered it quickly, so carelessly that he got tangled in branches that hooked and snagged at his clothing. Chapman's hat was torn off his head twice, both times hurriedly picking it up and roughly placing it back on his head. His curious nature was getting the best of him now and his thoughts were that this person could shed some light on this curious array of masterpieces in the middle of a forest. It took but a few moments for him to cross this thick patch of trees and brush. Emerging on the other side of the thicket, the first thing he saw was the back of an old granite statue of a young man. He barely took notice of the statue's details as behind it a short distance away was a small log cabin with smoke billowing out of a stone chimney.

Had he not noticed the smoke coming out of the top of the rough, multicoloured stonework he might have thought the cabin was an abandoned shack. The wood looked dark as it had greyed with time and the roof looked like it had been patched many times before. He could see no windows or doors from this angle so the door would have to be on the side facing the river that was in front of the cabin.

This was a lot to take in as the cabin lay to his left and in front of it was the river he had heard shortly before. It wasn't very wide; or deep but looked like it could be this cabin's only source of water. There were three more statues in front of him, plus the one of the man behind him. One was a deer at the river's edge, the second a giant moose on the opposite side of the river facing in his direction. The third granite masterpiece was a person but from this angle he couldn't tell if it was a man or woman. The hair was long and the shoulders not too broad and so he couldn't be certain at first. What caught his eye the most was the contrast of colors of the clothing that was draped over both shoulders. It was as if someone had carelessly draped wet clothing to dry on this marvellous work of art.

I suppose living amidst so many masterpieces in time one might lose appreciation for them. That's the first thought that went through Gary's mind as he walked past the cabin towards the riverside.

That's when he heard the splashing of water and what again sounded like a voice humming. At the river's edge sat a figure hunched over, next to a few rocks that also had a few pieces of dripping wet, unidentifiable clothing on them. At a glance the figure had a narrow waist and wider, feminine hips. Her feminine voice confirmed this as she hummed her melodic song, which Gary didn't recognize. She was bent forward; one hand bracing herself on the rock next to her and her other hand he assumed was in the water, perhaps washing something he but couldn't see from this angle.

Walking towards her he blurted with excitement. "Excuse me miss, but are you the one who carved these amazing statues?"

"Leave now, we don't want any visitors," the soft voice said in a firm tone as she froze in place holding her garment in the cold river water. "Were perfectly fine living here by ourselves," she added.

"But I want to buy a few of your statues," Chapman blurted out in haste as he walked towards her. "Name your price," he added, extending a hand towards her. "My name is Chapman, Gary Chapman," he continued ignoring her comments as he was so used to getting what he wanted.

"Martha?" he heard a man's voice coming from what he had thought to be an empty cabin. "Who are you talking to, sweetheart?" the voice asked.

Gary froze in his tracks and looked towards the cabin for any sign of life that he might have missed in his haste. After a brief moment from this new perspective he saw stirring inside what looked to be the doorway of the cabin.

"It's nothing, Henry. I was just talking to myself again," the woman's voice exclaimed loudly.

Gary turned and took another step, still intent on introducing himself to the woman. When she turned to face him, he gasped. She was stunningly beautiful, with piercing green eyes. Her high cheek bones and perfect face was breathtaking. In that brief moment he also noticed her thick long dark hair writhed about as if it had a life of its own. Some strands rearing up as if coming to attention with what looked to be small tiny eyes looking directly at him. By then he felt himself frozen in his tracks and in his last few brief moment of consciousness he came to realise that she was the one who made all these incredible statues but not with any chisel or in fact with tools of any kind. But he realised this too late to save himself as he felt his consciousness slip away.

"I'm almost done washing the clothes, Henry and then I'm coming to make dinner," she said while she and hundreds of beady eyes on the ends of what resembled snake-like creatures on her head, instead of hair, looked directly into the face of this new granite statue. After a moment she reached over and picked up the wet clothes sitting in a heap on the rock behind her and she draped what looked to be a man's shirt over Gary's extended arm, now made of solid grey granite. "I'm sorry you had to find us," she whispered softly.

A shirtless Henry emerged out of the cabin holding an empty basket in his hands in front of him. "You want me to get some carrots from the cellar?" he asked.

Martha took a moment to look at her handsome companion before turning to fetch the garment she had dropped by the river side when Gary showed up. She held it up looking at the fresh dirt in dismay and dunking it back in the river to wash this new filth off the otherwise clean grey shirt.

"Ouf," she heard Henry exclaim sharply.

She turned to see him holding his chest while standing next to the newest granite statue of an aging bird watcher. "When did you have time to make this one?" He inquired "You haven't carved anything in years."

"Come, let's go get some carrots," she said taking the basket from Henry's grasp.

"Wait now, hold up," he replied. "What is it?" he asked as he ran his hand over its arm up to the face. "It's a man, isn't it? And he is wearing a hat," he said as he continued running his hands over the granite masterpiece. "Binoculars?" he added in an inquisitive tone.

"Oh, Henry, I haven't been this happy in a long time. I'm so happy you came into my life when you did. I thought I would be lonely forever," said Martha, smiling as she watched her lover feeling the granite with both hands.

"You make me happy too," replied Henry as he ran his hands over the statue adding "I just wish I could see more than just shadows so that I could appreciate these amazing statues you carved."

With tears welling up in her beautiful green eyes she spoke softly. "You will never understand this, Henry but I am so ugly that you couldn't stand the sight of me if you could see me. I know that doesn't make much sense but just know that it would be impossible for you to love me like you do."

Henry, taking his focus away from the statue, walked towards the sound of her voice. He could see but a shadow where Martha stood in the contrast of bright daylight and touched her face with his hand. "You're right about that not making sense, but if my not being able to see means I get to know your love then I don't want to see."

He affectionately ran his hands in her now limp, thick hair and she touched his arm as she smiled, knowing she would only know his love while he lived out his mortal life.

"You always get so emotional when you show me one of your new carvings," said Henry.

Sleepy Meadows

1

Lying in her bed, Agnes could feel sweat roll off her taught skin. She had shed her thin wisp of a blanket long ago, the heat and humidity in her bedroom too much for her to bear. Her short silky nightgown barely covering her dark brown skin, she struggled through the heat in an attempt to sleep as much as she could. The dampness of the bedding beneath her made her even more uncomfortable as she awoke yet again. At that moment she felt his presence even with her eyes still closed. He had come to call on her yet again.

Opening her eyes, she could see his silhouette against the large window and the glow of the moon in the night's sky. The wispy white curtains that framed the edges fluttered gently in the breeze. In the fog of her sleep-clouded mind she wondered when he had arrived. How long had he been standing there watching her? She wanted to speak, to ask those questions but found herself unable to. The thoughts of his touch again came over her and she soon could think of nothing else. She closed her eyes, her body writhing at the thought, she ran a hand over her young firm breast, feeling her nipple harden.

Letting out a soft moan she opened her eyes to see him now leaning above her. She felt the weight of his body cave the mattress slightly, causing the bed to creak. The moonlight behind him makes it so she could only see his form and not the details of his face. For a brief moment she remembered, in his late-night visits, she had never seen his face. She closed her eyes in anticipation and felt his lips on her forehead followed by her neckline as he kissed her gently. Making his way to her chest trailing down to her breast she felt her passions rise as he placed a hand on her hip. He showered her taut belly with gentle kisses as he made his way even lower as she moaned in anticipation. Her body now tensing with desire; she runs her fingers through her mysterious lover's thick hair, pushing him lower yet. Her body suddenly feeling alive like never before, she let out a loud moan vocalizing her pleasure.

2

"Are you alright, Agnes?" Caregiver Maureen asked as she turned on the lamp next to the bed. Agnes was quivering under the layers of multicoloured blankets, her small wrinkled, age spotted leathery hands clenching the blankets under her chin. Beads of sweat were forming on her forehead and her silver hair was damp with perspiration.

"It was him again," said Agnes as she looked up at Maureen with abnormally bright eyes.

"Did you have the dream again, Agnes?" asked Maureen who dabbed at the beads of moisture on her forehead with a tissue.

"You know I could feel him, Maureen. It's like he was really here. You do believe me don't you?"

"Of course, I do. I know you're not a liar," she said as she smiled at the old woman, the kindness beaming from her expression as she made eye-contact with her patient.

"I'm hungry," said Agnes as she relaxed, pushing off the blankets.

Maureen pulled the blankets up again knowing full well her favourite old lady would soon feel chilled again. "It's only five thirty, Agnes. Try and go back to sleep. Breakfast will be in a few hours, ok."

Frowning, Agnes lay back and pleaded, "But I'm hungry now! Would you be a dear and get an old woman some cookies and juice. Please?"

Maureen rested her hand on Agnes's arm and smiled softly. "You know I can't say no to you now, don't you? I'll be back in a

27

few minutes with your cookies and juice."

Watching Maureen as she walked out, Agnes spoke softly not to wake the others, "Thank you, sweetie."

3

"Who was that?" asked Jenna in a whisper as she met Maureen in the hallway of Sleepy Meadows Rest Home. Maureen smiled at her as she turned and walked into the small kitchen next to the nurses' station. Jenna followed her taking her armload of dirty linens with her.

"Agnes had her dream again. I gotta bring her a snack." Maureen smiled as she busied herself getting the date cookies and pouring orange juice.

"Really, How is she?" asked Jenna as she plopped herself into a kitchen chair.

Maureen smiled as she put the carton of juice away. "Bright like the other times. She knew my name."

"Wow, that's amazing," said Jenna slouching in her chair and letting the linen droop a bit in her arms.

"Remember the last time she had her dream? She was vibrant all the next day almost. She only started forgetting later that night."

"Oh, I remember all right. The first time it happened two months ago I almost fainted. The contrast between the days before to that day was just too much. I thought she was possessed at first. Scarred the shit out of me!" Jenna said as she got up, watching as Maureen, with the juice and cookies walked down the hall.

Jenna stood still in the hallway as she watched her co-worker enter Agnes's room and heard the old lady say "Oh Maureen, you're such a sweetheart. Thank you!"

4

Agnes sat in her chair at the breakfast table, her aches and pains not so bad this morning. She smiled bright as they brought her a bowl of warm oatmeal with sliced banana in it. A white-

28

haired elderly man in pyjamas under a housecoat with thick glasses approached her table, slightly dragging his slippered feet as he smiled and began to speak. But before he could, he paused when she surprised him by speaking first.

"Good morning, Father Richard," she smiled as she scooped up a large spoonful of oatmeal and gobbled it up.

He reached the chair and pulled it back to sit next to her as he spoke. "Agnes my dear, you look well today."

Still chewing on her banana and oatmeal she replied "Thank you, Father. I do feel well. Hungry, but well." As they heard a loud snore coming from behind them, they both looked at each other, exchanging knowing glances.

"Just Richard, Agnes. Please, I'm not a priest anymore. Remember?" he said, setting his own bowl of oatmeal down before him. He picked up his spoon in his pale white bony hand and scooped a spoonful as he watched Agnes already begin to scrap the bottom of her bowl. With a mouthful he looked at her and spoke "You've got quite the appetite this morning."

Agnes scrapped the last bit from the bottom of her bowl and stopped to lick her spoon leaving a smear of oatmeal on the dark skin of her chin. "Oh yes, and I'm still hungry," she said.

Twisting to look around, Richard tried to see if any of the staff would notice him in his attempt to catch their attention. At that moment an age spotted hand placed a bowl of oatmeal before the tiny old woman saying "Here, you can have mine. I'm not hungry this morning." Walking past the pair, the old man in dress pants and long sleeve shirt did this without as much as a glance backwards.

"Going to bed, Victor?" called Richard.

They could hear Victor dragging his feet, his shoes scrapping against the floor as he slowly walked on. "Yes, I'm very tired."

Agnes scooped up a large spoonful of the oatmeal and ate it. She tilted the bowl to scoop up more and paused. "I wonder what time Lenard will be home tonight." She took a large spoon-full and popped it in her mouth.

Richard sank a little in his chair as he let his disappointment wash over him. Agnes' moment of clarity was already fading slowly but he could see that she felt physically very well at this moment. At least this gave him some comfort.

5

Sitting on a bench in the staff room changing her shoes, Maureen was getting ready to head home. She couldn't help but smile at the thought of how Agnes had made her day. Her eyes shining brightly as Agnes said Maureen's name had overwhelmed her with a happiness that she rarely felt in her job. Taking care of people who were sometimes lost to the world sometimes took its toll on her spirits.

Sitting up, she took the chain that had fallen out of her white uniform and ran her fingers over the pendant. A cross of silver given to her by her mother on the day of her confirmation, many years ago and she had worn it almost every day since. She sat quietly, grasping this symbol of her faith between her thumb and forefinger. She sat deep in thought until the opening of the door startled her.

A tall black man dressed in a white uniform had walked into the staff room.

"Darcy, did you hear about Agnes? She's having one of her good days again," she said with a wide joyous smile.

"Great! Terrific!" said Darcy sarcastically as he opened his locker, pulling out his work shoes and sitting on the bench.

Shocked, the smile on Maureen's face faded quickly as her forehead crinkled into a puzzled look. "What's that supposed to mean?"

Darcy slipped a foot into a white work shoe, sat up and without looking at her spoke. "It makes my job so much easier when they're completely lost. You know how it is, Maureen. It's just easier that way," he said, bending down to tie his other shoe.

Maureen quickly snatched up her purse, muttering "Fucking asshole" under her breath and stormed out of the staff room.

She could barely hear Darcy call "What?" as she headed down the hallway.

6

The laundry cart's wheel squealed slightly as Peggy pushed it down the hallway of the Sleepy Meadows Rest Home. Making her rounds to change the bedding was a duty that not many liked. Knowing full well she was the new girl, the rest of the staff had pawned off this task on her. And since only being four weeks into her new job, the last thing she wanted to do was complain about something she felt was no big deal.

"Hi Florence, how are we today?" she asked with a large smile that the residents loved so much.

Sitting in a chair near the window, Florence sat starring outside at the changing leaves of the fall season. "I miss Cecile," she said in a soft trembling voice.

Pausing in the middle of stripping the bed, Peggy looked over at the old woman by the window and replied. "I'm sorry about Cecile. He was a lovely man with such a lively laugh. I wish I would have had time to know him better. We all miss him too you know, but he's with God now."

"That's what Victor told me last night," replied Florence. "I haven't slept a full night since his heart attack you know. But Victor comes by to keep me company some nights."

Placing the dirty linen in her cart, Peggy returned with an arm full of fresh smelling clean ones and placed the stack on a chair next to the bed. "I can ask Dr Williams to prescribe you something to help you sleep if you want. I'll ask him to come by and see you when he comes by later today. Ok?" she said as she stuffed a pillow into a pillowcase. Peggy turned around as she heard someone come in behind her. Darcy was wheeling in a wheelchair with a folded bathrobe placed neatly in the seat.

"It time for your bath, Florence. They asked me to take you there," said Darcy, stopping the wheelchair in front of her as he produced a fake smile.

"I'm too tired. Tell them to come and get me tomorrow," replied Florence without taking her eyes off the red leaves in the tree outside.

Darcy's smile faded as he took the bathrobe out of the seat. "You know I can't do that, Florence."

Spreading the bedspread, Peggy spoke "She didn't sleep well last night."

Darcy looked at her with a crumple forehead. "I'm just doing my job is all," he said turning to the old woman "Please, Florence."

The old woman started to get up but stumbled back into her chair. Darcy walked around and reached for her arm to help her get up, but the bitter old lady swatted his hand away with hers and struggled to her feet. Slowly she turned, grabbing hold of the arm rest of the wheelchair. Darcy grabbed hold of the handles and steadied the chair as best he could. She dropped herself into the chair, a loud popping sound echoed in the room as her hip joint popped into place. Florence let out a groan as she felt a wave of pain from her arthritis wash over her. Beads of sweat appearing on her forehead as Darcy release the brake on the chair, pushing it out of the room while glancing backwards as he rounded the corner.

Jenna, with her purse in one hand and a coat draped over her arm popped her head into the room. "There you are," she said to Peggy who was just finishing the bed. "You don't have to worry about Victor's bed. I did it last night."

"Oh. Thanks! He's still in bed so I wasn't sure how I was going to change his sheets," replied Peggy.

Jenna smiled "I know. Victor always sleeps most of the day. That's why I did it last night. He says fifty years of working graveyard shifts will do that to you. And after six years of working them myself, I already believe him." Both ladies laughed briefly at the truth in the sarcasm. Peggy watched as Jenna walk away while she turned her cart around in the hallway. "See you later, Jenna."

7

Standing at the sink in the small kitchen, Maureen; back to work for her next shift was rinsing a plastic glass. She placed it in the dishwasher among the other dirty dishes; closing the dishwasher she stood motionless for a moment.

"What are you doing?" said a voice behind her. Maureen, clearly startled, turned and smiled at Jenna.

"I was just trying to remember what Amanda told me earlier. Florence saw Doctor Williams today and he gave her something to help her sleep. I was sure Amanda said she had not given her any yet." She held up a pill bottle and gave Jenna a serious look. "I think she gave her one before she left. And I just gave her another one."

"Two won't harm her, Maureen. She could sleep through a Tornado, sure but it won't hurt her," said Jenna in an attempt to reassure her co-worker.

"I can't believe I did that. I think I'm gonna throw up."

"Florence will get the best night's sleep she has had in years. That's all." Jenna took the bottle from Maureen and walked away saying "I'll put them with the rest of her meds, so you won't have to worry about it again."

8

Standing in a meadow of tall grass spotted with bright yellow flowers was a young woman, her long blond hair flowing in the gentle breeze. Her pure-white sundress glowing in the bright warm sunlight as she ran her hands over the top of the grass. There was peace and tranquility here that she had not felt in decades. The few white fluffy clouds were sailing gently through the otherwise clear blue sky. A sense of familiarity washed over her as she looked over and saw a young man standing on the horizon facing her. She was dreaming again, and she knew it. She had gazed upon this youthful face but mere hours ago when reminiscing through an old photo album of her youth.

"Cecile?" she asked, knowing full well it was a young version of her husband standing before her.

"Yes, Florence; it's me," spoke the man as he smiled and began walking towards her.

"Oh, Cecile! I've missed you so much the last few weeks." She spoke softly as she felt a tear run down her cheek. At that moment she noticed her shadow rapidly growing before her. It stretched out over the tall grass like a blanket of blackness enveloping everything it touched. Spinning around, she saw the sun disappearing quickly over the horizon as the light grew dim. The dark clouds began appearing and blackening the sky and she could feel a sudden dampness in the air weighing down on her. Her sundress clung to her youthful body as she felt the air become warmer, making it hard to breath. Soon there was no blue in the sky but only dark clouds and growing darkness. She turned her gaze to the horizon before her only to find that Cecil was nowhere to be seen. He was gone. In the blink of an eye it was now nighttime. The dark black clouds parted, revealing a full moon just above the area where Cecile had stood mere moments ago. The glow of the moon pulsed brighter for a moment and when it dimmed again, she could see a man standing on the horizon. She knew this was no longer Cecile but someone else. Someone dark and sinister, and yet she felt no fear. She could only make out a dark silhouette against the moonlit sky. At that very instant she felt the ground move under her feet and the sky spun above her. Feeling a sudden rush of blackness overcome her senses, her knees buckled underneath her. As a rush of warmth came over her, she felt a moan escape her lips as she awakened from the dream and opened her eyes to see the shadowy figure standing directly before her. She felt a hand on her side just below her breast and all went black before her eyes.

9

Upon opening her eyes, Florence saw Maureen standing above her with a worried look on her face.

"Florence? Are you ok, Florence?" she asked with a worried tone in her voice.

The elderly woman beaded with perspiration, still in a drug induced haze of slumber and mumbled something incoherent at first. Maureen made out two words out of the entire sentence. One being "dream" the other being "black". Without the rest of it she had no way of knowing what this was about. Maureen stood for a moment as she watched Florence drift off to sleep again. Her breathing steady and calm now as a small smile spread across the old woman's face.

"Is she alright?" she heard a voice ask shaking her out of her own haze of worry. Maureen saw Richard standing in the doorway in his black housecoat holding a cup in one hand and a book in the other.

"She's fine. What are doing up, Father?" she asked as she straightened Florence's blankets before walking out of the room.

"I was getting some tea. I get bouts of insomnia, but the tea usually helps." Maureen took hold of Richard's arm and began to walk with him to his room. "Tell me, Father Richard, how do you like living here so far?"

"It's fine. All the staff are lovely. But I wish everybody would stop calling me Father Richard. I haven't been a priest for a few years now."

"Sorry, Father. I mean Richard. We don't mean any disrespect."

"I know that," said Richard with a gentle smile as he turned into his room. He placed his half empty cup of tea onto the nightstand between the bed and his chair. The very chair he likes to sit in to read, getting lost in books that were frowned upon when he was a man of the cloth.

Maureen sat on the edge of the bed. "Can I ask you something, Richard? I mean you don't have to answer if you don't want to."

"I have no secrets, my child but you might not like my answer," said Richard as he put on his thick reading glasses.

"Every other resident in this place has a least one crucifix hanging in their room, rosary beads on their nightstand and pictures of Jesus on their walls. I was just curious that you, a retired priest had none of that."

Richard laid his book in his lap and fiddled with the bookmark protruding from the pages before looking up at Maureen. "I'm not retired my dear. I left the priesthood. You see in my life as a priest I have seen too many things. Things that can make you doubt your faith." Richard shifted a bit in his chair, and when he saw Maureen wasn't too shocked by what he has just confessed to her, he continued. "I've come to the realization that there is no God. And I couldn't go on lying about it. They let me live among them for almost five years after I quit in hopes that I would find my faith again. But after all that time they saw that this would not happen and so they asked me to leave."

"Surely you don't really mean that. Do you?" asked Maureen.

"What part? The one about the fact that there is no God? I do believe there is much evil in this world. And maybe, just maybe, there was a God at one time. But I don't think he exists anymore."

Maureen absentmindedly found herself feeling the crucifix she wore through the fabric of her uniform.

"Don't worry about me, Maureen. I'm fine with my decisions," he said, removing the bookmark and placed it on the nightstand.

"Let me know if you need anything. Anything at all," she said as she got up. She paused at the doorway. "Oh. And one last thing, we have a small chapel right here in Sleepy Meadows if you ever want to go."

Smiling, she left before Richard could reply to her comment.

10

Alone in the sombre light of the dining area, sat a white-haired Florence in a wheelchair, patiently waiting on breakfast. As Maureen walked by and saw someone sitting in the dimly lit room, she turned and found the light switches making the room bright again, matching the brand-new day.

A brief moment of worry crossed her mind as she remembered the double dosage of sleep medication from the night before.

"Florence? What are you doing here all by yourself? Are you alright, sweetie?"

"I'm starving. What time is it?" asked Florence as she glanced towards the kitchen.

Maureen sat in a chair next to the old woman. "Breakfast isn't for another hour, sweetie. Who brought you here this early?"

"Nobody brought me. I came by myself," replied an impatient Florence.

"With your arthritis, you could have fallen and hurt yourself. We wouldn't want that now would we?" said a sympathetic Maureen.

"My bones don't hurt very much this morning. I'm just so hungry," said Florence with a deep expression of sadness on her face.

"Wait here and I'll bring you something. Ok, sweetie?" Maureen got up and walked toward the kitchen.

A hopeful Florence brightened as she spoke "See if they have any fruit cups. The ones with the cherries. And some pancakes!"

"I'll be back in a minute," replied Maureen.

In a hushed tone, a sharper than usual Florence spoke knowing full well Maureen couldn't hear her from the kitchen. "I'd love some pancakes with some maple syrup. I'm starving."

Maureen returned a few minutes later with a plate of pancakes, sugar free maple syrup and a fruit cup. She placed them down on the table, along with utensils, barely setting them down before Florence snatched them up with a big smile on her face.

"Thank you, Maureen. You've always been my favourite," she said as she cut a large square of pancake, dipped it in the bowl of syrup and put it in her mouth.

Turning towards the kitchen, Maureen walked away dabbing at a tear as she spoke "I'll get you some juice to go with that."

11

Having finished his breakfast and on his way back to his room, Victor took a detour making sure to walk past the ex-priest's room. Stopping at the doorway of Father Richard's room and looking in, he could see feet sticking out from behind the wall. Richard sat in his favourite quiet place. Most likely with a book in hand like he always did after breakfast. Richard had only been living at Sleepy Meadows for a short time but by now everyone knew he always had a book in hand. His was the only room that didn't have a television. He had asked for it to be removed on his very first day.

"Richard?" said Victor with an inquisitive tone.

There was a pause, he saw the slippers move a little and a robed man with wispy white hair peaked through thick glasses from behind the wall. Victor could see the book still clutched in the ex-priest's hand with a bony finger inserted between pages.

"Yes," he answered.

Victor stepped into the doorway and asked "It is you, isn't it? The same Richard who was admitted to the hospital after being run over by a truck forty or so years ago?"

What little of Richard's face Victor could see took on a perplexed look as he replied "What? How would you know that?"

"The same Father Richard who had the most miraculous recovery, you don't recognize me do you, Father Richard?"

"Should I, Victor?" he asked, ignoring the fact that Victor kept calling him Father. He inserted the bookmark into his book noting his page carefully. "At seventy-nine my memory isn't quite as sharp as it used to be."

"Until I recognized you, I thought I didn't know a soul in

Sleepy Meadows. Or even the entire town of Carlton for that matter. You know, the locals say nothing ever happens in Carlton."

"Oddly enough, that's also why I came here. To leave my old life behind, now I'm just Richard. A simple old man who likes to read as much as he can," said the ex-priest as he set his book on his nightstand. "Come in, Victor."

Victor walked into the room and pulled a chair from a small table in the room and sat down facing Richard. "I overheard the nurses talking about you after breakfast this morning. How you used to be a priest but didn't believe in God anymore."

"I suppose I shouldn't have told Maureen that part." Richard looked down at his feet in shame as he continued. "But I've never been one to lie."

"Is it true that you don't believe in God anymore?" asked Victor.

Richard looked Victor in the eyes and spoke. "I do have days when I think it would be easier if I still believed. But I also can't lie to myself either. I have seen too much sin in my lifetime. No man is perfect and so according to God we would all go to Hell now wouldn't we. All of us!"

Victor looked Richard in the eyes as he spoke with conviction. "God is not religion. God is not the Bible. I know they teach you different when you become a man of the cloth but that is not it."

"Do you believe in God?" asked Richard.

"God does exist, but not like most men think he does," replied Victor.

"I see a crucifix under that shirt of yours. How can you say that and wear a symbol of religion like that?"

"This," said Victor as he fished out a simple leather string from his shirt exposing a golden pendant of Jesus on the Cross. "I too have been studying religions, Father. And Jesus, the Son of God, really did walk the earth. I can tell you that for certain. But again, he was not the saint we all believe him to be. But he really was crucified even though it had nothing to do with the sins of man."

"I know many scholars of religion that would argue that fact," replied Richard.

"As do I, trust me!" said Victor as he got up and put the chair back in its original place at the small table. "Well, I'm getting very tired and need to go get some sleep."

"It was nice talking with you, Victor," said Richard reaching for his book.

With his back turned to Richard, Victor paused and asked "I have one more question for an ex-priest. If I may be so bold as to ask this question in hopes to get an honest answer."

Richard sat book in hand. "I'm an honest man, Victor. What do you want to know?"

"It's about confessions. Now that you are no longer a man of the cloth, are you still bound to your oaths of secrecy, or have you cast those aside as well?"

"I am an honest man, Victor. But I do still feel bound by the trust placed in me by those who confided in me. Those are things I will take to my grave, God or no God."

Satisfied with that answer, Victor left the room without saying another word.

Richard sat quietly for a moment as he recalled the beginning of their conversation. Victor had not explained how he knew about his past. How could he have known these things? He had told no one at Sleepy Meadows about the details that Victor knew about him. He would have to speak to Victor again. But only later as for now he wanted to know what happened next as he cracked open his book yet again.

12

The sound the man's shoes made on the old cobblestone street echoed against the stone buildings on this otherwise quiet afternoon. A feeling of eerie silence swept over the man as he noticed the place was devoid of any signs of life. A strange thing he thought, especially for such a beautiful sunny, summer's day in the streets of London. The lone walker paused as he looked up and down the seemingly abandoned streets. He pulled out a silken handkerchief, wiping the sweat from his brow as he adjusted his bowler hat.

A familiar sound came from behind him. A wagon pulled by a single horse suddenly appeared, gliding past him. No driver sat on the wagon. Odd, thought the man. At that moment he heard a sound from above. A quick glance in that direction reveals nothing. Then a sound behind hind now causes the hair to rise on his neck at full attention. But in the blink of an eye the blue sky and sun were gone, the sky now dark and full of stars. He felt a sudden chill in the air as his breath appeared before him in a mist. Before he could form a rational thought in his head, he heard the sound again from above. He turned, looking up towards the rooftop of the stone building he stood next to only to see a shadow of a man hurtling through the air towards him.

13

At that moment, a fully clothed Victor awoke, sitting up in his bed. He rubbed a cold hand on his neck for a moment, looking about the room. His thick curtains made the room a sombre blend of shadows for the middle of a sunny fall day.

"Are you alright?" A woman's voice spoke from the doorway.

"Yes, yes I am. Just a bad dream is all," replied Victor as he lay down again, turning on his side. Peggy stood at the door for a moment, watching. She was waiting for Victor to maybe stop breathing or show signs of a heart attack. When she heard snoring, she calmed herself and walked away.

14

The first thing Peggy saw as she made her way into Richard's room was his book laying on the floor by a slipper covered foot. The first time she had seen this, panic had welled up over her that very instant. She had thought her worst fears had finally come true. In her short time working at Sleepy Meadows, her fear was finding one of her aging resident's lifeless body. The first time she'd seen it she had dropped the tray of medications, scattering an array of multicoloured pills all over the floor. Today she walked in casually, placing the tray of medications on the small table in the room. She proceeded to pick up the book while looking at the cover. A battered copy of *I, Robot* by Isaac Asimov in her hand made her wonder why a man of God would read such science fiction.

"It's a really good book," said Richard as he wiped drool from his chin.

"You like this stuff?" she asked as she fetched Richard's medications.

"There are so many books I never read while I was in the priesthood."

With a smile she handed him his medication. Richard swallowed the pills, washing them down with a cup of water.

"How's Agnes today?" asked Richard. "I didn't see her at breakfast this morning."

Peggy picked up her tray and turned to face Richard. "She isn't well. I don't understand it because she has had so many good days lately and her appetite had improved too."

"That's a shame. Is she still asking for Lenard?" asked a concerned Richard.

"She's completely lost. Damn I hate that Darcy! He says to me this morning; 'Agnes's cheese finally slid completely off her cracker.'" Peggy frowned showing her disgust. She looked down at the tray with a look of sadness as she continued. "She's got bad bruises. Darcy says she fell yesterday when he went to get her."

Richard's shoulders slumped low as if discouraged. He fiddled with his book before looking up at Peggy. "How long has Victor been living here at Sleepy Meadows?"

Peggy, while still holding her tray in front of her replied. "A couple of years, maybe more. Why?"

"It's just something he said to me, that's all. My mind isn't as sharp as it used to be you know."

Peggy smiled and shot a quick glance at the book in his hand saying. "Well it's sharper than mine if you understand that kinda science fiction."

Richard smiled as she walked out of the room. He took a moment to reflect on their conversation before opening his well-used book. Thinking about Agnes and how much he liked her. He felt bad that it had come to this, but this is what it had to be he thought. Setting his bookmark down on his lap, he opened the book and let Isaac Asimov take him to another time.

15

Victor sat quietly in his room fingering his rosary when he heard the sound of shuffling feet at his doorway. Without looking, he knew who stood in his doorway.

"Hello, Father Richard. What are you doing up at this hour?" asked Victor.

"I thought you didn't believe in religion?" asked the ex-priest.

Victor paused, looking at the beads in his hand. "I don't. But they bring me comfort," replied Victor as he laid the light brown wooden beads in his lap.

Standing at the door with his hands in the pockets of his robe, Richard spoke. "I have been struggling for the last few days, trying to understand what you said to me. How you knew about the time I got run over by that drunk driver and nearly died."

"Father Blanchard. The drunken priest who ran you over and never even noticed," said Victor as he watched Richard's face grow pale. "You had a punctured lung, two broken legs and you were bleeding internally. You should have died that day."

"I know," said Richard. "Everybody always told me it was a miracle that I survived. The only part I remember is having the worst nightmares of my life during the weeks I spent in and out of consciousness."

Victor gestured for Richard to come in. He pointed towards a chair by the small table. "You also had severe head trauma as well."

"I was in the hospital for months. Give or take, I can't really remember how long it was," said Richard as he sat in the wooden chair by the table.

"One thing I do remember is an orderly. A man whom, now that I think of it, reminds me of you. My memory of that time is a bit hazy, but you do look very much like him. Was he your father perhaps?" asked the ex-priest.

"What do you remember about him?" asked Victor.

"I remember that he visited me often. Especially after he learned that I was a priest. He would sit with me and talk to me about God. I don't remember much about it because I was still in pretty bad shape and very heavily medicated."

"Anything else?" asked Victor.

"The memories are really very fuzzy. I remember pieces but I know he visited often. I remember he would talk to me. I remember the day that I became lucid; he asked me if I would hear his confession."

"You told me no. You said you didn't feel well enough yet to hear it even though you already had," said Victor.

"I don't understand?" replied a confused Richard.

"I would talk to you when you were unconscious. Tell you things."

"That was forty years ago. I have no memory of that," said a confused Richard.

"Thirty-seven years ago to be precise," replied Victor.

"I'm pretty sure I would remember you."

"You knew me as Patrick Dubois," replied Victor.

"Patrick?" replied Richard with a slight French accent in the pronunciation.

"Yes. But I am Victor now."

"I don't understand," replied the perplexed former priest.

"Can I count on you to keep my secret, Father?"

Richard just stared on in confusion as if Victor had just spoken a foreign language. Both men remained silent for a moment until the former priest broke the silence first.

"I don't remember much about Patrick. I do remember that he was not a young man thirty-nine years ago."

"Thirty-seven. Thirty-seven years ago," said Victor. "And I've never forgotten you."

"Thirty-seven years ago I was in my early forties and Patrick was an old man."

"Yes I was. Quite old." Victor smiled as he picked up the rosary from his lap and ran it through his fingers. "Quite old indeed."

"How can that be?" asked Richard.

"Did you hear about Agnes?" asked Victor.

"Yes. Yes I have. Peggy told me she is not doing well."

"I don't think she has more than a day or two left. Sad really, but she'll have a good day tomorrow," said Victor as he got up from his chair. Looking down at the still seated Richard. "Will you keep my secret like I asked?"

"Yes. Yes of course," replied Richard as he struggled to get up from the wooden chair. "Do you know about Agnes's bruises?"

Victor paused for a moment, fingered the rosary in his hand, turned his back to Richard and spoke. "Yes. Yes I do. She is quite lost and has been rather difficult the last few days. She must have stumbled trying to get out of bed again. Maybe even fell."

"Most likely," added Richard as he fixed his slipper and made his way out.

Victor turned on the light in his bathroom as he watched the fallen priest walk out of sight. "She'll have a good day tomorrow. She deserves that much."

16

Lying in her bed, Agnes opened her eyes and saw only darkness surrounding her. Her mind in a fog, she was unable to tell where she was and that began to frighten her. Shivers ran down her spine when she felt a presence in the room with her. In this complete lack of light she could only suspect it to be the mysterious silhouette of a man. An unidentified stranger that had repeatedly visited her but she had never seen. Holding her breath, she listened carefully for anything that would confirm her suspicions. In that moment, the cobwebs smothering her thoughts seemed to fade away. She clutched at her blankets pulling them towards her chin. Even though her blankets were thick she felt a hand come to rest on her thigh. A sudden calming feeling of familiarity washed over her. Somehow she knew her mysterious visitor had returned. Her consciousness swooned about her and soon, sweat beaded on her brow and upper lip. Her chill now gone, the dizzying darkness swirled around her for a moment until her mind grew clear again.

"Lenard!" shouting as she awoke from her dream. Her eyes adjusting to her dimly lit room of the Sleepy Meadows residence to see a silhouette standing by her bed.

17

"It's Victor, not Lenard," the man said.

"I know that you old fool. Lenard's been dead for a very long time now," said the bright and alert silver-haired old lady. "I was dreaming but I can't remember much about it."

"I just wanted to make sure you're ok. Are you?" asked Victor as he reached for a tray that rested on the nightstand.

"Yes, yes. I'm fine. Hungry, but fine," said Agnes as she struggled to sit up. "When did I get so damned old?" she asked impatiently struggling to sit up.

Victor helped her prop herself up and placed some pillows behind her. He watched her sink in them as if tired out from the effort it took to sit up. Sitting on the edge of the bed, he placed the tray in front of Agnes. "I brought you some of those soft raisin cookies you like and some tea," he said with a smile.

The old woman smiled as her eyes widened. "Oh thank you. Lenard would have liked you, Victor. You're such a kind man."

Victor smiled as he watched her savour each bite. With a cookie in each hand, chewing with glee as she hungrily looked at the four other cookies in the plate before her. Agnes would have a good day just as Victor predicted earlier that night. A long conversation followed about Lenard and how they never had children because it was God's will. How instead, she had spent most of her life teaching young children and loved every moment of it. Soon an hour had passed before caregiver Amanda had found the pair enthralled in conversation.

Walking in with an arm-full of linens, Amanda spoke. "Victor, you little devil. You're keeping our sweet Agnes awake. She needs her rest more than you."

A bright-eyed Agnes snapped back with a sly grin. "Oh shush, girl. I haven't had this much fun chatting up a storm in a lonnnng time."

Amanda froze in her tracks as parts of the linen slipped from her grasp and dangled towards the floor.

"It's ok, Agnes. I have a few things to do anyway. I will see you at breakfast," said Victor. As he exited the room, he could hear the women talking behind him. He could hear Agnes ask Amanda if she had ever told her about her lovely, late husband Lenard.

18

Darcy walked into the staffroom only to be greeted by the sound of laughter. After a rotten morning he was thinking his mood couldn't possibly get any worse only to be proven wrong as he arrived for his shift.

Amanda's arms were flailing about wildly as she spoke to Jenna. "I know. I couldn't believe my ears at first!"

Opening his locker, Darcy spoke. "What are you so freaked out about?"

Jenna replied. "Agnes. She is having a good day today. A very good day!"

"Really?" asked Darcy.

"I know. Jenna didn't believe me either until she saw for herself."

"Yeah, well don't get too excited like the last time because it won't last," said a sour Darcy while changing his shoes.

"You asshole! You always have to ruin things don't you," said Amanda as she slammed her locker shut and stormed out.

"What?" Darcy said while pretending as if he didn't know why she was upset.

"Victor asked if you could come by his room later to help fix his curtain rod," said Amanda.

"Yeah, whatever," replied Darcy. "If I have time."

19

Darcy is a tall dark mid-thirties man, whom after years of working at Sleepy Meadows, was well known by all. There are many kind-hearted employees and then there are those few who are just doing their job. Darcy is one of the caregivers that most residence know to tread lightly around. Quick tempered, he is a very impatient man, often getting angry with the residents when they don't comply. Many grew to fear his bouts of aggression. Unless you spoke to the ones who are subjected to illnesses that affected the memory. In those cases, they often forgot that Darcy was an impatient man and sometimes were left with reminders in the form of bruises. Sadly, many of those reminders would soon be forgotten where they came from. Many of the staff suspected he was sometimes abusive and would not have tolerated it if they knew the truth. Nobody had ever caught him in the act, and the residents were too afraid to speak up. Agnes's latest set of bruises on her dark brown skin were not a result of her clumsy weakened self. They were a result of her feeble attempts to resist Darcy's efforts to take her to her bath time. But one resident knew this. One of the few who was still very keen of mind, even though he was older than any of the other residents by a great many decades.

Standing in the doorway, Darcy saw the old man sitting in his chair and staring up at the curtain. It had come apart from the rod a bit on the left side and hung limply, exposing the window beneath. Below it was the wooden chair that normally sat before the matching small table in the room.

"How'd you manage to do that now, Victor?" asked a clearly unimpressed Darcy.

"I tried to fix it but every time I get up on the chair, my head starts to spin and I feel like I'm going to fall," said Victor meekly. "Maureen made me promise to wait until you could fix it for me."

"She would do that now wouldn't she? Sweet little Maureen." Darcy stepped up onto the chair. "I should take this all down. I don't know why they let you put up this stupid blanket anyway. Sleeping all day and staying up all night is for young kids, not an old man like you," said Darcy as he placed the last hook back into place pinning up the dark thick blanket. "You happy now, Victor?" asked Darcy as he felt a hand on his ankle. Looking down he saw Victor who now had his cold, surprisingly strong hand wrapped around his right ankle.

"Yes, yes I am," said Victor as he grasped Darcy's belt with his other hand as a sharp searing arthritic pain shot through it. Victor quickly lifted Darcy so his feet no longer touched the chair and throwing him down with all his might. For a split-second, it was as if Darcy weighted the same as a small child. He hit the tile floor hard, bones snapping in his right arm as he tried to break his fall. Dazed from hitting his head, he groaned from the pain in his arm while looking up at Victor. The old man knelt next to him on the floor and placed both his aching hands on either side of Darcy's head, lifting slightly and then bashing his head on the hard floor. A snapping and crunching sound echoed in the room as blood flowed from the fresh wound he had just inflicted.

Still kneeling, Victor watched the blood pool around Darcy's lifeless head. He groped his wrist in an attempt to sooth his arthritis. He lazily ran his index finger through the pool of blood, lifted it and stared at the blood for a moment as it dripped down the finger, before inserting it into his mouth. His eyes closed, savouring it like someone might savour a bowl of home made icing. Getting up to the sound of popping, aching joints, Victor made his way to the door of his room only to pause and look back at Darcy's lifeless body. Reaching into his pocket he felt the beads of his rosary with his fingers.

"God forgive me," he spoke softly under his breath. Walking out of the room, Victor stopped in mid step just as he turned into the corridor as his eyes caught a glimpse of something on the floor before him. A book lay facedown with a bookmark protruding out of the well-read pages. He bent down to pick it up. Popping joints echoed in the hallway as he straightened. Turning the book over and reading the text on the cover.

I, Robot by Isaac Asimov.

"Good morning, Victor. Did Richard loan you his book?" asked Peggy as she came from up the hallway.

"Peggy. Dear, I'm sorry to have to tell you this but Darcy's had an accident in my room while he was fixing my curtain for me."

Rounding the corner, her knees buckled at the sight of all the blood. She never expected it to be this bad.

"Oh my God!" she uttered aloud without realizing she had vocalized her horror at the sight of Darcy. She ran out as fast as she could.

Victor looked at the book in his hand and then down the hall behind him suspiciously.

20

The next morning Maureen sat across the table from Jenna in the staff room with a sad look on her face. "You know, Jenna. It sucked having to find out on Facebook that Darcy died."

"I know. That's how I heard too. By noon the whole town of Carlton was buzzing with the gossip."

Maureen added "I feel bad for saying this, but he wasn't my favourite person, you know."

Jenna patted her hand saying "Don't feel bad. He wasn't very high up on my list either, deary."

Maureen sipped her tea and asked. "I wonder how Victor is?

It must have traumatised him to have that happen in his room."

Jenna smile slightly. "Victor? He's fine. He worked in hospitals most of his life. He seen more blood and death than all the staff of Sleepy Meadows combined, I think. At least that's what he implied when I asked him how he was." Jenna took a gulp of coffee from her cardboard cup with the brown plastic lid. "It's not Victor I'm worried about. It's Richard that worries me."

Looking down into her porcelain cup, Maureen added "I know. As a priest, he's seen death a lot too. But, he used to have God to help him deal with it. And finding Agnes dead in her bed must have been hard for him."

"Dead. And after the best day she had in years," added Jenna.

Maureen sipped the last of her tea and looked into the empty cup. "I've never gotten use to losing our seniors. I mean you get attached and they get to be like family." Brushing away a tear, she got up to put her cup in the kitchen sink.

21

Peggy tugged at the clean sheets, making sure they weren't too tight for the next resident who would move into Agnes's old room. Pausing to smell the fresh linen, she stuffed one of the pillows into a pillowcase.

"Peggy," a voice called behind her, startling her so much she fumbled with the pillow, catching it before it hit the floor. She turned, hand to her chest as she felt her heart race. Richard stood in the doorway.

"You scared me," she said with a smile, laughing at herself.

"Sorry to bother you but have you seen my book?" asked Richard. "I seemed to have misplaced it."

"No I haven't, Father Richard." She spoke with a serious look. "But I do have something for you. Agnes, before she died, she asked Victor to make sure that you got this." She reached into the pocket of her uniform and pulled out a balled-up hand. Taking the ex-priest's hand in hers and turning it palm up. She opened her hand and out fell a clumped up blue rosary.

"She said it was her late husband's. She wanted you to have it." Peggy closed Richard's hand gently over it and looks into his eyes. "I hope that's ok. He asked me to give it to you. It's one of the last things she asked him to do when they last spoke. Not long before she passed away."

Richard didn't speak as he placed the rosary in the pocket of his robe and left the room.

A few moments later, with his hand in his pocket fingering the beads, he walked into his room to find *I, Robot* sitting on the pillow on his bed. Puzzled, he looked about as if expecting to see someone standing there but there was no one. Shrugging to himself, Richard scooped up the book and sat in his chair, removed the bookmark and without looking away from his page, placed the bookmark on the nightstand.

22

The next morning, Peggy walking past the dimly lit dining room, noticed a lone person sitting at the end of a table near the kitchen. The old lady stared toward the kitchen in anticipation, as if waiting for someone to come out at any moment. Squinting, Peggy walked closer to see who it was. She made her way towards the wall were the light switches were. In a moment of recognition, she spoke. "Florence? Is that you?"

"Oh, deary!" Florence looked confused in that moment.

"What are you doing here all by yourself?" asked Peggy meekly.

"I'm starving. What time is it?" asked Florence with a look of confusion.

"It's almost breakfast time, you poor dear. I'll go see if I can get you something right away, sweetie."

"Blueberry pancakes!" said a smiling Florence as she fished her teeth from her pocket and picked the lint off them. Muttering she said to herself "I'd love me some blueberry pancakes with butter and syrup right now."

Peggy emerged shortly from the kitchen with a plateful of exactly what Florence had asked for. She was smiling at Florence as she set the plate down before the old lady.

"Oh, thank you!" said Florence as she scooped up the fork and knife, the confused look was gone now that she had food before her. And not just any food, her blueberry pancakes with butter and maple syrup. Her favourite syrup, which was made right there in her home town of Carlton!

Peggy pulled a chair and sat near Florence. "I guess it pays to be a regular at this fine restaurant, huh Florence. I didn't even have to ask. He'd already had it made for you."

Finding residents sitting there waiting to eat had become a regular occurrence. So much so that most of the cooks came in early and always peaked into the dining room to see if anyone would be anxiously awaiting their breakfast that day. Today it was Florence's turn it seemed.

Florence smiled at Peggy with a mouthful as syrup dribbled down her chin.

"Did you sleep well, deary?" asked Peggy. "Are the pills helping?"

Florence swallowed her mouthful before replying. "Oh yes. I sleep soundly now. I never even woke up when Victor came to see me last night."

A warm feeling washed over Peggy when Florence smiled again. For the first time since her husband Cecile's passing, she looked happy. And even though it might only last a few moments of blueberry bliss, Peggy would sit here and enjoy every moment of it. This is the reason she loved her job.

23

Richard could feel the arthritic pain in his crackling joints as he walked towards Florence's table. She sat sipping tea in front of a slew of empty plates, bowls and saucers. But before reaching her table, he stopped at the table next to her where Victor sat alone. Before him was a full and untouched bowl of oatmeal, he sat sipping what smelled like herbal tea.

"Good morning, Father Richard," spoke Victor emphasising the word father without turning around.

Richard paused before speaking. He looked straight ahead not wanting to look at the man seated next to him. "Agnes didn't really ask you to give me her rosary did she?"

"No, she didn't. But how would you have known that?"

Richard's right hand reached into his pocket, past the book to finger the rosary that was clumped up underneath it. "Her rosary was brown; not blue."

"I didn't think you knew that."

Richard, still looking in Florence's direction, spoke. "I saw what really happened to Darcy."

Victor's calm demeanour didn't change. "I had to. While I still had the strength, I had to." Victor set down his cup of tea before him. "Are you going to tell on me?" he asked.

Ignoring the question, Richard replied "How could a man of God do such a thing?"

Victor, tea in hand, replied. "I couldn't let him hurt Agnes again." Squeezing the thick porcelain cup with mounting anger, a snapping sound echoed as he looked down to see the cup's handle, broken into four pieces before feeling a jolt of pain shoot through his wrist and up his forearm.

Richard walked away, smiling at Florence as he grasped the chair next to her.

"Mind if I join you?" He pulled the chair out before her reply.

"Father Richard. Please do," she said with a smile as she watched him sit next to her.

For the first time in a long time, Richard didn't mind that she had called him Father. He had no idea why he was ok with it as his faith had not been restored. Especially after witnessing Victor, a man of God, kill another man.

"You must have been hungry this morning by the looks of all these empty plates," said Richard.

"I was famished." Florence smiled calmly. "Have I ever told you about the time Cecile and I went to Disneyland?"

24

Late that night, Richard watched Maureen as she walked down the hall with an armload of clean towels. She rounded a corner and disappeared into Agnes's old room. Had someone already moved in he wondered, as he made his way down the hall to investigate.

"Oh dear!" A startled Maureen exclaimed as she saw Richard standing in the doorway in his black housecoat holding a cup in one hand and a book in the other.

"I didn't mean to startle you," he said as he peered into the room. "Has someone moved in yet?" he inquired.

"A Miss Palmer is moving in tomorrow. Poor old girl has Alzheimer's and the family can't take care of her anymore."

"Have you seen Victor?" asked Richard. "He's not in his room."

Maureen picked up the dirty towels and walked to the doorway. "He never is this late at night. He always wanders the halls and visits those who can't sleep. You want me to tell him to go see you?"

"That's ok. I'm going to finish my tea and read a little. Maybe I'll check on Florence first though."

"Ok, Father Richard. Just don't wake her up. Ok?"

"Oh, I won't," replied Richard.

25

All was quiet as Richard peered into Florence's room. He expected to see her sleeping, alone in her room. Instead, to his surprise, he saw Victor standing next to the bed. He was in the process of fixing her blankets while Florence slept soundly. Victor was already looking directly at Richard as if he had heard him coming. Large beads of sweat glistened on Florence's face as she shivered in her bed.

"Is she sick?" asked Richard.

"She'll be fine in a few minutes," replied Victor.

Richard, not knowing what to think about that statement

could only ask. "How do you know that?"

"Trust me, Father Richard." Victor spoke with a slight scowl of annoyance.

Richard gestured, book in hand, towards Victor asking. "Is- is that blood on your shirt?"

Victor looked down to see a few spots as big as dimes, maybe even nickels on the front of his shirt. He ignored this comment, walked over and placed his hand on the ex-priests back guiding him towards the door.

Richard stopped at the door, looked Victor in the eyes and spoke. "I've been meaning to talk to you about the morning that Darcy died. About what I saw."

Victor, expressionless, replied. "Why don't you and I go sit down somewhere quiet so we can talk? I'll get us some tea and come by your room."

26

Upon entering the ex-priest's room, Victor noticed the blue rosary hanging off the wood ball of the headboard. Fighting back a grin, he carried the tray containing tea and date squares to the small table in the room.

"Sit. Please," Richard said as he gestured to the second chair he'd set out especially for Victor.

After setting the tray down on the table, Victor spoke as he sat. "Tell me, Father Richard, what is it that you saw that day?"

Richard spoke softly. "I'm not sure what I saw. Maybe my old eyes played tricks on me because I could have sworn I saw you lift him up, so his feet were not touching the chair he stood on. Only to throw him like he weighed nothing, like he was nothing but a plastic doll." Shifting uneasily in his chair he continued. "I've seen much larger men than you, younger and stronger, who wouldn't be able to do what I saw you do." Victor sat quietly watching Richard carefully as the former priest continued speaking in a hushed tone. "And then you cracked open his skull on the floor like it was a soft melon." Richard looked at his old hands and then looked at Victor. "My joints ache. I can't even open a prescription bottle anymore. I don't have the strength."

Victor picked up his cup calmly as he spoke. "He was hurting Agnes and others too. Some of these people are lost to the world now and don't know any better. Why should they have to suffer at the hands of that bastard?"

"Do you think God will forgive you for that?" asked Richard.

Victor smiled slightly at the thought of a man who had lost his faith, now asking about his. "Do you?"

Ignoring the reply, Richard pointed to Victor's swollen knuckles and asked. "How could a man of your advanced age, with arthritis as bad as you have it? How could you possibly manage to kill a large brute like Darcy?"

Victor sipped his tea. Looking up from his cup at the old man before him and asked "Can I trust you to keep my secrets?"

"Yes, of course," Richard said.

"Swear to God?" asked Victor.

"If it makes you feel better to hear me swear to your God then why not. Yes, I swear to God."

Victor glanced at the rosary hanging from the bed post and sipped his tea. "You know, Father Richard, this is not the first time we've had this conversation." Victor watched Richard take up his cup of tea as he added. "But I suppose you were heavily medicated the first time we spoke thirty-seven years ago."

Richard replied, "I vaguely recall the time I spent hospitalized, especially the early weeks."

"You see, I'm not like the other residents here at Sleepy Meadows. I'm from London, England you know."

"London? But you don't have an accent?" said Richard inquisitively.

"It took a very long time, but I eventually lost it. I'm very old, much older than anyone in this place you know."

"Victor, are you ok?" asked Richard as he sipped his tea.

Victor spoke as he watched Richard's reaction carefully. "I'm what most would call a vampire, Father Richard. Although nothing like in the books you're reading or in the movies; I don't turn into a bat you know."

Richard, speechless and dumbfounded for the first time in his life said nothing as he fumbled his cup of tea, which was now near empty. Victor took the cup from Richard and set it down on the tray. He smiled at Richard. "No, Father Richard; I am not crazy. I really am a vampire. You see, Father; vampirism is more like a disease." Victor glanced towards the door to make sure no one could hear him.

Richard spoke. "But you're a man of God."

Victor took on a more serious tone as he continued. "Yes. Yes I am a man of God. God is real. And just like vampires, He isn't what most of mankind thinks Him to be."

Richard shook his head in disbelief as he pointed a finger at Victor and smiled. "If you really are a vampire, then what are you doing in this place? And vampires don't have arthritis."

"Don't they? I didn't realize that priests studied vampirism." Victor smiled. "I know it's hard to believe. Especially since what I am telling you is not what popular fiction has ingrained in your mind. Vampires are not immortal gods. The disease does slow down aging, but it doesn't mean you get to live forever. And you're not immune to all the problems that plague the normal man either. Yes. Yes I have arthritis. I wish I didn't."

"But you have no fangs," said the ex-priest. "Vampires have fangs. How else would they drink blood? And I've seen you up during the day." Richard waved a finger at Victor pointing. "You have a crucifix under your shirt for Christ's sake! Do you really believe that you're a vampire?" asked Richard.

"I know it's hard to imagine since men have made vampires out to be evil monsters. We're infected people and that's all. Yes, I have a rosary and I pray for forgiveness everyday for the things I have to do to survive." Victor sat forward on the edge of his chair and looked Richard in the eyes as he spoke. "I don't know how it happens, but the fangs come out just enough when I feed. The teeth don't grow but the gums push them out. Daylight doesn't kill vampires. But our flesh is dying and the ultraviolet rays speed that up. That's why most of us shun the light as much as we can."

Richard suddenly felt like he would be sick. His head spun and his stomach churned. Panic arose in him as he could see in Victor's eyes that he truly believed what he was saying.

"I'm dying, Father Richard. Maybe not as fast as some of the residents in here but my body is shutting down." Victor spoke with conviction. "My body is rejecting the blood and I can't feed like I need to. My body is dying."

Richard leaned forward and rested his hand on Victor's and spoke with sincerity. "Vampires don't die, Victor. You're not a vampire. Would you like me to talk to someone for you?"

Victor pulled his hand away from Richard and sat back in his chair. "You asked me the same thing thirty-seven years ago when I told you then. I'm not crazy, Father. You see, vampires' age and they die. Most can only get the disease at a young age when the body is stronger. Otherwise it can't survive. And young vampires need to feed more often and it becomes like a lust." Victor hung his head, looking at his feet as he continued. "I was young once. And like most young, you feed too much and innocent people die because of your need to feed. But as you get older, your body begins to breakdown and you don't need to feed as much. That's what allowed me to find God again. Beg his forgiveness for what I had done." Victor reached into his pocket and pulled out his rosary and ran the light brown beads through his fingers. "When I aged and my lust subsided, I made a vow never to kill again." Looking up at Richard's expressionless face, he continued speaking. "I began looking for ways to feed without killing. That's when I met Luanne. She was a nurse at the Boston General Hospital. She was one of the many nurses who took care of the comatose patience. Finally, I had found a way where I could feed without killing. Not long after I began volunteering to sit with terminally ill patients which gave me access to what I needed. I've never killed since. Not until Darcy came along anyway."

Richard started to rise from his chair but stumbled back into it. The room spun around him and he could no longer feel his legs. He tried to speak, but an incomprehensible slur was all that Victor heard. His glasses slipping off his face almost falling to the floor before Victor caught them in one swift motion.

"I put one of Florence's sleeping pills in your tea. I'm sorry but I need to do this so you believe me. You're going to have a bad dream and when you wake up, you will feel incredibly hungry. You might even feel better than normal. I never understood why, but in the elderly it has a bit of a rejuvenating effect."

Richard began to stand again and this time, Victor helped him get up. He stumbled forward slightly as he felt Victor's strong grasp hold him up. "Let's get you to bed, Father," said Victor as he helped the ex-priest to his bed.

Richard wouldn't remember lying down in his bed. Sleep came before his head was rested on his pillow.

27

The smell of all the old wood washed over him as he saw that all the pews were filled to capacity. On the pulpit before him rested his sermon, written in Latin just like he used to do. Raising his hands before him, the robed Father Richard spoke. His voice was muffled, inaudible even to his own ears. Looking down where his sermon had lain now sat a book.

The Adventures of Huckleberry Finn by Mark Twain.

His arms still up with his palms towards the sky he paused in mid-muffled sentence. Looking up from the pulpit only to see the pews now completely empty and void of life. He lowered his arms slowly. The book on the pulpit was also gone. As the room began to spin, the priest tugged at his collar as beads of perspiration appeared on his brow. He turned to see a dark silhouette of a man standing in an otherwise brightly lit church. The dark man took a step closer just as the room grew dark before Richard's very eyes.

28

"Dear God!" uttered Richard as he woke in a panic. He shot up into a sitting position; groggy from awakening in such a hurry. A slight burning sensation in his left arm soon had him pulling up the sleeve of his pyjamas. On the inside of his left arm he found two small puncture marks. Richard rubbed his eyes as he realized that they were in perfect focus even though his glasses sat on his nightstand. Not having been able to see without his glasses in over twenty years, he sat in wonderment staring at the tiny marks on his arm. That's when the hunger pangs made him look at the clock on his wall; he still had an hour to wait until breakfast.

"Pancakes!" Richard said aloud as he found himself with a sudden craving for pancakes. With syrup made right in Carlton. And he wanted them now.

29

Richard sat before a slew of empty plates, completely stuffed, having eaten twice what he normally ate for breakfast. Leaning back in his chair, and suppressing a burp to be polite, he noticed Victor approaching him.

Victor spoke as he set down his tray containing his oatmeal and tea. "I noticed you forgot to put on your glasses this morning, Father."

Richard's hand immediately felt for them on his face as he smiled. "Yes. Yes I did. I'm so used to needing them that I can still feel them on my face, even though I am not wearing them."

Victor sat down. "Don't get too used to it. You'll need them again by later today, tonight at the latest."

Richard leaned forward, clasping his hands together before him and resting his arms on the table as he spoke softly. "I had a dream last night, a horrible yet peaceful dream. A man came to me. I couldn't see who he was. But I know it was you."

Victor ran his spoon through his oatmeal as he spoke. "I can't explain the dreams. I've been living with this a very long time and have learned a lot but I don't know what causes the dreams." He took a spoonful and put it in his mouth. Swallowing, he continued speaking. "I think it might be the same thing that rejuvenated you. I'm not sure."

He paused and set his spoon down. Dazed, he stared blankly into his bowl before him. "I too have dreams. Every single night I dream of the day I was cursed with this wretched disease. I was a young man walking the streets of London when he fell upon me."

"I don't understand how you've never gotten caught. Nobody has ever told anyone what you did to them. How can that be?" asked Richard.

In a hushed tone, Victor replied. "It wasn't always like it is now. But that's why I now have to feed on those who are not well anymore. They don't understand what has happened." Making eye contact with Richard, he continued. "Really, I give them good days in return. Tell me you don't feel good right this minute. Tell me your aches and pains are almost non-existent right now."

"I do feel remarkably good, physically that is. But emotionally, spiritually, I can't say the same." Richard paused as if in deep thought and asked. "Will I turn into one now? Will I become a vampire too?"

"No," replied Victor without hesitation.

"How do you know that?" asked Richard.

Victor watched Richard's expression as he spoke. "Because I didn't take enough blood from you. I don't know how it works but I need to take a lot of blood for the person to change. I haven't had to feed that much in a long time you know." Victor smiled slightly and sighed as he saw a look that he believed to be disappointment on the ex-priest's face. "I'm really very old. And tired; very tired." Victor sipped his tea and waited for a caregiver to walk past them with her resident so they would not hear him continue. "Besides, some are immune. And you would have turned thirty-seven years ago when I fed on you then. I know because I tried to turn you then." Victor watched as Richard's face grew long and pale. "I thought you would die from your injuries otherwise. I think I helped save your life. The internal bleeding wasn't as bad because of me."

"Immune?" was all that Richard could ask in the shock of what he had just been told.

"When I saw you here for the first time, I recognized you," said Victor. "And so I took it as a sign from God. But I don't know what He is trying to tell me and I was hoping you could help me figure that out."

Richard got up from his chair and pushed it slowly back under the table. He stood behind it for a moment in silence before speaking. "Maybe. Or maybe you're a sign from God to me." Richard inserted his hands in the pockets of his housecoat as he walked off. He paused and glanced back at Victor who sat in stunned silence as he pondered the ex-priest's words.

30

The door of the staffroom burst open as Peggy ran in. "There you are!" she exclaimed when she saw Jenna and Maureen as they were getting ready to go home.

"What are you so excited about?" asked Jenna with a huge smile. "Got some juicy gossip, don't you?"

"You'll never guess," said Peggy.

"What? What is it?" replied Maureen.

Peggy was smiling as she wiped away a tear. "Richard. I just saw him go into the chapel."

Maureen smiled at the thought and then the smile vanished as fast as it had appeared. "I wonder what brought this on? I hope he's ok."

31

Entering the empty chapel, the first impression the ex-priest had was how much it reminded him of the very first church he celebrated mass in. On a smaller scale, a mere quarter of his church, it had the same wood moulding to everything he could see. There were fewer pews than he though it should, but he knew this was to leave room for wheelchairs. The smell of the lemon-scented cleaner was strong, almost overpowering the smell of the wood varnish itself. Paintings on the walls made to imitate stain glass windows. Unlike all the churches he had been in, this one had cream coloured leather padding on the pews. And for this reason, he found them remarkably comfortable on his old stiff, arthritis-riddled body as he sat down. He felt at ease in the chapel, even though he was sitting in a pew and not standing at the pulpit.

"I don't know if you're real anymore. I haven't in quite some time now," said Richard as he looked up at the ceiling. "But I do feel that maybe you've sent Victor to me to test my faith. If you are real that is. And a part of me wants to believe what he tells me. But a part of me doubts it can be real." Richard pulled the blue rosary from the pocket of his robe. Holding it in his left hand, he slowly ran the beads through the fingers of his right. "Just like I doubt you are too. But right now, I feel maybe you are real. And sending Victor to me is your way of reminding me that you are."

Richard slid himself out of the pew and onto his knees. A few loud popping sounds came from his joints as he knelt, grasping the wood of the back of the pew before him, steadying himself. Once in the kneeling position and with his rosary intertwined in-between his fingers, Richard leaned his head forward as he had done a million times before. Only today, those words that he had said throughout his life escaped him. Try as he might, he could not recall the Lord's prayer.

He whispered "I'm lost. I've lost my way. Please help me find my way back."

Richard scrambled backwards as he slid himself back into the pew before trying to rise to his feet. Struggling on what were now numb legs only to fall back into the pew. Twice. He did succeed at the third attempt at getting to his feet and with blue rosary in hand he walked to the door before stopping in his tracks. With a look towards the large crucifix at the far end, he spoke.

"Maybe I'll come back and see you tomorrow."

Reaching out with an age-spotted hand; he pushed open the wooden door. Exiting the chapel, he saw Peggy turn away quickly, as if she had been waiting for him to exit the chapel. Which is exactly what she had been doing and he knew it. As he watched her round a bend and disappear into a room, he tried to place the blue rosary into his robe pocket. Hearing the clatter of the rosary hit the floor; he stumbled and looked down to see that his arm had barely moved. Looking at his hand he couldn't understand why but it felt as if it tingled all over. Like a million tiny needles prickling all over his hand and running up his arm. The rosary was on the floor before him and when he tried to step forward, his leg refused to cooperate as it stayed in the same place. His body lurched forward as he lost his balance and fell forward. His sight became blurred before he hit the floor. His mouth opened in an attempt to cry out but nothing came out but gargled incoherent sounds. The last thing he saw he was white stocking covered legs in small white sneakers running towards him. Hearing garbled shouts around him. Lying on the floor, Richard felt numbness envelope his senses as everything grew dark around him.

32

One week later, the staff room was empty of all the incoming staff. Empty, except two of the tired outgoing souls from the graveyard shift.

"Do you think God was punishing him?" asked Maureen as she sat changing her shoes.

"Don't be silly," replied Jenna as she slipped on her jacket followed by her scarf. "Although, you have to admit the coincidence is a little unnerving to say the least."

Maureen stood up from the chair she sat in and pulled her jacket from her locker. Slipping it on as she spoke. "Dr. Williams told me Richard will be back later today."

Jenna closed her locker. "How is he?"

"Well after five days, he recovered some mobility, but he is wheelchair bound now. Not strong enough to walk on his own." Maureen buttoned her coat and slipped her purse on her shoulder. "Only thing is Dr. Williams said his mind is starting to go. He says the stroke is the cause." She paused, inserting her hand in her pocket as she fingered her keys thinking of home. "For the last few days he thought he was back at Boston General Hospital forty or so years ago. Apparently, he had been in the hospital after being hit by a truck."

Jenna and Maureen gave each other knowing looks as they exited the staffroom, neither of them saying anything. Not wanting any of the residents to overhear them as they made their way out to the parking lot. Jenna took a deep breath, smelling the crisp fall air as she walked to her car. Maureen, with her hand in her pocket, pressed the remote, listening as her car started up.

"Dr. Williams said Richard can barely speak now. But the interesting part is that he thinks he's still a priest." She smiled slightly as she continued. "Now he wants to be called Father Richard and gets upset if you don't."

Jenna pressed her remote, unlocking her car door. She opened it and stepped behind the door as she spoke. "That's quite ironic."

"Yes. Yes it is," said Maureen as she turned and walked towards her car. "See you on Facebook!" she exclaimed.

33

Standing in the doorway, Victor watched as Richard lay in his new hospital bed with the side rails up as he snored gently. He couldn't help but notice the ex-priest looked to have aged twenty years in the last week. His thin white hair looked even thinner now, dishevelled. The lines on his face seemed deeper. Much deeper than before and this scared him. He had never realized what a lonely existence he had until Richard came along. It had been a very long time since he had been able to speak openly with anyone. Talking with the former priest had helped him appease the guilt he felt about feeding on the feeble residents of Sleepy Meadows. Victor slowly walked in and stood next to the bed, watching his friend for a moment before speaking.

"Richard?" he said softly. "Richard?"

Slowly Richard stirred as he opened his eyes. His speech slightly muffled he spoke. "Patrick? Is that you? Have you come to chat again?"

Victor's felt his hope sink as he heard the words spoken by Richard. At that moment he heard footsteps nearing the door behind him as caregiver Amanda entered the room.

"Did he just call you Patrick?" asked Amanda.

Victor sighed. "Yes. He's confused and doesn't remember me."

"How are you, Richard?" asked Amanda as she stood next to the bed.

"Father Richard. Please call me Father Richard. I can't wait until I can leave this hospital and get back to my parish."

"You need rest, Father Richard. Would you like me to bring you something to drink? Are you hungry, Father?" Amanda smiled gently.

"Tea. Tea would be nice. Thank you," said Richard.

Amanda walked past Victor on her way out. "I'll be right back with some tea. I'll see if he needs to use the bathroom or something in a minute."

Victor replied only by smiling slightly, trying not to show the sudden sharp pain in his side. After Amanda had left the room, Victor spoke. "I'll let you get some rest and come back to check on you later, Father Richard."

Victor turned and walked towards the door as he heard Richard reply, "Thank you, Patrick. You're a kind man. We will continue our talk later then. And your secret is safe with me."

Upon hearing this, Victor paused in his tracks for a moment before walking out.

34

While wandering the halls, Victor overheard Amanda talking to another caregiver from the evening shift. Standing at the entrance of a room in the Lost Ward, his sharp ears heard their conversation from around the corner and down the hall.

"He's still in pretty good shape so he won't have to change rooms. Not yet anyway. Not unless he gets worse." He heard a shuffling of feet before more was said.

"Yeah, he is definitely not ready for the Lost Ward," a female voice said.

"I hate it when you call it that," he heard Amanda say.

"Sorry," the voice replied as Victor walked into the room that he had stood before. The resident of this room would know brief clarity before the next morning came.

35

Later that night as Victor watched from a room in what many knew as the Lost Ward, he could see a stretcher being placed into the back of the Carlton ambulance. A scene he had gotten very accustomed to while living at Sleepy Meadows. The flashing red lights had caught his attention as they shone through the curtains and onto the walls around him. A creaking sound distracted him for a brief moment as he turned to see Lorraine, snuggled under her freshly tucked blankets as she began breaking out in a heavy sweat. Victor had fed tonight, taking what little his dying body would allow him to. Lorraine would have a good day tomorrow. However brief it would be, her day would be better than usual. In the past, this helped him to feel better about taking from these lost souls, but not this night.

A few hours later, Victor would overhear Maureen talking with Jenna while at the caregiver's station.

"Who did the ambulance take?" asked Jenna. She had spoken softly but Victor's sharp ears had still overheard her.

"You didn't hear?" he heard Maureen respond. "Father Richard. He had another stroke."

"Oh, dear God!" exclaimed Jenna.

Victor felt his spirit sink to a level he had forgotten was even possible as the reality of the situation swept over him.

36

It would be a week before Victor would see Father Richard again. This time the Father would be in his new room (which had been recently vacated) in the Lost Ward. He sat in a wheelchair as he drooled on himself, completely lost to the world around him.

"You don't remember me, do you?" asked Victor.

Richard could only mutter a garbled reply that Victor barely understood. It had sounded like Richard had asked if it was time to go to church yet. It sounded as if he had been asking his parents in a childlike manner of speaking. Victor's spirit sunk as he slowly walked behind the wheelchair and grasped the handles pushing it forward. As he slowly exited the room, he spotted Amanda coming down the hallway.

"Where are you two going at this hour?" she asked.

"I'm taking the good Father to the chapel for a few minutes." Victor smiled at Amanda. "I think it will do him some good. Both of us actually and I promise we won't be long."

Richard mumbled an incoherent reply that no one understood as Victor pushed the chair down the hallway.

37

The room was quiet as Victor sat with the sleeping man, who not so long ago had called himself an ex-priest. A book lay in Victor's lap like it had ever since Father Richard had returned from his stay at the hospital. A blue rosary inserted in it to mark the page. Since Richard's last stroke, during his nightly visits, Victor had been reading to him each night.

The Adventures of Huckleberry Finn by Mark Twain.

One of the books Richard had loved as a child and had wanted to read again but had not. One of the many things he had learned about Father Richard from the caregivers who loved him dearly. Too many books I want to read he had said to Maureen one night. The sound of Victor's voice seams to lull Richard into a deep slumber. Victor had lost track of time many decades ago. Having had Richard to confide in had been a blessing. A comfort he had not had for a long and lonely length of time.

Victor's head tilted slightly as his old, but incredibly sharp ears heard scuffling footsteps from down the hallway. He waited quietly until he saw Jenna round the corner, entering the room.

A slight smile as she spoke in a hushed tone. "Reading to Father Richard again?"

"I was," replied Victor as he took the book in his hand and looked at it. "I don't know if it's the book or my voice but it sooths him. Helps him sleep well I think."

"I'm sure it does. You're a good man, Victor," she said as she stood next to the bed. She noticed a plate of date cookies on the nightstand. Next to it was a tall glass of orange juice with a white straw floating high, like it would fall out at any moment.

Victor looked at Richard as he spoke. "I brought those for Father Richard. I thought he looked hungry."

Jenna smiled as she pushed the straw down into the glass.

"He will have a good day tomorrow," said Victor. "Yes. I think he shall."

"Why do you say that?" inquired Jenna.

"It's a feeling I get sometimes," replied Victor as he smiled meekly.

"Let me know if you need anything, Victor."

"Thank you," said Victor as he watched the young woman leave the room.

"Yes my friend. You will have a good day tomorrow," said Victor as he stood from his chair, aching joints making popping sounds. A sharp pain in his side reminded him of his body shutting down.

38

The shades were drawn tight as caregiver Maureen sat on top of her blankets wearing her comfortable pyjamas. The second-floor bedroom of her home slightly dimmed in the early morning sunlight. Her laptop resting on her lap, she scrolled through her Facebook wall catching up on the previous evenings' posts. A bloop sound caught her attention as she was alerted of having one new message. A few clicks later she saw the message was from her co-worker, Jenna.

The message read, "You still up?"

"Yes, just winding down," replied Maureen.

"Did you hear?" replied Jenna.

"What?" asked Maureen.

"Father Richard. He's awake and talking today. His speech is slurred and he thinks he's in the hospital in Boston again."

"Wow, really?"

"The weird part is Victor predicted it. He told me so last night," wrote Jenna. She added another message before Maureen could reply. "Yup and he had quite the appetite today."

Maureen replied. "I wonder how Victor knew he would be better today?"

"I don't know but I'm going to ask him tonight," replied Jenna.

"Thanks for letting me know," replied Maureen. "I need to get some sleep now or I won't be much fun to work with tonight... lol"

"Me too, ttyl," replied Jenna.

Maureen couldn't help but smile as she logged off and shut down her computer. Knowing that Father Richard was having a good day today lifted her spirits. Putting her laptop aside she fluffed up her pillow and got under the blankets. She closed her eyes, a slight smile still on her lips as she tried to clear her thoughts, focusing on getting some sleep.

39

Maureen sat in the staffroom. Alone, she slipped on her shoes for her last shift of the week. A smile appeared on her face again as the memory of Father Richard's good day came back. Her only regret is that she had not been there to see it herself. He had faded back into the land of confusion that was his true self by afternoon. All remnants of his good day completely gone now like it had never happened. Maureen was startled as the door to the staff room burst open abruptly as Jenna hurriedly walked in.

With a blank look, Maureen spoke first. "What's the hurry?"

Jenna cracked open her locker as she kicked off her sneakers and sat down to put on her white work shoes. "I went to talk to Victor before my shift."

"And?" inquired Maureen.

"He wasn't in his room," replied Jenna.

"He must have started his rounds earlier tonight," said Maureen. "Or he might be with Father Richard reading to him again."

"True. I guess I'll see him later," said Jenna as both ladies left the room to begin their graveyard shift.

40

Later that evening, Jenna made her way from room to room. She was in what many called the Lost Ward, checking on her sleeping residents. She couldn't help but hope to stumble upon Victor during one of his usual visitations. She had been to Father Richard's room twice already and would be there again momentarily. All in all, this had been a rather quiet shift so far and this was good since Jenna felt drained, more than ready for a few days off. As she rounded the corner into Farther Richard room for the third time this evening, she couldn't help but feel a momentary feeling of relief. Just as Maureen had predicted, there sat Victor. Book firmly clutched in his hand which was also wrapped in a blue rosary. His head slumped down and his eyes closed tight.

"There you are!" exclaimed Jenna in a soft tone, not wanting to wake Father Richard. "Sleeping at this hour?" she said inquisitively. She couldn't help but think this was out of character for Victor. She walked quickly across the room and laid her hand on his shoulder.

"Victor," she said, gently nudging his shoulder to wake him. That's when she realized how cold he felt. Victor always felt somewhat chilled but never this cold she thought. She shook him slightly.

"Victor?" said Jenna as she touched his cheek with the back of her hand. Cold as ice she thought. Feeling his neck for a pulse, she found none.

"God no!" she exclaimed. Pausing for a second in disbelief, before she could leave the room, a voice startled her.

"Is- is he dead?" she heard a slurred voice say. Turning she saw Father Richard sitting up in bed with his brow covered in large droplets of perspiration.

"Yes!" she blurted out before she could even think about her answer. Father Richard looked bewildered and confused as he sat up in his bed.

"Poor Patrick," said Father Richard who held his glasses in his hands instead of placing them on his face. "He was a confused and troubled soul."

In a state of shock, Jenna didn't register what Richard had said to her but instead she ran from the room and down the hall. These would be the very last coherent words Father Richard would ever utter in the last few months of his life.

41

"Finally, a day off after a seven day stretch and what a week," wrote Jenna as her status update on her Facebook wall. She sat with her laptop at the kitchen table, her hair still damp from the shower and wearing her favourite pyjamas. She intended on wearing them all day, not planning to leave the house. Sipping hot coffee as she caught up on her friend's Facebook updates.

A bloop sound alerted her of a new message. The message was from Maureen.

"You're finally up. I got gossip!" the message read.

"Miss me already did you?" Jenna typed in response.

Maureen replied, "My cousin Douglass McKinnon just got back from Vegas late last night."

Jenna replied "I still can't believe Victor died so suddenly. Other than low blood pressure and arthritis, Dr Williams said Victor looked to be the healthiest resident we had." Jenna sat back sipping her coffee as she waited on Maureen's reply.

"Can you keep a secret?" asked Maureen.

"Of course," replied Jenna.

"Victor died early Thursday. Douglass only got back late Friday. He only went in to work on Saturday."

"So?" asked Jenna impatiently as she got up to get more coffee. A bloop sound made her hurry back to the table, spilling a li

"Victor's funeral arrangements clearly said he wanted to be cremated on the same day he died."

"Bad timing is all," replied Jenna. "Is Douglass worried about complaints from the next of kin?"

"There is no next of kin," replied Maureen. "But that's not the part that freaked Douglass out."

"Ok, now you're pissing me off! Spill it already... lol" wrote Jenna in her reply.

"After being in storage at the funeral parlour for two and half days, Douglass said it was like looking at a corpse that had been dead for weeks."

"What does that mean?" asked Jenna. "Was the cooler in the storage unit broken?"

"I asked him that and he said that it was fine. But the decomp freaked him out. He had never seen anything like that before."

"Did he call Dr Williams to have a look at the body?" asked Jenna.

"No. He is supposed to follow the residents pre-made funeral arrangements to the letter and so nobody is supposed to know this," replied Maureen. "Which is why I asked if you could keep a secret."

"I'm sure Dr Williams wouldn't mind in a case like this. It was just bad timing."

"Too late anyway. The cremation is already done. He didn't even want to tell me about it but I pried it out of him. Can you believe it, he was afraid I'd tell someone," wrote Maureen.

"Well you did!" replied Jenna. "You told me."

"lol" replied Maureen.

Bill and Frank

We both walked quietly on this grey day in the middle of May. It had rained again all last night but it had stopped early in the morning. Everything was still damp and soggy and nothing would dry without the sun coming out. But still, spring was upon us and all around the grass was now a dark shade of green. Also, the trees had begun to bloom, which meant the sweet smell of spring was in the air.

The both of us had remained quiet since leaving the truck at the abandoned Hennessey farm. All you could hear was the occasional bird and the sound we made as we traveled up the neatly groomed trail. The crunching of fine gravel as the two of us walked slowly, not in a rush to get to our destination. We would come here a lot and walk from the old farm up this trail and down to our favourite fishing hole, Jagged River. On this day I had left the fishing gear in the truck, and I think we both knew why.

Less than a week ago we had found out that Frank had cancer and didn't have long to live. This was all I had thought about since that day. We had worked together for the last ten years since we graduated the academy together. Not only were we partners, but we had become the best of friends and had been pretty much inseparable ever since.

We did everything together including going fishing every spring. We spent many days at the old Jagged River sometimes not even catching anything. The river was so quiet and peaceful compared to the noise of the city. After riding in the squad car all week we would look forward to the quiet times at the river.

We went there all summer, often spending hours there lost in the sounds of the rushing river. We would listen to the chirping and fluttering of birds in the dense thickets and trees all around us.

The entire time we walked I could feel the hard steel of my .22 Glock against my back, tucked inside my jeans. It was hidden by my light blue denim jacket so Frank wouldn't see it. Somehow I think he knew what I was thinking as he never even made eye contact with me the entire walk up to the river.

I had not been sleeping well in the last few weeks as I knew something was wrong. I would have never admitted it to anyone, but I had never really had many friends growing up and so this made our relationship even stronger for me. I think most of the guys on the force knew it too. Probably why they teased me all the time, saying how Frank was the better officer of the two of us. The better driver. How I couldn't do anything without him.

A big part of me knew they were right on that last part. This is why knowing Frank was dying was tearing me apart.

We sat next to the river on the damp grass for what felt like hours as I lost track of time. It was abnormally quiet. You couldn't hear any birds or anything, only the rush of the river, which was still a little high from a combination of all the recent rain and the melting of the snow.

Frank had his back to me and hadn't even glanced in my direction since we got here. I was completely exhausted not having slept at all for the last few days. I was ashamed to admit it to anyone but my emotions were getting the best of me. For the last half hour I had sat here with my pistol in my hand with tears running down my face. It had taken me a very long time to even take the safety off and a part of me knew it was selfish of me as I couldn't bear to watch Frank die a painful slow death.

After quite some time I was finally able to gather up the courage and I aimed my Glock at the back of Frank's head. I could feel the warm tears running down my face and my hand trembled, but I knew I couldn't back down now or I would never have the courage to do this again. Meanwhile, Frank never even looked at me and I felt he probably knew what was about to happen. I was a crack shot but with my emotional state I was afraid of missing and not being able to muster up the guts to take a second shot. It had to be a clean shot and I knew it and so I struggled with my emotions.

A loud crack broke the silence and was heard echoing through the forest but only the wildlife and the sudden flutter of birds acknowledged it. Gunshots were not all that uncommon a thing to hear deep in the woods behind the old Hennessey farm.

Sobbing at the thought of what I had just done I was weak from the stress of it all. Frank lay in a pool of his own blood soaking the grass and pooling onto the ground around him. The ground was already so wet that it was not absorbing any of the blood. The puddle grew larger and larger right in front of me.

2

A second crack echoed through the forest that morning before all went quiet. A few of the brave birds who had not fluttered far after the first shot suddenly flew away from the commotion not knowing that this would be the last shot they would hear that day.

3

The sun was finally out today after the last week of sporadic rain they just had. Everything was starting to dry, and people were out and about again. The rays felt wonderful, beating through the windows of the police cruiser as Sergeant Jake McGinnis drove through the Stonevalley city streets.

Suddenly his cell phone rang, and he found himself digging through his pockets and searching through the garbage and sections of newspaper on the seat of his police cruiser for the resonating device. The Sergeant got the call on his cell phone which was odd as the thing usually never rang during the day.

"Sergeant McGinnis," Officer Nowlan's voice said. "We need

you at the fishing hole at Jagged River pronto. We have a situation."

"Why are you calling me on my cell and not the radio?" asked Sergeant McGinnis.

"Didn't want this getting around like wildfire, Sergeant but it's Bill and Frank, you better get over here quick," replied Nowlan before hanging up.

What was that all about, wondered Jake? Not wasting any time as he turned his cruiser around and turned on the lights, speeding through the streets heading out of the city.

What the hell did Bill go and do now? I had asked him to go see the counsellor thought Jake as he weaved through traffic. He couldn't help but think he should have forced him to go. Ever since Frank was diagnosed with cancer, they all had seen the change in Bill. He had become very withdrawn and quiet and most of his fellow officers tried reaching out to him to let him know we would help him get through this. But to all it was obvious that he was devastated.

Arriving at the scene, Jake was greeted by Officer Nowlan.

Nowlan spoke first. "You know Bill's neighbour Jenny Baker, her sons found the bodies. We took them into the city not long after to talk to a counsellor as they were pretty messed up."

"Bodies?" replied Jake inquisitively.

"Right down here by the river," answered Nowlan.

It took a moment for Jake to get over the shock of the scene and he stood dumbfounded for a few moments staring at Bill. He was barely recognisable as he had clearly put the gun in his mouth and blown his brains all over the bark of the tree he was leaning against.

When the Sergeant finally did speak he said, "I can't believe it came down to this. I knew Bill was heart-broken but I never saw this coming, dammit. What a tragedy for his family and the force," exclaimed Jake.

"Dammit, I told him we would get him a new dog. Best damn team we ever had on the canine unit."

Pre-ordering Murder

1

The sun rose gradually in the sky, indicating the oncoming day as it crept in the large windows on a quiet Saturday morning. The beautiful mansion sat on a slight slope in the Hollywood Hills amongst other equally large and impressive landscaped properties. From inside the spacious home, the aroma of freshly brewed coffee filled the kitchen and the office to its left. All was quiet except for the sound of clicking from an old-fashioned computer keyboard, echoing in the office and throughout the home. Breaking the silence, an electronic voice suddenly spoke from within the house's security system.

"Welcome, Douglas," the unnatural, electronic female voice said.

The clicking of the keyboard ceased and all went quiet.

"Hello?" said Douglas as he swivelled in his office chair to face the kitchen. Puzzled as to why the security system would have greeted his arrival when he was already home working in his office. He turned and faced his computer again; making sure the Autosave program was saving the notes on the script he was reading in his documents. Opening the house monitoring software he was puzzled that it now showed an arrival time of 10:22 AM on the list of activity. Problem was it also showed his arrival with his wife Rebecca at 11:43 PM the previous night and that he had never left. Rebecca was the only one who was noted as leaving (for the spa) at 7:45 AM that morning.

"Damn firmware glitch," he muttered reaching for his iCom device and getting out of his chair. He walked towards the kitchen, "Call Safehouse Securities," he said as he lifted the flat, transparent device to his ear. A blue glow formed on the inside left of the otherwise crystal clear device, he heard it ring on the other end just once and then the glow faded.

"What the…" he muttered as he looked at the device inquisitively. That's when he heard footsteps.

2

Outside the home on the sidewalk a young, spandex-covered woman jogged by with her iBuds firmly inserted in each ear. In perfect sync, each tiny wireless speaker played a new remix of an old Indi song called *Slumber* originally done by an artist called The Sublime Rocker. With her volume up high she never heard the first two gun shots that echoed loudly inside the home. There was a slight delay while the woman kept jogging on her way and then a third shot could have been heard had someone been there to hear it. Then all was quiet as the jogger turned up a street and vanished from sight.

3

As the short, shapely brunette walked toward her silver Lexus, her high heels made clicking noises on the asphalt. She slid her thin purse straps over her shoulder and glanced back. Her shapely hips swaying, she knew she would catch the two men she had just walked past in the act of gawking at her. Something the ex-model turned actress was very used to. Attention she actually craved, to be honest. She truly loved being the object of their desire even if she would rather not admit to it. Her tight green dress hugging her luscious curves as she strut her stuff, smiling at the men. Being desired was much more exciting than being had for her.

"Door," she said as she approached her car. The car detected her presence, squawked as the alarm deactivated itself and the door popped open slowly. She slid her shapely legs into the vehicle sitting at the wheel. The car sensors knowing she was now on the inside proceeded to shut the door slowly.

Placing the palm of her right hand onto the dashboard she

simply said "Home," and the engine started up. Once running, the navigation system took but a split second to find its location at the Paris Hilton Hotel and Spa and its destination. A seat belt harness slid from inside the seat forming a semi-circle around the young woman's slender waist and also at the shoulders. Each semi-circle joined to the other half in the middle. As she opened her purse and started digging inside it, the car's wheels turned, and it pulled out into traffic. Finding her lip gloss applicator, she turned toward the mirror whose sensors detected her motions and pivoted towards her so she could apply a fresh coat of soft red cherry glaze that complimented her dark complexion.

Hearing a soft chime, she reached into her small purse again to pull her iCom and saw a text message from Tony that read "Delicious as always, I'm already looking forward to next Saturday's spa appointment".

This made her smile as she pressed her thumb onto the upper right-hand corner of the device. A soft blue glow just around the edge of her thumb appeared instantly. A keypad appeared onto the front of the device where she typed the words.

"My pleasure, literally!!!" is all she wrote. And then with a swipe of her thumb, a menu appeared, and she quickly deleted the conversation between her and Tony. Looking up as she felt the car slow down and make the turn onto her street, she put her phone away and fixed her hair. The car pulled into her driveway and slowed to allow the garage door to fully open and then came to a stop next to her husband's gold Lexus. She gathered her things and went to the front door of the house. Sensors closed the garage door as she walked away from it. Motion sensors detected someone on the path and a sudden aroma of lilac flowers filled the air. Detecting the chip implanted in her right hand the door unlocked and opened before her.

"Douglas?" she said as the door closed behind her.

"Welcome, Rebecca," the unnatural electronic female voice said. Ignoring it, Rebecca spoke. "I was thinking we should go to dinner later…. Douglas?"

Walking past the kitchen counter she set her purse down, assuming she would find her husband asleep on the couch in his office as usual. The sight of her dead husband lying in a pool of blood was too much for the young woman and she let out a shrill shriek that echoed loudly throughout the entire house. Her voice trailed off as her sight went dark and she collapsed to the floor in a state of unconsciousness.

4

The salt and pepper haired Dupres sat alone in the passenger seat of his car typing up a report. His antiquated laptop sat on his lap as he filled out the old style G20 forms from the case he closed two days ago. He checked to make sure the Autosave was saving his document before he closed the laptop and took a sip of his coffee. A blue light began blinking on the dashboard as it made an electronic "bloop" sound.

"Hello," spoke Dupres activating the on-board iCom system.

"Detective Dupres," the female voice said as a semitransparent holographic image popped up. The attractive Captain sitting in her office with her awards covering the wall behind her.

"Captain Silverson," he said with a coy smile appearing on his lips.

"You know that kid you busted in January? Remember him, Derek White who hacked into the mainframe at the University and stole all those kid's banking information by hacking into their chip information databanks," said a stern faced Silverson.

"Yeah, what about him?" asked Dupres his smile vanishing as he spoke.

"He walked today and on a technicality of all things."

"How the heck did that happen?" inquired a frustrated Dupres.

"You know how I keep telling you to stop using that outdated laptop and get a virtual keyboard like everyone else. You know how I keep telling you that if you had the iKey you could use the new G30 forms that half fill themselves out."

"Yeah... so, where are you going with this, Captain?"

"You put the wrong damn date, you idiot. He HAS an alibi for January of 2028," said a clearly angry Silverson.

Dupres opened his old laptop, opened the file he was working on and without speaking a word he changed the date from 2028 to 2029.

"It's not just the date but some of the data is corrupt too. Just thought you should know before the big bosses get the I.T. guys to take away that laptop of yours. And before that punk Arvin calls you to rub it in," said the Captain before cutting off the call.

"Fuck me!" muttered Dupres as he picked up his coffee. He took a large gulp and spilled some on his shirt and tie. The dashboard's blue light flashed again and was accompanied by a "bloop" sound.

"You couldn't wait could you, Arvin," he said impatiently looking for a napkin to clean off some of the coffee.

"What are you talking about?" replied Arvin as the rectangular flat and semitransparent holographic image popped up yet again. This time it showed the handsome young man sitting in his own car.

"Never mind," said Dupres. "What's going on?"

Using his index finger Arvin poked at the bottom left hand corner of the hologram and a side widow appeared showing an aerial view of Arvin's location. A dot appeared indicating his exact position in front of 6350 Rogerton Drive in Hollywood Hills.

"Get your ass over here, partner. We got ourselves an old-fashioned homicide and we need an old school detective."

"Bite me!" said Dupres.

"That's exactly what I mean. Even your expressions are old-fashioned." Arvin Walls shut down the iCom before Dupres could offer any other witty old-fashioned comebacks.

"Drive, emergency mode. Location 6350 Rogerton Drive in Hollywood Hills," spoke Dupres as he tucked away his old laptop while the car's seat belt harness slid from inside the seat forming a semi-circle around his waist and at the shoulders. The roof's holographic lights activated and the car pulled out on the nearly empty road and sped off.

"Fuck," said Dupres as more coffee spilled on his lap as the car made a fast, but controlled turn.

5

Having parked on the street Dupres walked towards the yellow holographic "tape" that surrounded the entire property. An electronic voice spoke the words "Noting the arrival of Detective Dupres," and a small portion of the yellow holographic ribbon changed to green right before the detective. As he walked through it he glanced to his side and saw a reporter get a mild shock from the yellow barrier as he got his arm too close to it. This made him smile slightly but he tried not to show it. Brushing at a newly discovered coffee stain on his pant leg he walked past a few beat cops who whispered amongst themselves.

"Dupres, Get any coffee in you?" asked the reporter bitterly as he put his thumb in his mouth in an attempt to sooth the sting. He had clearly seen Dupres smiling when he got stung from the electronic police line ribbon and hadn't appreciated it one bit.

"About time you got here," said Doc Brown. "You do know what day it is right?" added the coroner with a smile. "What year?"

"It's time for you to go help Marty and the kids," replied Dupres as he walked past the chuckling coroner.

"It never gets old does it, Dupres?" asked Doctor Roy Brown.

"Never will either," replies Dupres.

Arvin, who clearly was not a subscriber of the classic movie iNetwork had a puzzled and not an amused look for a brief moment. "You'll never guess whose house this is? I mean was," said Arvin as he met Dupres on the steps of the Hollywood mansion.

Without the slightest of pause in his reply Dupres said

85

"Douglas Fairbanks," as he walked past the young Detective. He stopped in his tracks and turned to look back at Arvin. "Was? Fairbanks is dead?" he asked.

"I forget what a movie buff you are," replied Arvin.

"How did he die?"

"Shot to death."

"Really? Hey, did Florence call you?" asked Dupres.

"Captain Silverson? No, why?"

"I was just wondering," added Dupres, "It's not important. I assume they've already taken a 3D scan of the house?"

"Of course they did."

"Good."

As they walked into the kitchen, Dupres picked up the spherical 3D image hologram generator and pushed his right-hand palm down onto its side. A small blue light brightened and then a 3D full scale image suddenly appeared and filled the room showing the entire layout down to the smallest details. He could tell from the imaging that the body had not been moved yet. In the kitchen floor the hologram showed a second body of a young woman in a green dress with a paramedic hovering above her, blocking Dupres' view of her face.

"Who's that?" asked Dupres gesturing with his head at the hologram image of the second body that was no longer there.

"Fairbanks' wife, Rebecca. She found the body and must have fainted. It was her implant that dialled 911 and not his." Arvin walked towards the body and knelt beside it. Dupres released the device and the hologram vanished. He stepped in behind the now kneeling Arvin and looked over the body.

"Don't touch anything," shouted Roy Brown, who was more commonly known as Doc Brown, as he hurried in stumbling with his kit.

"You could have gotten here sooner had you come here in the Dolorian," said Dupres.

Brown ignored him as he knelt making his knees pop. He set his kit down and fumbled it open. "I can't remember the last time I had to do this. Ever since seven years ago when they tried to blow up the Empire State Building and they passed that law making Facebook tracking mandatory. Well let's just say with the government's microchip implants following your every move and logging the data in Facebook, there haven't been very many murders I tell ya."

"That's the problem, Doc. His chip is gone," said Arvin as he pointed to the late Douglass's hand, which had been cut open.

"How could that be? It should have alerted 911 as soon as he got shot. Maybe even before if his heart rate increased enough to set it off," added Doc Brown. He coated his hands with liquid gloves; they dried quickly, turning into a thin silicone coating.

"Assuming the chip was removed after he died are we?" asked Arvin.

"Yeah, well that's why we're here I guess, right, Watson?" asked Dupres.

"I guess that's makes you Sherlock then, right?" asked Arvin as he watched Doc Brown pick up the late movie producer's hand and examined the rough cuts to the top. They appeared to have been done to remove the implant. One cut even pierced through and came out on the inside of the hand.

"I'm surprised you knew that one," said Dupres, obviously referring to the Sherlock comment.

"He didn't until last year when Douglass here remade it. I was just glad he got to do it and not that Bill Connors with his animation crap," muttered Brown as he dug through his kit, clearly looking for something specific.

"That's one thing we agree on, Doc. I would much rather watch real actors any day over that computer animated crap they got these days."

"One of you put this on," said Doc as he handed the canister of liquid gloves to Arvin who then handed it to Dupres. Brown pulled another canister out of his kit, shook it a little and began spraying a light mist over the body.

"What's that?" asked Arvin.

"It's a type of glue to keep any evidence from falling off the body when we turn him over," said Roy as he got up to make sure he sprayed all over thoroughly. "I haven't had to use this in a long time."

Dupres sighed loudly; making sure everybody heard him before applying the gel gloves. "I hate this stuff," he added as the liquid hardened.

"Ready? Help me turn him over," said Doc as he started to grab hold. Dupres leaned in and they turned the late Fairbanks over, the rubbery pool of blood now congealed with the spray also turned over with him.

"Good thing for the ceramic tiles. It will make collecting the blood so much easier," said Doc Brown as he picked up his spray and misted the body again on the other side.

"Shot three times," said Dupres, gesturing towards the body.

"You really are Sherlock incarnate aren't you?" said Brown without even a hint of a smile.

"Sarcasm never did suit you, Doc," replied a grinning Dupres.

Having wandered off, Arvin spoke "I wonder what he was working on?" He stood at the arch entrance of the late producer's office looking it over from a distance.

"Fairbanks and Connors were in a bidding war to pre-sell the remake of King Kong," explained Dupres.

"Of what?" asked Arvin.

"King Kong," said Doc Brown. "Thanks for constantly reminding me how old I am."

"Yeah, he hardly remembers the days before they pre-sold movie theatre tickets before they were even made," said Dupres as he joined his young partner in staring into the producer's office. Both men were looking for clues as to what might have happened.

"Guys, I'm not that young. But what is King Kong anyway?" asked Arvin as he poked at a thin old–fashioned, paper book with a single finger. Not wanting to contaminate potential evidence he read the title out loud. "Dark Tales for Dark Nights."

Dupres was looking at an old stack of books on a shelf while he spoke. "The script was written by that has-been writer from Carlton, Pierre C Arseneault. He had a good career until he started hanging out with Charlie Sheen. It all went downhill from there."

"Well good thing is we already have a suspect," said Arvin pointing at a note scribble on a notepad. On it was a note written in black ink, most likely with the pen lying on top of the notepad.

"William P. Connors' price for King Kong. $ 50,000,000.00 for an animated version."

Nudging the pen aside Dupres said, "I heard Douglas's price was double that and that he almost had it all in the bank while Connors only has a quarter of his raised."

"That's motive for sure," added Arvin. Doc Brown was still standing over the body when he signalled two paramedics over to help him bag the body. As they did this he spoke "It still doesn't explain how he could be killed without his implant alerting 911."

"Good point, Doc. Arvin; you call that kid Shawn at the precinct and have him look for Fairbanks's implant. It's gotta still be transmitting wherever it is; especially since it never alerted 911".

"Does that make me Sherlock?" asked Doc Brown as he walked behind the paramedics wheeling the stretcher outside.

Arvin pulled out his iCom and made a quick call, blurting out instructions quickly. As he put his iCom back in its holster he nudged Dupres and asked, "Which one did you pre-order from?"

"Fairbanks of course."

"Me too," replied Arvin as he poked at the old-fashioned keyboard that activated the hologram that was the monitor.

6

"Thanks for agreeing to meet us on a Sunday, Mr. Cooper,"

said Dupres as he walked into the C.E.O.'s office. He was being followed by Arvin who was busy checking out Amanda. A slender, attractive brunette in a form-fitting business blazer and skirt who was not his type but she was certainly distracting him at the moment. As Cooper's administrative assistant she had announced their arrival and let them in, closing the door behind them.

The slim, grey-haired man in the expensive retro silver suit walked out from behind his desk to great them. He spoke as he extended his hand, offering a handshake even before reaching the men. "Under ordinary circumstances, I would insist that my staff take Sunday's off. It's a rule of mine. But these are not ordinary circumstances, so I have had my best team come in to figure this thing out." He walked over to a bar on the side of his office and stepped behind it. The office was quite modern and had little other than the tools necessary to do business. No art on the walls or even a picture of his family decorated the room.

"Can I offer you gentlemen any refreshments, coffee or tea? Water perhaps?" he asked, reaching for cups.

"No thanks. We're fine," answered Dupres before even glancing back at Arvin.

Cooper put the cup down and said, "I know what you're going to ask me and I don't have an answer for you yet." He walked around to his desk gesturing for them to sit in the chairs before it. Dupres began to sit and was startled when the chair's sensors activated, and it automatically adjusted itself to his height.

Arvin smiled and spoke. "He doesn't get out much," gesturing towards Dupres with a pointing thumb.

"That's an old-fashioned expression," replied Dupres glancing at Arvin.

"For an old-fashioned guy," said a smiling Arvin as he turned his attention back to Mr Cooper.

"So, Mr. Cooper. Can you explain to me why we had to come down here instead of your office sending us the files we requested as usual?"

"Well, Detective Dupres, it's not that simple this time. You see, we do have to make sure that what we share with you will not become public knowledge. If the media got a hold of this it would be utter chaos."

Arvin spoke. "It should be as simple as you sending us the data we asked for."

Cooper shifted uneasily in his seat, clearly not comfortable with what he had no choice but to share with the pair of detectives. After a brief pause, he spoke. "Let's go down to the lab shall we. There's something you need to see for yourself to fully understand what I am going to tell you." Cooper got up and walked to a blank wall. Upon approaching the wall, a panel split open in the middle revealing a private elevator behind it. Stepping in, Cooper spoke aloud saying the floor number he wanted.

Dupres shot a glance at Arvin as all three rode the elevator down quietly. The elevator came to a smooth stop and the doors opened to reveal a large room. As they walked off the elevator, Arvin looked around at the outer walls, which were a dark grey. The interior walls were mostly made of glass. Some clear, some frosted, and many had hologram monitors projected behind them. The room was filled with electronic equipment that even he, being a Tech junky, had never seen before.

"Is this where they design the implants?" asked Arvin.

"Yes, this is one of our labs where we do research, product testing, and development. The implants used to be made in China until three years ago when the labour unions started forming. Now they're made in Canada and the U.S. only, but designs are made right here in this very room," said Cooper as he directed them towards the back of the lab.

"Shouldn't we go through some sort of thing to remove static before coming in here?" asked Dupres.

Cooper chuckled a little. "Not necessary. We had to make them safe before implanting them. We couldn't have simple static, or better yet a mild shock injure the subject the implant was in now could we."

"Subject?" replied Arvin inquisitively.

"The person in question, you know what I mean," replied a slightly annoyed Cooper. "Here they are. Let me introduce you to our trouble shooters."

Walking into a separate room in the back they saw three people working. Both detectives half expected to see them in white lab coats, but each of them was in normal street clothes. All three stopped what they were doing to turn to great the guests. They knew it would have to be important for Mr Cooper to interrupt them after all that has happened.

"This young man is the head of our R&D department, Grady Baxter and our lead programmer, Alli Lebel. I believe you already know our newest addition, who is now heading up our new software security department, Derek White."

"We've met," said Derek as he looked up at Dupres.

"Are you serious?" asked Dupres looking at Cooper sternly.

"Yes I am, very serious. Derek here helped identify flaws in our firmware databanks that we were not aware of. Also, I made him an offer her couldn't refuse. Right kid?" He slapped Derek on the back hard enough to make the young man wince as the sound echoed in the room. "Are we getting anywhere?" he asked looking his team over briefly.

Alli spoke up. "Let me show you what we have so far," as she flicked away at a modern sensor keyboard which popped up a large holographic screen a few feet in front of her. She added "This is the activity grid for Mr. Fairbanks via his implant's recorded data, which is stored in Facebook's databank." The screen showed a 3D graphic of the room that just looked like a series of lines. There were blue and red lines that went in all directions forming a layout of the house. A few keystrokes later she zoomed into the kitchen area.

"If you have the data, why didn't you just send it to us like usual?" asked Arvin.

"It's not that simple," replied Cooper.

Alli continued. "That morning, Mr Fairbanks got up at 8:46 AM. Shower, coffee and breakfast and then he went to his office. At this time his wife was already gone to the spa and that's correct as per the chip data. The only time this shows him getting up is when he went to the bathroom at 9:46 AM. Then he went back to his computer where he remained until 10:24 AM. But now the system also shows him arriving at 10.22 AM."

"Wait a sec, how can there be two?" said Dupres pointing at the holographic screen that showed two locator chips signals.

She zoomed out to show the entire area. "That's what we don't understand. We scanned the area for other signals and found nothing. Nobody else was there but then out of nowhere, Fairbanks appears at his own door and comes in."

Derek piped in excitedly. "It's a clone implant, has to be. Some of the hackers out there have been trying to make this happen for a while but nobody has been able to yet."

Shooting him a glance Dupres said "Well someone did it, one of your friends maybe?" This made Derek's smug smile disappear.

"The new signal is showing up as Fairbanks and the recordings are somehow overlapping. At least it does up until about 10:23. That's when the new Fairbanks draws a gun. It's a legal gun, but no registration shows up for it and the chip activating it shows up as Fairbanks's." Alli shifts the scan and shows the chip locators coming towards each other. "The scan shows the two signals coming closer and then the original signal weakens and disappears, thus causing the dropped call that the real Douglas was in the process of making. When it did the legal handgun registered as being fired a total of three times. Following this the new signal is shown going to the kitchen. We assume he got a knife from the kitchen. It then returns to the body where it hovers a bit and then leaves the building and vanishes once outside."

Cooper turned to Dupres with a very serious look. "You have to understand that we can't give you this data. Nobody can know this is even possible."

"That doesn't change the fact that a murder was committed here," added Dupres.

"It would have to be someone who knows this type of technology. Someone who works for Cooper Technologies, or has in the past," said Derek.

"That's what we thought until you hacked in the databank and stole information from us," Alli added as she picked up a small spherical object off her desk that was a quarter of an inch in diameter. "Most people don't even feel it in them. Forget they have it," she added. "Were not sure how yet but it's as if the chip's signal was not only duplicated but also interrupted or hacked. I'm not sure how it could be done without that split second making it think something was wrong and alerting 911."

"It almost has to be a firmware glitch, that's the only thing I can see," added Baxter.

"A heck of a coincidence that it would act up only at this moment, wouldn't you say?" asked Arvin.

An angry Alli added "There is no glitch in my firmware, thank you very much"

"I mean no offence, but I still say it's a firmware glitch of some sort. I'm going to run some scenarios to see what I can come up with," added Baxter.

While no one was watching him, Arvin looked the short and curvy Alli up and down. "We're compiling a list of suspects and as soon as we have a warrant, we will need you to check the locations of them all."

"The first being Connors," Dupres added as he looked at Derek. "Who did you pre-order from?"

"Fairbanks," said Derek.

"Fairbanks," said Alli. "But Baxter ordered from Connors because he likes animated actors."

"Well they might as well be since everything else will be animated. Unless Fairbanks had a hundred-foot ape actor that we don't know about," a grinning Baxter said in his defence.

"Well, keep digging and let us know what you find out," said Dupres as he turned to leave.

"Will do," replied Baxter.

"It was nice meeting you all," said Arvin as he shot a glance at Alli as she got up from her chair. He looked her up and down again and she didn't seem to mind this from the handsome young detective. Not until she caught a clearly jealous Derek watching.

"I'll send you our list of current suspects in the morning," added Arvin.

"Let me walk you out," said Cooper.

7

"How can you eat that slop?" asked Arvin as they exited the last old-style dinner on the edge of the city.

As Dupres walked through the doorway, a mechanical voice spoke. "Payment received, Mr Dupres, thank you and please come again"

"No offence but who still eats old-fashioned eggs, bacon and toast anymore? You should try the new Hostess Complete Cereal."

"I won't put that manufactured crap in me," said Dupres before getting down to business. "Did you send the list to Cooper?"

"Actually no, I wanted to talk to you first. The list we have is very short at the moment."

Both men got into the squad car. No sooner than Arvin had shut his door than Dupres said "Station," at the cars navigation system and the car engaged, strapped the men in and drove off. While looking straight ahead and in deep thought Dupres began listing off the names of the suspects whom he wanted to get their chip data.

"The first name on the list is William P. Connors. He would benefit the most from the death of Fairbanks."

"Agreed," said Arvin as he punched the name into his onboard computer.

"Second name is that has-been Pierre C. Arseneault. Rumor has it that he wanted Fairbanks to make the movie, but I think he may have been paid to say otherwise. He never publicly stated it but I'm sure he never liked animated actors. Besides, he knew them both and might have inside information."

"True," replied Arvin as he tapped away on his keyboard while looking at his hologram monitor. The car was still cruising along to its destination as both men worked inside it, completely ignoring the world outside. The car slowed down in traffic while the traffic flow changed in their favor.

"Rebecca Fairbanks, let's make sure she was where she said she was. She stands to inherit a lot of credits,"

Arvin looked at Dupres. "Agreed. You really want to add Derek White to the list don't you?"

Dupres added "I don't trust that kid. To quote that has-been Arseneault, once a crook, always a crook,"

Arvin smirked. "I think he was quoting someone else when he said that. Anyways, I've already contacted the three major motion picture companies about getting access to the list of people who pre-ordered the movies,"

"That's going to be quite the list," said Dupres as he scratched his scalp through his salt and pepper hair.

The younger detective shut down his computer as they pulled into the station parking lot and the car slid into its assigned parking space. "Well I figured we would look for patterns. People who repeatedly pre-ordered from either producer regularly. I mean our list of suspects is quite short otherwise."

"To quote Arseneault again, we only really need one suspect, the guilty one."

"Good point," added Arvin as he started to get out of the car. At that moment a blue light began blinking on the dashboard as it made an electronic "bloop" sound.

"Hello," spoke Arvin activating the on board iCom system.

"Detective Dupres, Arvin," the female voice said as a rectangular flat and semitransparent holographic image popped up. Captain Silverson was sitting in her office with her awards covering the wall behind her.

"Captain," said Arvin.

"So, who are we arresting?" spoke the Captain.

"Nobody just yet," said Dupres.

"What? With today's chip technologies you're telling me you don't know who killed Fairbanks yet?"

"No, Captain. As a matter of fact, we don't. The chip data was hacked and the people at Cooper Tec haven't figured out how or by whom yet," replied Dupres.

"So we have an old-fashioned murder case," said Silverson as she leaned back into her chair.

"Not quite," said Arvin. "Everybody around him is still chipped and so we can narrow it down by process of elimination. We're compiling a list of suspects as we speak and should know more soon."

"Good then, keep me posted," said Silverson.

"Of course, Captain," said Arvin as the com shut down and the call ended.

"Let's go grab some coffee and make some calls," said Dupres as he got out of the car.

8

Moments after getting coffee before heading to the station both men were now in the car when a sudden "bloop" sound was heard coming from the onboard iCom system. A blue light began blinking on the dashboard as it made another electronic "bloop" sound.

"Arvin here, can I help you?" he spoke at the device. The holographic screen materialized quickly to show a slim, grey-haired man in a dark grey suit jacket.

"Cooper, what have you got for us?" asked Dupres.

Cooper leaned towards the camera and spoke in a less than enthusiastic tone. "I'm afraid I've got some bad news for you.

It looks like some data has been tampered with. And not just now either. It goes back awhile. Connors is one of them and so is Fairbanks."

"Really? How can that be?" asked Arvin.

"We don't know yet. Alli just told me this minutes ago. I just wanted to let you guys know for now but we should know more later today. All I ask is that you tell no one about this."

"Ok, thanks. Keep us posted," said Dupres.

As the holographic screen faded away Arvin chuckled. "You're so old-fashioned. Keep us posted he says,"

"Bite me," replies Dupres.

Arvin burst into laughter.

9

"Thanks for agreeing to see us on such short notice, Mr Arseneault," said Dupres, standing in the door of the modest Hollywood home.

"No problem, Detectives. Come on in," said Pierre. He gestured for them to come in, scratching his bald head as he walked past the detectives. "I don't understand why you haven't arrested anyone yet. The chip data must have made it pretty easy."

"It's not that simple this time," said Dupres.

"Really? Do tell, how so? You do know that writing a modern-day murder mystery became a thing of the past when those things became law. I mean someone gets killed, right. The cops check the data and minutes later you arrest the killer. A writer can't do anything with that now can he? Not to mention, no more serial killers to write about."

"I supposed not but that isn't really a bad thing," said Arvin as they followed the writer into his office. Pictures of the writer's career highlights adorned the walls. One wall was covered with pictures of him posing with various small-time celebrities and politicians at various events. Arvin pointed out one picture that stood out of Pierre with Charlie Sheen to Dupres who barely acknowledged seeing it.

Seeing this, Pierre spoke as he sat behind his desk. "And just for the record I only ever attended one of his parties and someone slipped something in my drink. I woke up naked in the neighbour's guest house with a twenty-year-old large breasted porn star and I was labelled as a party animal ever since. I suppose the pictures of me having sex earlier that night with Lulu, the midget porn queen didn't help any either."

Arvin tried to stifle a smile. "The video of you singing Sinatra in your underwear was worse."

Dupres walked over to a shelf that spanned the entire back wall and began looking at the collection of old-fashioned DVD's and books in astonishment. "You have quite the collection here. Pretty impressive. No Blu-Ray?"

"A few, but I prefer DVD's."

"I've been collecting Blu-Ray myself," says Dupres as he scanned the titles on the shelves.

"Well I don't see the point when you can just watch it anytime on iMovies. For a few credits the file is simply made available to you. Anyway, we know you pre-ordered a hundred copies of King Kong from Fairbanks when the bidding first started and so killing him would be foolish. That's not why we're here. We're curious and want to know about the relationship between Fairbanks and Connors. You knew them both didn't you?"

Arvin sat down in a chair facing Mr Arseneault.

Pierre shifted in his chair and smiled as he spoke. "Most people think they hated each other and were bitter rivals. That's a popular misconception on the part of the public mostly because of the media. And I supposed they might have done that to themselves too. Nothing fuels sales like a little healthy competition between rivals."

"What's that supposed to mean?" asked Dupres as he pulled a DVD off the shelf and began looking it over in amazement.

"Well let's just say there was a time when Fairbanks and Connors were more than just friends."

"Please explain," asked Arvin as he leaned forward, sitting on the edge of his seat.

"You see, Fairbanks and Connors were lovers. And while they were lovers they concocted this plan to monopolize the movie industry. Since both of them were the most in demand producers they held a lot of power and they both knew it. So no matter who met the pre-order price first they would split the profits. But since Fairbanks always made more money he knew his wife would never let him split it evenly. She threatened to expose their plan to the media and that would have ruined them both." Arseneault shifted in his chair and added "But then the agents found out about the plan and greed really set in and that's when everything went to shit."

Arvin sat back in his chair and reflected on what he had just heard before speaking.

"Well I don't think that rules Connors out as a suspect, as a matter of fact I think it makes him even more of one. What do you think Dupres?"

"Huh, what? He's got Doc Hollywood, the Back to the Future trilogy and every Planet of the Apes movie ever made."

Arvin glanced back and turned to Mr Arseneault and shook his head in disapproval.

Dupres picked a DVD off the shelf and flashed it to the other men and said "He's got The Green Mile"

"You'll have to forgive my partner. He's a movie buff," said Arvin.

Dupres put the DVD back on the shelf. "Oh and I do agree by the way. He is still a suspect even if they were lovers and potential business partners. But we should have the data from Cooper Tec this afternoon and so we should be able to eliminate most of the suspects." Pulling yet another DVD off the shelf he smiled and added "Didn't think I was listening did you, kid"

"Well we thank you for your time, Mr Arseneault," said Arvin.

"My pleasure," replied Arseneault as he walked over to show Dupres a few treasured gems in his collection.

10

As the detectives walked back to their car Dupres stopped in his tracks and pulled out his iCom, which was already glowing blue. Putting it to his ear he said "Dupres here, what's up?"

Arvin stood watching and listening to a one-sided conversation consisting mostly of Dupres saying "yup", "aha" and "ok". "Who was that?" asked Arvin as he watched his partner put his iCom back into his pocket.

Dupres spoke with a scowl of an expression on his face. "Derek White. He wants us to come to Cooper Tec to show us some of the data they found so far."

"You don't like him much do you?"

"Don't like him. I don't trust him. I bet this all leads back to him and his friends. What was Cooper thinking putting a kid like that on the inside?"

11

One hour later, Arvin and Dupres found themselves in Cooper Tec, riding down to the lab again with Cooper at their side in his private elevator. The red electronic numbers counting down as the three men descended to their destination.

"I hope you got something for us this time. The captain is getting impatient," said Arvin.

Dupres glanced at Arvin and spoke looking at Cooper. "Don't mind my partner. He's never been a detective without the chip technology and so has never done any real detective work before." He slouched a bit and added in a muttered grumble. "Although I'm not really sure this even counts as real detective work anyway."

Cooper looked up at the numbers changing on the digital holographic pad above the door as he spoke "Don't you worry guys. I wish we didn't have to go through this and I could just hand over the chip data as usual. This might cripple Cooper Tec if it gets out."

Cooper impatiently pushed through the doors as they opened. Alli met him as he walked in and demanded. "Are you sure Mr Cooper?" as she glanced at the pair of detectives.

"No. But it's not like we have a choice in the matter."

"Fine then," she said impatiently as she led them to a computer terminal. Derek sat at the sensor keyboard before a holographic screen full of data files. Baxter, sitting at a second terminal next to him, was sipping on a banana flavoured soft drink while examining technical data. It appeared to the detectives that he was looking at chip design specifications on the holographic screen before him. Before saying a word, Derek swivelled his chair and glanced at Cooper who nodded in approval even though everyone could see he was not a happy man.

"When we started digging into the Fairbanks murder, we found overlapping signals and that his chip had been cloned. At first this looked to be an isolated incident but when we did some more digging, we uncovered that this was not the case at all."

Cooper's shoulders seamed to sink a little. "It's been going on for years," he said as he stood, not taking his eyes off the screen.

Dupres stood quietly looking on as Arvin asked. "What does this mean exactly?"

Alli spoke in an annoyed tone "It means someone has been cloning chips and forging data for a long time now. Most of the files that come up as being tampered with are all celebrities and a few politicians too."

Derek randomly clicked on files and read out the names "Douglas Fairbanks, Rebecca Fairbanks, William P. Connors, Charlie Sheen are just the tip of the iceberg."

"Looks like half of Hollywood is on this list," said Baxter.

"More than half is on this list... the important ones are anyway, actors, writers, producers and directors," replied Derek. "With your permission, Mr Cooper I would like to bring in a few friends who might be able to figure out how this cloning thing was done."

"Hackers for lack of a better term," said Dupres while looking at Derek.

Cooper gave Derek a light pat on the back. "Maybe, but I'm sure they might know things we don't. Angles we might not think of. Do it!"

Baxter got up and gestured Cooper to the side as if to ask without asking if he could have a word. Something Cooper recognized and followed Baxter into a quiet area where they could speak without being heard. Baxter shifted his gaze back towards the people they had just walked away from as he looked Cooper in the eye and spoke calmly. "I don't trust Derek, never did. And I don't like the idea of bringing in more of his kind either. Did you forget the damage he did to Cooper Tec's reputation already?"

"No I didn't. But right now, I think we need to see what his friends have to say before this goes public."

"Well I don't like it one bit."

"You don't have to Baxter; it isn't your neck on the line now is it?" asked Cooper as he walked away from Baxter. "Derek, call your friends and meet them in security. I'll get them set up with guest passes and access to workstations." Cooper walked towards his private elevator, the doors sensing his approach and opening for him.

Baxter spoke as he walked past everyone. "I'm going to lunch now and should be back when your friends get here."

Dupres nudged Arvin's arm as he spoke. "Baxter, hold that elevator."

Arvin turned to Derek. "Keep us posted," to which Dupres chuckled as he got on the elevator with Baxter.

Derek now alone with Alli placed his hand on her arm and asked her a question. "Alli, can I trust you?"

Alli smiled at Derek as she replied. "Sure!"

"My friends did try and figure out how to clone the tracker chips but I lied when I said they could figure this out."

Not knowing what to think at Derek's comments she inquired. "Really? Why would you lie about that to Cooper? That's not going to help you get ahead in this place."

Derek took her hand in his. "I need you to trust me. I'm play
ing a hunch and there is no time to explain."

12

Both men were now alone in the underground parking garage. Arvin approached his car and spoke "Doors," watching
them open slowly as he stopped to look behind him.

At that same moment, Dupres had stopped and reached into
his pocket and pulled out his iCom, which was glowing blue. He
put the phone to his ear and spoke impatiently, as if the person
had bothered him during something important.

"Dupres here!"

Arvin stood next to the car watching Dupres go through his
usual array of "yup", "aha" and "will do". Arvin saw him look at
the phone with a stunned expression as the blue glow faded
away.

"That was strange. It was like my phone died on me." Dupres
put the phone back in his pocket and started walking towards
the elevator. "Derek says he wants to talk to us in private."

"Did he say what about?" inquired Arvin as he followed
Dupres, glancing behind him at the closing doors of his vehicle.

Dupres reached out and pressed the elevator button. "He
said he found something and would rather show us in person.
Probably wants to confess."

Arvin, with his hands now planted deep in his pants pockets
said, "I wouldn't be so sure; I think you're misjudging this kid."

"Tell that to the people who got their bank accounts cleaned
out by your innocent little kid," said Dupres.

"Maybe you're right but I'm not convinced yet. I mean this all
goes way to far back. Way before he was ever an employee of
Cooper Tec."

"Good point," replied Dupres.

"Just keep an open mind," said Arvin as the elevator stopped
and the doors slid open.

"Perfect timing," said Dupres grinning as he saw Baxter standing alone in the elevator.

Before anyone could say anything else Baxter pointed a handgun in a bandaged right hand at the men before him. Dupres noticed right away that the bandages of the hand holding the gun were quite bloody. He also noticed the handgun's sensor was armed and the light underneath the barrel was green meaning it could be fired at will. Not only was the gun legal but somehow a computer technician's chip was allowing him to use it.

Arvin reached for his own gun, pulled it out of its hip holster and pointed it at Baxter in a quick motion, like the old gunslingers in the western movies. He squeezed at the trigger twice to no avail and only then did he notice the light on the back of the police issue Glock was red instead of the green it should be.

Baxter smiled at Arvin for a brief second before he shot him in the chest. The impact of the gunshot made the young detective stagger backwards a step, now off balance he fell flat on his back.

Dupres took a step forward but not before Baxter could squeeze the trigger again. Dupres felt a searing pain in near his left shoulder, the blood quickly formed around the bullet hole on his beige suit jacket as he reached Baxter, now inside the elevator. Dupres made a desperate grab for Baxter's gun hand with both of his. He clasped his hands quickly over Baxter's and the gun went off while aimed at the ceiling. The wound in his shoulder left him with no real strength in his left arm, so Dupres did almost all the squeezing with his right hand, causing bolts of pain to shoot through Baxter's right arm. The struggle was short lived as the gun went off again, this time the bullet penetrated the meat of Dupres right thigh, making him collapse to one knee in the doorway, stopping the doors from closing at that same moment. Still in the kneeling position, Dupres pulled his gun from his hip holster while Baxter stepped over him, making his way out of the elevator. He ran past a prone Arvin and disappeared amidst the cars not far away.

"Fuck!" said Dupres as he looked at the red light on his Glock.

"Oh my God!" he heard Amanda screech as he saw Cooper's assistant quickly run over. She had emerged from the second elevator just at that moment to the sight of the two bleeding detectives. She pulled her iCom from her pocket. "Mr Cooper, I need you to come down to the parking garage right away. First level and hurry."

"Baxter killed Arvin," said Dupres as he pulled himself out of the doorway of the elevator letting the doors shut.

A coughing sound and then a weakened voice spoke. "Who said I was dead. Although I will be if the paramedics don't get here soon." This was followed by more coughing. "Hey, Dupres, you're a movie buff. I bet you're disappointed that there was no high-speed chase scene."

Dupres laughed at the thought. "High speed chase, the cars navigation systems would have just shut down as soon as we tried to do a few crazy moves." He leaned back as the blood stain grew on his shirt underneath his suit jacket. The elevator doors opened, and rustling sounds of people could be heard as the paramedics arrived.

"Fuck, over here... me first," said Arvin as he lay in a small pool of blood. "I think the bullet went right through me," as he lifted his head off the concrete trying to look at the wound showing it to the paramedics as he began to cough.

"I'm next," said Dupres as a paramedic came to assess his condition.

The elevator doors opened again, and they heard a voice. "What's going on here?" said Doc Brown as he emerged quickly followed by Cooper, Derek and Alli. Brown put his kit down next to Dupres. "911 said your chip signals both went out and so we assumed you were dead. Both of you... and Amanda's signal is the one that was set off."

"How's Arvin?" asked Dupres looking behind him to where he was now being hoisted up on a stretcher.

"I'm pretty sure the bullet missed his lung somehow," said

a paramedic as they wheeled him onto the elevator. The paramedic standing next to Dupres spoke. "I think yours is worse actually, we gotta get you to the hospital."

Doc Brown slapped Dupres on the back and chuckled as the detective winced in pain. "I've never been so happy to not be needed before."

Arvin spoke as he was being pushed into the back of the ambulance "Derek, you need to go track Baxter and see where he's going."

Dupres was being made to lie on a stretcher.

Alli spoke "Run? Where to? He's got three tracker chips. Actually, make that two tracker chips now so how far could he get?" she said half asking. Reaching into her pocket she pulled out a small silver orb and looked at it. Dupres could see it was still bloody and so he guessed this was just recently removed and this explained the bloody bandaged hand.

Cooper stepped in behind Derek and Alli placing a hand on each one's shoulder. "I need you guys to see if you can trace whatever cloned chip he is using to have access to get away. He had to have one to be able to drive a car."

Alli smiled at Derek. "My money says he cloned Dupres' chip. Your gun isn't registering your chip is it?" she asked. "And that would also explain why we thought you were dead and how he stole your car."

"And why my phone died on me," added Dupres.

13

Three days later Baxter was said to have been seen on a small island off the coast of Hawaii with Charlie Sheen and Lulu the midget porn queen. Sheen's publicist said these were merely rumours as the star was on set filming Scary Movie 17.

14

The hospital room seamed quiet to Arvin as he lay in his bed in a cloudy daze. Sleeping on and off throughout the day due to the heavy pain medications and being so groggy he lay very still enjoying the numbness he was experiencing at this very moment. The bullet, by some small miracle, missed his lung and gone straight through him. Having been in an induced coma for days due to infections and complications he was only now spending some time in the land of the living. And with this being his first day awake his hospital roommate had been so kind to loan him a book to read, to help pass the time he had said. Another of Dupres's old-fashioned expressions thought Arvin as he lay with his copy of "Dark Tales for Dark Nights" laying on his chest with a bookmark protruding at an angle from the middle of it. His roommate Dupres lay in his own bed with his own newly autographed copy of "Sleepless Nights" on his bedside table. On the opposite side sat a vase containing a colourful mixture of flowers on his dinner tray, which had been pulled away a bit. They must have been recently delivered he thought as he didn't remember them being there when last his eyes stayed open for a while. That's when he saw Dupres' eyes open.

"You awake?" he asked.

"I am now," replied Dupres.

"Who are the flowers from?" asked Arvin.

"Don't know, I must have been sleeping when they brought them."

At that moment they both heard the shuffling of feet at the door and a familiar voice.

"You guys are finally awake," said Derek who was standing at the door holding the hand of a lovely young woman. In the haze of having just awoken Dupres had not recognized the smiling Alli right away. She not only held his hand but also clutched his arm like a girl in love, smiling all the while. Derek also glanced at her with a large smile and love in his eyes. Dupres couldn't help but think this kid might be all right after all.

Alli nudged Derek making him blush a little before speaking up.

"Cooper wanted to come by and thank you guys for not

hanging him out to dry. But being the head of a worldwide tech giant he is quite busy. Especially with all that happened after we uncovered Baxter's years spent doing favors for all those Hollywood celebrities he idolized so much."

Alli spoke proudly smiling all the while. "Derek managed to find the layered data that Baxter had been hiding for them."

Derek smiled at Alli and corrected. "We-we figured it out."

"Cooper was so impressed that he offered Derek the lead developer job," spoke Alli.

"Congratulations," said Arvin.

Alli looked at the flowers and read the card. "Such pretty flowers. Florence, is that your wife?" she asked.

"Captain Silverson sent you the flowers?" said Arvin with a sudden rise in curiosity very apparent in his voice.

Dupres, changing the subject quickly, asked their visitors if they have been watching any of the entertainment shows since Fairbanks was murdered. They discussed the fact that even though Fairbanks died, Connors still didn't get the movie deal. The movie was scrapped and most likely won't be made after all.

Alli's smile vanished. "I watched the interview with Connors and he said that Baxter and he were good friends. And Baxter had become bitter towards Fairbanks since he no longer wanted anything to do with him."

Dupres turned to Arvin smiling. "Oh and Arvin, I forgot to tell you. You're going to be a star." To which Arvin gave him a puzzled look. "Arseneault stopped in yesterday while you were still sleeping and said he backed out of the deal to write the remake of King Kong because he pitched a new idea for a movie to the studios. He is writing a story about the Fairbanks murder called Pre-ordering Murder."

"Are you serious?" asked a shocked Arvin.

Dupres looked at Arvin and grinned. "Yup, the script isn't even written yet and they've already started pre-selling the movie."

Flljan, Flljan

1

With both hands clutching the steering wheel of her small hatchback, Margaret sat leaning forward with her face buried in-between her arms, sobbing uncontrollably. Her cheeks soaked with tears as she sat, her spirit finally broken in a long time. Her plain blue jeans and modest looking, off-white top matched her matted down long hair and sneakers. Most women her age still wear trendy clothes and walk around in their high heels, but not this mother. Some might notice the lack of mascara running down her face. That was because she had given up looking after herself long ago and dedicated her life to her son, Andrew.

"I can't take it anymore, Andrew," she said softly with her face still buried in her forearms. "I can't... I don't know how anymore," she sobbed. Tears flowed freely down her cheeks.

In the passenger seat, Andrew was overly agitated today and she had no idea why. He'd been this way for the last week.

"Flljan, Flljan!" he said loudly as he rocked his upper body back and forth shaking his forearms with contorted hands as he always did when he got excited. His white bike helmet that he wore most days in the car was coming loose and needed fixing before it fell off. If it fell off and he got too excited he might hit his head in the side window like before.

"I don't understand what's gotten into you this week. What is it, Andrew? I wish you could tell me?" she said as she sat up brushing her tears off her cheeks. Looking at him now she could hardly remember the boy he once was three years ago before it all happened.

Andrew was calmer now but still repeated the words he always said when excited. "Flljan, Flljan," he said while rocking himself back and forth in a calmer fashion while staring at the dashboard.

"Why can't it be like before?" she said aloud as she took a tissue and wiped the boy's nose. Not unlike one would do to a three-year-old. Straightening his helmet, she clutched his face as he stopped rocking, her touch calming the boy down like it always did. She often tried remembering him the way he used to be before Dr. Holbrook came into her life. The intelligent boy who used to make his parents proud bringing home A's and B's on his report cards. The same boy that his father now insisted should be in a special care home where he would have staff to look after him at all times of the day. A thought that Margaret would have never even consider not even to save her now broken marriage.

It's hard to even picture him like that anymore after all these years she thought to herself as she straightened up his shirt and jacket, which were getting all twisted up with his constant rocking back and forth on the drive home.

While glancing in her rear-view mirror to see if anyone had pulled up behind her as she sat at the intersection Margaret straightened herself while she spoke quietly. "You know what, Andrew. Today would have been your graduation day."

To which Andrew murmured something incomprehensible at first. "Mmmmmaaaahh... Flljan, Flljan," he muttered as he began softly rocking back and forth again.

2

Three years earlier a young and vibrant fourteen-year-old Andrew wearing his number nine jersey was on the ice for his last hockey game of the season. With the game tied in the last period, Coach Price knew he would face criticism from most of his player's parents. But to win at this point he had to put his best kids on the ice and even though they wouldn't admit it they all knew he was right. Most of them would complain about his not giving their kids ice time. Not being fair to their children, putting his favourites on the ice including his own son Troy. They all knew he was trying to give them what they wanted. Bragging rights of winning the tournament, something they hadn't had for the last six years.

Truth be told, he wanted to win badly and so he played the kids that had drive and loved hockey. Especially when it meant winning the tournament against the Stonevalley Hornets who was their rival team. His Mappletown Rockets had lost the last three tournaments out of six to them and he would be damned if they would lose this one too.

The hardest part was that these kids from two small communities went to the same amalgamated school. The rivalry was always fuelled in a social scene full of cruel kids.

"Come on, Corey, Troy, Andrew, get that puck!" he shouted, clapping his hands in support as the kids rushed by their bench. Number thirteen, Troy, rushed the boards pinning a Hornet against them filling the crisp air with the sound of clashing hockey sticks as they struggled over the puck. With a flick of his wrist at the right moment Troy stole the puck and sent it gliding towards Andrew who was in a shoving match with a Hornet. Steven, the star player from the Hornets was more concerned about keeping Andrew from getting the puck than getting it himself. In the heat of the moment he was focused on pushing his rival away from it. But a sure-footed Andrew out-skated the opposition most of the time and did it again. Quickly he skated away with the puck that had bounced off Steven's skate while he wasn't looking.

On a breakaway with two full minutes left on the clock he headed for the net with confidence that left little Scotty Newman, the Hornets goaltender sweating bullets and shaking like a leaf. With a bluff to the right Andrew shot to the left and with a deafening cheer from the crowd he scored his second goal of the night. You could feel the excitement in the air as the townsfolk cheered for their hometown Rockets.

With a minute twenty-two left on the clock now it was up to the boys as all they had to do was keep the Hornets from scoring and they could win. With the score now at four to three in their favour there were many nail-biting moments but the Rockets did their part in keeping the Hornets from reaching their goalie. The few times they got the puck and it looked like they would get their chance they would get outdone by Andrew's ability to glide on the ice. Other parents would often elbow Jeff or his wife Margaret and jokingly say he was NHL material. The couple always beamed with pride as they watched their son play hockey, for he was a natural.

Like something out of a feel-good sports movie with thirty seconds left on the clock Scotty stopped the puck from entering the net. This would have given the Rockets a guaranteed win had they scored but Scotty pulled off yet another save. He held the puck for a brief second and then shot it to number thirty-six, which was Andrew's rival if he was to have one. Steven, who was big for his age of fifteen had the puck and would make his parents proud and tie the game. Or so he thought, but the smaller Andrew's skating abilities would prevail making thirty-six look bad yet again. Something he had done many times this night and the home crowd loved it.

When the clock ran out the score was still four to three making the Rockets the winners of the tournament. Most likely Andrew would win most valuable player with the most goals and assists this season. A fact that made Steven even angrier as not only did Andrew make him look bad tonight but he would also take the trophy that had been his for the last two years.

Dropping their gloves, sticks and helmets on the ice Andrew and his teammates celebrated their win with loud cheers, pats on the back, hugs and high fives. Having just won the right to celebrate did not sooth the bruised ego of the opposition. Especially not that of their star player, number thirty-six. Steven being a sore loser, a fact that was compounded by the screams and boos of their own so-called supporters including his own parents. Angry, he quickly skated towards Andrew who had his back towards him and out of blind rage he checked number nine in the back, sending the smaller Andrew flying forward onto the ice. Caught off guard he was thrown violently forward on the ice, his bare hands sliding out from under him on the slick ice and hitting his head hard.

After witnessing such an act of unsportsmanlike aggression the entire hockey arena grew very quiet with everybody holding their breath as they waited for the boy to get up off the ice. Something he would never do on his own as he lay still on the ice. Soon after convulsions started, the gathered coaches and referees called for a stretcher.

"You're gonna be alright, Andrew," the panicked coach Price said trying to reassure himself more than anything as he knelt on the cold hard ice next to the twitching star player.

3

Three weeks later an exhausted Margaret was sleeping in the quiet lounge at the Regent Hospital. Her son in a coma, Doctor Holbrook had prepared her for the worst —that Andrew might never wake up. The brain damage was so severe that until the swelling went down they had no idea what his chances were. Something his mother couldn't accept was that she could possibly have lost her only son.

Sleeping so lightly curled up in the Lazy Boy she heard footsteps near her but after weeks of this she had become accustomed to the staff milling about while she rested. She learned to easily ignore the sounds of their soft soled shoes as they went about their business.

"Mrs Griffard?"

At first she thought she was dreaming when she heard the soft voice that sounded far away yet near her all at the same time.

"Margaret?" This time the voice sounded more inquisitive

than before.

Choking on her words the boy's mother spoke with a dry broken voice. "What? What's the matter? Was I snoring too loud?"

"It's Andrew... he's awake," replied the voice.

"What?" said the groggy and confused mother. She sat up in her chair trying to process what had just been said to her.

"Your son... he's awake."

"Really... oh my God!" Margaret rose from the chair shaking, weak and feeling like she might faint.

Nurse Jenson took her by the arm and walked with her to Andrew's room as the tears flowed down her cheeks.

Andrew lay in his hospital bed, his hair having almost grown enough to hide the surgical scars by now. A sullen faced Doctor Holbrook standing by the bedside greeted her as she approached the bed to see her son's eyes open for the first time in weeks.

As Doctor Holbrook spoke, he gently touched her forearm and gave her his best bedside manner. "Mrs Griffard, the swelling is almost all gone and even though the damage is not as severe as we had thought, your son has suffered brain damage and most likely will never be the same again. Now we don't know for sure yet how much damage is permanent, but the damage is done and there is really nothing more we can do now but wait."

Margaret spoke softly touching her son's hand. "Andrew?" She touched his cheek and sat on the bedside. She watched as her son's eyes rolled in his head and he tried to speak. "mmmmuhhh... gaaaa... flllll."

"Just ask the nurses to page me if you need me, Mrs Griffard," said the doc as he left the room.

"Ffffllljan... Flljan, Flljan....muuuuhhhh... Flljan," said Andrew before seemingly falling asleep again.

4

Three years later while still sitting at the intersection of

Thomas Avenue and Avery Street. Margaret wiped the tears away and looked out at the intersection of Thomas Avenue and Avery Street.

"All the people must be at the school auditorium for graduation today," said Margaret. She spoke to her son like the accident had never happened even though knowing full well he would not reply. She simply could not break the habit.

"Let's get home before the traffic gets crazy, huh," she spoke adjusting her seat belt and sitting up straight. Using a clean tissue, she had crumpled in her lap she wiped the drool on her sons chin and she smiled her best smile at him to comfort him.

White helmet now adjusted and strapped in place his mother turned her attention to getting home again. They were no more than a few blocks away and she was thinking that once home she would be able to give him his new medications to help calm him down. Andrew had been very excitable today and she couldn't figure out why. She never had abandoned her grocery cart in the middle of the store before but today he was just unbearable.

"We're going to call Doctor Holbrook to make an appointment later. Remember we went to see him last month, Andrew?"

A mere block later Andrew started rocking back and forth again, harder and faster than before. He looked very upset and began speaking very loudly "mmmmmaaaahh... Flljan, Flljan!"

"What has gotten into you today?" asked Margaret knowing full well he would never answer anything other than "Flljan, Flljan".

Andrew, shaking his forearms as he rocked so hard that his helmet came loose and fell at his feet. "mmmmmaaaahh... Flljan, Flljan."

An angry and upset Margaret reached before him with her arm in front of her son trying to stifle his constant rocking.

"Andrew... stop it, stop it now you hear me," she shouted as her car ran the stop sign. She never saw the full-sized king cab truck full of teenagers coming.

5

Little Scotty Newman, who had barely grown since his days playing for the Hornets as goaltender had taken his dad's work truck without permission on his graduation day. He would have barely saw the small red car over the hood of the large truck had he been paying attention to the road. With the winch making it even more difficult to see anything right in front at first, he couldn't see what he had just hit. He had been too busy trying to stop his friend Steven from texting Scotty's girlfriend with his iPhone. Steven had just taken it from the console and was threatening to send foolish messages to her with it and Scotty was trying to take his phone away from him.

6

Upon impact her head was turned so while looking at her son her sight was suddenly filled with fluttering white specs of light. The smell and taste of blood filled her nasal passages and mouth. Before she realized what was happening her life essence had already left her body. The impact had crushed the driver's side killing her almost instantly. The small light vehicle was flung across the road by the large heavy work truck and it only stopped when it slammed into a parked car. Without his helmet Andrew didn't have a chance as his head bashed into the side window so hard that it snapped his neck and crushed his fragile skull.

The chaos was over just as quickly as it had begun leaving parts of both vehicles all over the faded black asphalt of the intersection. The car, having taken the worst of it, was left in an unrecognizable heap of twisted red metal. Inside this heap were the bodies of mother and son clasping hands as Andrew in his last moment had reached out and put his hand over his mother's already cold hand before taking his last breath.

The truck had veered into a utility pole smashing the front end even more than the original impact. The balance of the truck was barely damaged as the larger vehicle clearly had the advantage in the encounter. This meant its passengers should have fared well had they all been wearing their seat belts like they should. Scotty who was wearing his had only minor injuries consisting mostly of bruises and sprains. Jean-Charles who was riding shotgun also had his seatbelt on but had broken his wrist trying to brace himself. Troy who was in the back had bounced around and was in pretty bad shape. Steven though, sitting in the middle of the back seat without a seat belt had been thrown through the windshield. His body had hit the wooden pole the truck now rested against. He lay on the ground barely showing any signs of life except the expansion and contraction of his rib cage showing he was still breathing.

7

Soon after, the flashing lights could be seen from up the streets in all directions as the ambulances and rescue truck were at the intersection. Officer Clarence and his partner were setting up a roadblock as the first ambulance left with two of the boys bringing them to the local hospital.

Clarence was stringing yellow tape across the road on the east side so no one would come too close. After a second police car drove up, Clarence spoke in a low tone to the new officer on the scene.

"Steven was taken to the hospital with what they think are pretty severe injuries. They think his neck is broken and he might be paralyzed."

Ducking under the yellow tape Office Petry's voice broke a little as she asked, "That's Margaret and Andrew isn't?"

"Yup. They never stood a chance in that tiny car. Not against this monster of a truck anyway."

Pointing, Petry asked "Who was driving the truck?"

"Little Scotty Newman. I gotta call this in so his parents can be notified before they hear about it."

He grabbed the radio from his belt and spoke into it. "Dispatch, this is Officer Clarence. I need you to send an officer to notify the families of the victims before they hear about it from strangers. License plate GUK 158. It's Margaret and her son Andrew." Pausing, waiting on a reply from the other end of the radio he walked towards the truck.

A female voice came on. "Clarence, maybe you should wait until both the ambulances have taken all the victims to the hospital."

"I know what you're thinking, Sharon but you know half these folks in the houses facing the scene are peaking through the blinds or outside on their cell phones. Most are probably already posting stuff on Facebook about this and I know I wouldn't want to find out that way if it was my son."

Sharon knowing full well he was right spoke briefly. "What's the plate from the truck?"

"It's a vanity plate. P H I L J A N. It's Philip and Janice Newman's company truck from Philjan Construction. Their son Scotty was driving it."

"Ok Clarence, I will have someone notify the families right away. And I have to agree that I wouldn't want to find out that way either."

Penny For Your Thoughts

1

Nestled on the corner of Twenty-Third Street and Main sat a very popular small gourmet coffee shop called B-Cups Café. The old stone building housed the place which was now famous for its rich coffee flavours and it had garnered a regular clientele. The bulk of whom had to walk there due to the complete lack of parking. The entrance was angled just so, giving it easy access to both streets it sat on. Most of the patrons worked nearby as it was nestled in the hub of downtown amidst all the little shops, travel agents, boutiques and assorted offices. This also meant that it saw a large amount of foot traffic in the course of a day. The Café was always the busiest spot on Main with almost everyone popping by for some form of caffeine at least once, if not multiple times a day.

Summer was here again, and the extra foot traffic would draw those who would pray upon the kindness of strangers. Many of the homeless were regulars, almost as much as the people who worked nearby.

One young man in his twenties was simply known as Stanley. In raggedy clothes he would often sit somewhere near the coffee shop and play his five-string guitar. It was a five-string guitar because Stanley couldn't afford to replace the second string from the bottom that had broken when the cops had forced him to move along a few weeks prior. Brenda, the owner of The Uppity Shoe Shop next door had called them as she thought Stanley was bad for business. Nobody knew Stanley's story because nobody ever took time to learn it. He was just there again this summer like the previous two summers, playing his guitar and singing for pocket change so he could eat.

Another of the many regulars was Delroy. Dressed in layers of dirty clothes and smelling a bit. Most everyone knew his story because he was more than willing to share it.

"S-s-spare some change?" uttered Delroy in a half stutter to anyone walking past him on the sidewalk. "The man c-c-cut me because of m-m-m-ma Tourettes. FUCK! I knows it."

Delroy was one of the unlucky city workers whose job got cut due to downsizing, which was blamed on one of the many recessions. An uneducated aging black man whom had been dicked around by the union for years was now on his own. His lack of a high school diploma kept him from getting hired anywhere he applied. And those times he got close to landing a job, he would get nervous and his Tourette Syndrome would kick in and his foul mouth would cost him the opportunity. Delroy would often get upset when things wouldn't be going well as he never could understand why he had to have a high school diploma to be a janitor. He had been a janitor for twenty-eight years without one but that didn't mean anything now. With no job, it didn't take long for Delroy to fall behind on the rent and the landlord showed him no mercy, throwing him out on the streets.

Penniless and having no living relatives to turn to it didn't take long for the city to swallow a man like Delroy whole. He soon found himself on the streets struggling to survive. Adapting quickly, he did the best he could.

But Delroy was no ordinary man. There was something very special about him that only he and his mother had known. This secret she took to her grave long ago and he never told a soul.

"E-E-Excuse me, Mista. Can ya spare some change? Help f-f-feed this old soul will ya?" he would ask the man in the paint smeared jeans and chequered shirt as he walked past him carrying a can of white paint. It was still early this day and traffic was heavy.

"W-W-What about you there, young lady? Can you spare a

few quarters so I's can eat?" he said to a young black lady in the business suit as she hurried past, not making eye contact. As Delroy turned to look down the street, his face lit up like he had seen an old friend.

"Hey there, S-S-Samantha," he said to a full figured, busty lady strutting her stuff as she walked by. "You ve-ve-vacuuming naked with the curtains open again?" he said half laughing with his head cocked to the side. He admired her generous curves as she stopped dead in her tracks. She twisted her body at the waist and looked over her shoulder at Delroy with a look of disbelief.

"How?" is the only thing that escaped her lips as she caught herself feeling embarrassed that someone other than Marty, her retired neighbour knew about the shows. On Wednesday nights when his wife was gone to her bridge club, Samantha would clean her place in the nude. While the lights next door would go out, she knew full well Marty would be standing in the dark watching her and it turned her on. But this was a secret only she and her white-haired neighbour knew about. So how did this strange homeless man know? Flustered and angry, she turned and walked away as Delroy smiled wide relishing in the moment.

He had first seen Samantha a few weeks ago when she had aroused his curiosity. The urge to use his gift on her had been impossible to resist. Today it would be Tony, a mid-thirties looking clean-cut and slender man. He wore dress pants, and stylish shirt and a pair of the trendiest of dress shoes he could afford. But there was something about him that caught the homeless man's attention. Not being able to resist these urges he approached him as he walked past.

"Hey you," Delroy said to the slender man. "Penny for your thoughts."

"What?" inquired Tony.

Before he knew it Delroy had grasped his wrist placing a penny in his hand and repeated what he had said previously. "Penny for your thoughts, Mista. P-P-Penny for your thoughts."

Tony jerked his hand away and gave the homeless man a dirty look as he walked into the coffee shop. "Crazy bastard," he said as he looked down at the single penny in the palm of his hand. He flung it to the sidewalk and pulled the door open, disappearing behind the glass door of the Café.

Meanwhile Delroy stood as if transfixed and oblivious to the world around him. Spasms began rocking his body as he suddenly felt like he had been zapped by a charge of electricity. Again and again his body swayed but he didn't fall, his feet planted firmly in place. Then it washed over him like a cool breeze on warm summer's day. With his eyes closed he could see it clear as day. Flashes came quickly as he saw cut up moments from Tony's memories.

A bowl of oatmeal, a banana for breakfast, a run in the park, then getting ready for work, he could see it all clearly as if he had been there himself. The day spent selling men's wear at Dutton's Fine Threads down the street. Sub sandwich for supper on the way home to free up his evening alone since his girlfriend is out of town. And then Tony standing in his girlfriend's black dress and high heel shoes admiring himself in the mirror. At bedtime he wore his girlfriend's silk baby-doll pyjamas. The homeless man stood there for what felt like an eternity while Tony's memories of the last day washed over him like they were his own. He never understood how he did this and why it didn't work on everybody. But he had learned to understand that special feeling when he saw someone who it would work on. Unable to resist the urge, he had to do it each and every time. The stronger the urge, the clearer the memories would be.

As Tony stepped out of the café with his tall double espresso in his hand, he made eye contact with Delroy who was now smiling from ear to ear showing rows of yellow teeth.

"You best not gain anymore w-w-weight, Tony or the be-be-black dress won't fit anymore," said the homeless man with a chuckling laugh.

Embarrassed, Tony hurried down the street trying to ignore the looks he was getting from the people. How the hell did he know this he wondered? Nobody knew his secret so how could he?

2

Four days later. People were making their way down the street mostly going to lunch from work; Delroy was still near the coffee shop asking for change as usual.

"Th-Th-Thanks, lady," he said as a grey-haired woman handed him a dollar and change. "I sure do prechiate it, Ma'am".

If all went well Delroy would have some money left over after buying supper that night. He just needed a little more and that's when he spotted the tall clean-looking man in the business suit. He had come out of the Going-Going-Gone Travel Agency down the street and was walking in his direction. The strongest urge he ever had washed over him in a flash. Delroy reached into his breast pocket of the raggedy shirt he was wearing and pulled out the entirety of its contents. A single penny that he always kept at the ready and as the man approached, he looked directly at him and spoke without a stutter.

"Penny for your thoughts, Mista."

Before the man knew what was happening, the homeless man had grasped his hand and pressed a penny into his palm.

"Penny for your thoughts, Mista. Penny for your thoughts."

As the man pulled his hand away, he spoke in a rude tone of voice. "Don't touch me, you filthy bum," he said as he walked off at a brisk pace.

Meanwhile Delroy stopped in his tracks with his back still to the man who was now walking away. He stood very still with his feet planted firmly like he had done on many occasions. A slight electric twitch and in a moment, he was transfixed and oblivious to the world around him. Spasms rocked his body as he suddenly felt like he had been zapped by a charge of electricity, again and again. Then it washed over him like a cool breeze and with his eyes closed he could see it clear as day. The flashes came quickly as he saw snippets of the man's memories.

He became aware of the man's name. Mark Holbrook. The flashes began simple with an evening watching a basketball game. Next morning, he had coffee while he read the newspaper, getting dressed for work and then leaving home. Rush hour traffic and then flirting with the coffee shop waitress that morning. Arguing with his wife on the phone and then booking a flight to Mexico for two on a web site. Arguing with the wife that afternoon and then crushing her skull violently using the brass antique vase from their mantel. The very last flash was of Mark standing over his wife's body. His face speckled with her blood and a look of satisfaction. It was the last flash because Delroy was awoken as if from a nightmare that was all too real.

When Delroy came to his senses he felt a sickening feeling in the pit of his stomach. He knew right away he had to call Detective Foster about this. He wasn't sure what he would tell him this time. Last time the Detective refused to take him seriously. But he couldn't let that stop him as his mother always told him he had this gift for a reason.

Maybe this was the reason he wondered. Pulling out a handful of change he selected a single quarter and returned the balance to the pocket whence it came.

Delroy first met Detective Grady Foster on a sunny afternoon in October a year before this day. Foster, an aging Detective in his late fifties had gotten a bit lazy in his job trying to pawn off cases to the younger guys in an attempt to simply coast by. A divorced heavy smoker, severely out of shape, Delroy felt a strong urge to make contact with him. He didn't get a whole lot from him except many flashes of cigarettes. Amongst these flashes he got was the Detective giving out his business card with his number on it.

Delroy never quite understood why the flashes came to him in the first place. He knew it was the contact that did it and not the actual act of giving the penny. But the penny was a reason for him to touch the person. An excuse to make the link he needed to make. And Delroy never forgot the flashes of memories he saw. He could still picture the card in the man's yellow cigarette-stained fingers.

Delroy held the payphone receiver to his ear as he heard a voice. "Detective Foster here, what's the problem?"

"The man's name is Mark. Mark Holbrook. Ya gotta f-f-find where he lives," said Delroy immediately not wasting any time getting to the point.

"Who is this?" asked Detective Foster.

"That ain't important, Mista. Ya gotta f-f-find where Mark Holbrook lives and go there. He killed his wife and is gonna g-g-get away with it if ya don't hurry," replied an impatient Delroy.

"I know you!" replied Detective Foster. "You're the guy who told me where to find the Bennett girl's body last winter after she got abducted."

"Never mind that, are ya gonna do-do-do it or not?" asked a frustrated Delroy knowing full well he would. He knew now this was why he had that urge long ago to make contact with the Detective. He would need someone to tell this kind of thing to.

"How did you know?" asked Detective Foster. "She hadn't even been reported missing yet when you told me where to find her. Who are you?"

"Look, are ya gonna help or not? I can't let this guy get away with this. My Momma wouldn't like it if I d-d-did, God rest her soul," said Delroy.

"Ok, how do you know this Mark Hallaback did anything wrong?" asked Detective Foster.

"It's Holbrook. Mark Holbrook. You listening to me?" asked an angry Delroy. "FUCK!" he exclaimed as his Tourettes kicked in.

"Ok, what did you say he did?" inquired Detective Foster.

"He killed his wife in their house. FUCK! Bashed her d-d-damn skull in with an ugly vase," added the homeless man.

"Ok. I guess I could send a car over and make sure everything is alright," replied the Detective. "What's the address?"

"I don't know the damn address. It don't work like that. FUCK! I only see stuff; certain parts. I know it's near the c-c-corner of English Avenue and Summer Street. And the house is nice," said Delroy. "Grey s-s-stone on the front with a white picket fence. Big Oak tree in the front yard."

"That's not much to go on," said Detective Foster.

"FUCK! He just bought 2 tickets to Mexico. Leaves in the mornin," added Delroy. "Bought them from the Goin-Go-in-Gone Travel Agency. I saw him coming out of their place earlier today."

"That might help me track him down," replied Foster. "Where can I reach you?"

"FUCK!" said Delroy just before hanging up.

3

"Damn it!" said Foster as he hung up his phone.

"What?" asked the young Detective Martin.

"Just got a lead on a possible murder. From the same guy who gave me the tip on the Bennett girl. After what happened last time, I almost have to believe him, right?" asked Detective Foster. "Do me a favour, Martin. Call a travel agency downtown called Going-Gone or something like that. I need to know if a Mark Hallaback; no... Holbrook; Mark Holbrook booked a flight to Mexico. I'm gonna go check this one out myself," said Detective Grady Foster as he grabbed his jacket and his half empty pack of cigarettes and headed out.

4

An hour later, Detective Foster sat in his car next to a half-dozen cigarette stubs on the asphalt of English Avenue looking at three different houses that fit the unidentified caller's description. Which would it be he wondered? I can't just walk up to the house and ask if anyone is dead inside, he thought to himself.

That's when he noticed the tree in front of one house was a willow tree and not an Oak eliminating one. No other houses in the neighbourhood had grey stone. It had to be one of these.

Suddenly out of one house walked a lady dressed in skintight yoga pants and a pink long sleeve slim fitting hoodie. She had an iPod, or something strapped to her arm with ear buds in her ears. She walked up to the edge of her driveway, did a bit of stretching, fiddle with her watch, probably setting a timer or something he thought and down the road she started jogging.

"Stupid people joggers are," he said out loud even though no one would hear him.

Via process of elimination, that left one house. He started to reach for the door of his car to get out when he noticed the garage door start to open. Just then he saw a silver Chevrolet Equinox come up the street and pull into that very same driveway he was looking at. The car slowly drove into the garage and stopped. From the garage exited a tall clean looking man in a business suit with briefcase in hand.

Foster started his car and pulled up behind the Equinox blocking his exit.

Getting out of his car, Foster spoke. "Excuse me, Mark Holbrook?" he said inquisitively.

"Yes?" replied Mark. "Who are you?" he said with an air of arrogance.

"My name is Detective Grady Foster. Can I take a minute of your time?"

A look of shock came over Holbrook's face for a moment. He quickly flung the briefcase at the Detective in a panic and bolted across the lawn.

Foster barely flinched as the briefcase hit him in the chest and bounced on the ground before him. Just at that moment he heard his cell phone ring and quickly pulled it from its holster.

"Detective Foster here. What's the problem?" he said putting the flip-phone to his ear while watching Mark disappears down the street.

"Foster, it's Martin. It took some convincing, but they caved and told me a Mark Holbrook bought 2 tickets to Mexico this afternoon."

"I figured as much. Listen, I already found his house and he just ran down English Avenue. Send a squad car to find him and tell them he is the only jogger wearing a business suit. I gotta check out the house. There's no victim yet so the guy's not even a suspect at the moment. I'll call you back in a minute," said Foster then closing his old flip-phone.

It only took a minute for the Detective to locate the spare key in the fake rock. It stood out like a sore thumb in the small pile of rocks under the cedar bush in the flower bed near the door.

"Hello," he said loudly as he walked into the house. Foster made his way into the living room and found Mrs. Holbrook lying under a blood-soaked blanket on the living room floor.

He quickly called it in announcing that Holbrook was now officially a suspect in a murder investigation. As he put his phone away, he couldn't help but wonder to himself who this tipster was. How did he know about this? What did he mean when he said, that's not how it works? *Not how what works* Detective Foster wondered.

5

Three days later, Mark Holbrook had been arrested for the murder of his wife. He had made no attempt to hide evidence as he had intended on leaving the country with his mistress before anyone would know she was dead.

Detective Grady Foster couldn't stop thinking about the caller that tipped him off about the murder. After a while he remembered what the man had said to him just three days past. Holbrook had bought tickets at the Going-Going-Gone Travel Agency. How did he know this? He was in the area and saw him leaving the place recalled Foster. Perhaps the caller frequented the area. It was worth a try as he needed to know who the mysterious tipster was.

Not long after, Foster stood under a small column of smoke near the agency, looking around the neighbourhood, a lit cigarette hanging loosely from his lips. Watching the people mill about he wondered how the tipster would have known this. That's when he heard a familiar voice from up the street.

"Excuse me, Mista. Can ya spare some ch-ch-change, huh?"

Could it be, Foster wondered? *No way,* he thought. It couldn't be this scraggly dirty looking homeless man. How could he possibly have known about Holbrook killing his wife in a suburb across town?

"Oh, thank you, miss. FUCK!" said Delroy as a lady gave him some change. "So-so-sorry, lady. I got's Tourettes you know."

A feeling of guilt came over the Detective about how he had been angry that the man hadn't given him his return phone number or address. His heart sunk a bit at the thought. He dropped what was left of his cigarette, butting it out with his foot while pulling out another and placing it in his mouth. While digging in his pockets for his Zippo he wondered what type of questions he would ask the man. If it was him in the first place. That voice; it sounded right he thought as he walked towards him nonchalantly.

"Hey, Mista. Can you spare some change so's I could eat?" said the dirty homeless man standing in front of the B-Cups Café.

Pretending he was walking past the homeless man, Foster reached out and grasped the man's wrist and placed a twenty-dollar bill in his palm. Using both his hand he closed Delroy's hand over the bill and for a brief second, they locked eyes. The homeless man's eyes seamed to roll back in his head briefly. Foster began walking away as if nothing happen. He glanced back at the homeless man who was just standing there. Like he was in shock or something with his arms draped down his side still oblivious to the twenty clenched in the palm of his hand.

Delroy saw flashes of the past day of the life of Detective Foster. He saw him smoking a cigarette while sitting on the side of his bed and another on the way to work. He saw countless cigarettes while driving to the station. He saw the Detective trying desperately to urinate while in lots of pain. He saw him taking pain killers afterwards. Mostly mundane flashes but in the last flash he saw a busy street with a homeless man asking a passer-by for change. He saw himself standing under the B-Cups Café sign asking a man for change. Delroy awoke from his trance-like state and turned his head to see Foster looking towards him in a cloud of cigarette smoke.

"You b-b-better see a doc about those kidney stones, Mista. They's hurt like a som-bitch," said the homeless man.

Foster paused and looked back at the man in stunned silence. How did he know this thought Foster as he turned to walk away again. The pain had only started two days ago and he hadn't told anybody yet.

Speechless

1

"Hey, retard," called out nine-year-old Garner Boucher during recess. He was standing amongst his mischievous friends, Quentin Monroe and Peter Willet. The school yard was crowded with kids playing. Some girls were playing hopscotch while another was skipping rope. Some boys were trading cards they had recently acquired from the local comic shop. Most were too busy to notice that at this moment not a teacher was in sight except the kids that were up to no good. Garner being one of them saw his chance to try and antagonize Devin Butler without getting caught.

"Say something will ya," said Garner as Devin sat in the dirt blissfully unaware of his presence. Devin usually sat alone, playing with simple things, and today was no exception. The boy sat with a large flat rock in both hands as he jabbed it into the dirt in front of him digging a hole in the damp, hard soil.

"Watch this," said Quentin as he drew change from his pocket. It was a combination of coins including twenty-two pennies, two dimes, a nickel and a quarter as well as some pocket lint now in the palm of his hand. Quentin flung the change in the dirt in front of the boy knowing full well how he would react. Devin dropped the rock and scampered on his hands and knees heading for the pile of change, picking it out of the dirt while the threesome of bullies laughed at him.

"Look at the retard," said the pointing Peter trying to get other kids to watch as Devin gathered up the last of the change he wanted. As he stood up, he looked at the handful of coins and put the change in the pocket of his dirty pants. He looked around as if he was unaware that the other kids were laughing at him. As usual he was content in his own little world and had just picked the dirt clean of all the pennies. The dimes, nickel, and quarter still lay half buried in the loose dirt he had recently dug up.

At that moment Jeffrey, Devin's older brother burst through a pack of laughing kids to witness his little brother being ridiculed again. Having heard the names, he knew they were picking on him.

"Stop laughing at him," he screamed at the crowd of his peers. "It's not his fault he can't talk."

"He's a retard," shouted Garner.

"He's autistic, NOT retarded," said Raylene McPhee as she made her way between the kids just as the bell rang indicating recess was over. She was not much taller than the kids were so she made her way through to see what was going on, knowing full well what she would find. Screaming boys and girls began running in all directions at first and then all funnelled into the one doorway back into the hallway of Carlton Elementary.

"I just stopped watching him for a minute," said the older sibling as tears welled up in the nine-year-old's eyes.

"It's ok, Jeffery. Devin's ok."

Jeffrey's younger brother stood smiling slightly while he fondled the pennies in his pocket making them jingle. Raylene reached out her hand to the boy as she bent a little trying to make eye contact. When she caught his attention, Devin straightened and took her hand then reached for his brother's hand too. Before taking hold of Devin's hand Jeffery made sure no one was watching. Unintentionally stepping on the quarter, a content Devin was completely oblivious to its existence as he walked on. The same quarter he had completely ignored while he picked up pennies all around the other shiny coins.

The bus ride home was quiet that day as usual. Garner and his cohorts sitting in the back of the bus thinking they were cool. Poking fun at kids on the bus and being mean to others.

Jeffrey and his brother always sat right behind old cranky Harold the bus driver who ran a tight ship. The older boy didn't like the smell of the cigars which the driver reeked of, but this always kept other kids from bothering his little brother. Especially since Harold kept a close eye on little Devin.

2

"Garner and Quentin were making fun of Devin again today," said Jeffrey as he picked at his peas with a fork showing very little zeal. A high-pitched whine came from under the table just before a few peas fell on the floor as Muffet, the forty pound mutt quickly cleaned the floor of anything and everything that happened to accidentally fall off a child's plate.

"Where were you Jeffrey when this happened?' asked his mother coldly as she sat her glass of water down next to her now half empty plate.

The boy's father shot her a glance. "Don't blame the boy for other kids being cruel to Devin."

Sitting motionless staring out the dining room window, Devin was already done eating his dinner, having left nothing but a few peas and half a string bean. Geraldine had barely begun speaking the words when the youngest of her sons got up and ran to the back door.

"It's ok, Devin. You can go play now."

He pulled on his shoes and ran out the back door of the home, letting the wooden screen door shut loudly behind him.

"Don't go far," screamed his mother as she walked to the back door watching him disappear into the thicket behind the house just past the shed. She pushed the door open and let the whiny Muffet out to chase after the boy. She heard the dog bark twice as he plunged into the brush at the exact same place as the boy had, just a moment before.

Standing by the door she spoke softly now. "I made another appointment with Doctor Melanson like Principal Sullivan asked."

The clinking of dishes echoed as her husband and older son cleared the table. "Do you remember what she said the last time we brought him to see Dr. Melanson?" he questioned as he scooped the leftover handful of overcooked green beans into the trash while she wasn't looking.

With a sigh of despair, she replied. "Yes I do, Linus. Trust me I do, but I also don't understand how a bright and intelligent boy who was very vocal would stop talking so damn suddenly."

"I know, Hun. Principal Sullivan said it sounded like he had a traumatic event. But Evee said he shows all the classic signs of autism."

Her shoulders quivered as she sobbed softly while she leaned against the door jam. Looking through the screen door she could see only trees and brush which filled their six-acre lot behind their modest country home.

"Thank you for clearing the table with me son, now please go do your homework," Linus said to Jeffrey as he patted the boy on the head as he watched his wife, feeling his own heart grow heavy.

"Why do I always have to go do homework when Devin gets to go play?" whined the boy. "It's not fair."

A moment later an overjoyed Muffet burst out of a thicket, bounded around the back yard in random patterns that made no sense to anyone. He stopped, stretching out his front paws in front of him with his butt in the air with a blur of a wagging tail behind him. He barked loudly towards the brush a few times and bounded into it vanishing into the newly grown greenery.

3

A few days later while sitting in their old dark blue Ford Escape, Linus and Geraldine were sipping coffee as they watched Jeffery play. This early on a Sunday he had the entire park to himself as he played on the park swings. They watched him attentively as they sipped the coffee they had picked up a short while ago. They watched his every move not wanting to take their eyes off him while they talked between themselves without ever looking at each other. They had brought Devin to see Doctor Evee Melanson as she had insisted on seeing him alone for a while in hopes that he might open up to her.

Evee could always get Devin's attention easily compared to most as he was fascinated by her. She knew this but couldn't figure out how to use it to her advantage.

"Your mother sent me an old video she had of you, Devin. She emailed it to me. You want to watch it with me?"

Getting up she turned her monitor on her desk a little so they could see it better from the chairs they sat in.

"It's you from about a year and a half ago," she told him as she took the cordless mouse back to her chair with her. Rubbing the mouse on her pant leg she revived it from sleep mode as Devin sat deep in his chair with his legs sticking straight out. This reminded her of how small he was for his age. He sat motionless with each hand on each arm rest as if waiting patiently for her to do something interesting.

After clicking on a few of the wrong icons she found the correct one on her third try.

"Are you ready?" she asked staring at him intensely, studying his every move and gesture. This was an attempt to read his body language since the boy had never spoken during the last three months, she had gotten to know him.

Pressing "Play" on the media player program the still image on the screen came to life. As the camera panned the room about a dozen children in paper hats surrounded a table as a young little girl sat at the end wearing a huge smile. A woman placed a large birthday cake with white frosting and six burning candles before her. A chorus of bad singers were in the midst of singing "Happy Birthday, dear Emily. Happy Birthday to you."

The little girl drew in her breath bracing herself with both hands on the table at each side of the cake.

"Make a wish," someone off camera said.

The little girl blew at the candles with all her might blowing them all out but one. An older Peter Willet quickly blew the last one out before a disapproving Emily.

"Hey," someone said.

"He's just a kid," a lady replied.

"Still," the other voice added.

Devin sat transfixed watching the video. Evee watched him just as intensely. He smiled when he saw himself on the screen.

"Happy Bird-day, Emilly. Here's yur present," the younger version of Devin had muttered with a large grin stained with grape juice.

Evee paused the video.

Devin turned to look at her, his smile fading away being replaced by a confused expression.

"You were five and a half on this video, Devin," said the doctor.

The smile returned on the boy.

"Are you ready to tell me why you stopped talking? Can you tell me what happened to you? I won't tell your mom or dad if you tell me not to. I promise!"

The boy turned his attention to the paused video and gazed at it. Seeing this Doctor Melanson hit play again and watched the rest of the short video.

4

Geraldine sipped her coffee while staring blankly at Jeffery as he swung back and forth like a pendulum on the swings.

"What I don't understand is even with all this. His refusing to talk and his change in behaviour, why is it his grades went up? Did you see the look on Principal Sullivan's face when he was telling us they tested him again because they didn't believe it at first? I mean come on. He's seven and is too innocent to even think of cheating."

"Some people say Autistic children – or maybe it's Asperger. Anyways, they say these kids usually are super smart in some ways," replied Linus.

Glancing at him quickly she added. "Yes, but straight A's across the board except for Phys Ed. Really?"

"Maybe he takes after his dad."

Geraldine smiled a real smile and then laughed a little.

"What? What's so funny about that?" he added content in knowing he had managed to cheer her up a little.

5

Standing in the parking lot with keys in his pocket Linus had an arm around his wife's waist. Devin, sitting in the back seat of the small rusty SUV could see his parents talking with Evee.

Doctor Melanson stood with her arms clasped together in front of her as she spoke.

"I really can't get him to open up at all. He has all the signs of Autism, but I can't explain why he didn't have them until last year. That is the part that confuses me the most."

Linus spoke to Evee but was looking at his wife watching her facial expressions "He's withdrawn from everything and stopped talking completely but oddly enough at the same time he is very independent. He dresses himself, feeds himself and is excelling in his schoolwork. I mean he never has to bring home homework. I used to think he wasn't bringing it but Raylene told us it's because he always does it while at school."

Meanwhile the boy climbed into the small space between the front bucket seats and sat in the driver's seat. He reached under some Butler Construction businesses cards and into the ash tray, which had never once been used for its original purpose. He began plucking out pennies, ignoring all other change they had recently acquired while purchasing coffee. Sixteen pennies in total. The boy looked at the palm of his hand, which contained all these pennies as if he had a fortune. He smiled as he examined the pennies in a daze when his father opened the door startling the boy. He clenched his hand into a tight fist as he climbed between the seats and threw himself into the back. Quickly he stuffed the pennies into his pocket before seating himself into his booster seat and buckling himself in. He ran his right hand over the coins that formed a lump on his thigh and smiled contently.

"Who wants ice cream?" asked their mother.

"I do, I do," replied Jeffrey who was already buckled in. He had done so while Devin had busied himself collecting the pennies. Devin just smiled and nodded an enthusiastic yes as he strapped himself in also.

"Last week of school next week then it's off for the summer, huh boys," Linus stated as he buckled himself into the driver's seat.

As he put the key in the ignition, he looked at his sons in the rear-view mirror. For a brief moment he could have sworn he saw Devin open his mouth as if he was about to speak. But he stopped as suddenly as he had begun and just stared out the window. What Linus couldn't see was Devin's hand resting on the pennies in his pocket. The father glanced at his wife and saw that she had not noticed this and felt it better than she not know.

"Ice cream it is then," he said as he started the SUV listening to everybody cheer. Everybody was vocalizing their happiness except little Devin. He simply smiled looking at them all briefly and then turning his gaze outside again as if removing himself from this very moment in time.

6

As the vehicle pulled up to the house, a lazy Muffet lifted his head from the cool grass where he lay in the shade of a maple tree. He shifted his ears about as if analyzing all the new sounds that he was hearing. Recognizing the familiar sound of the family chariot, he lay his head down again as if going back to sleep.

"He must have been running around chasing birds again," said Linus gesturing with a crook of his head as he walked to the back of the Ford Escape. Meeting his wife at the back Linus pressed the keyless remote and popped open the back hatch.

He smiled at his wife while she looked at the boys as they gathered their comic books and candy before bolting towards the house. She turned to find a man with love in his eyes as he watched his wife, the same woman he had fallen for years ago and was still madly in love with.

"What?" she asked, finally noticing him staring at her.

Her husband simply leaned in and gently kissed her on the lips. He didn't say anything and didn't have to as a tear welled up in her eye as he turned and opened the hatch fully. She felt the love he had for her in moments like this and wondered how she was so lucky to have found such a caring man.

"I got it," she said, grabbing the last of the shopping bags.

As he watched her push the hatch shut, he replied. "Don't you just love these old-fashioned paper bags Ernie Woodman uses?" Linus was referring to the oldfangled grocery store that was still old-fashioned because he was too cheap to renovate.

When both parents entered the house and were setting the bags down in the kitchen, they could hear the footsteps upstairs as the boys were already in their rooms.

7

"What did you get?" asked Jeffrey as he stood in the doorway of Devin's room holding his copies of the latest Spider Man, Iron Man and Superman.

Devin sat on the edge of his bed smiling as he pulled his comics from the bag laying them on the quilted duvet his mother had handmade while she was pregnant with him. He held one in his hands as his eyes scanned the cover art in vivid detail for a moment before turning to show his brother.

"Walking Dead comics? Mom let you buy those?" Jeffrey said.

Devin nodded as he turned the comic over again to admire the cover pic of a zombie biting a man's arm as he struggled with the undead creature.

Truthfully, Devin had put a Spider Man comic on top of the

pile, so she had not noticed the rest of his books as the cashier rang them in. The young boy flipped the book open and began to read it intensely as his brother went to his room to do the same.

A short while later while lying on his back, little Devin sat up quickly turning his attention to the window looking outside. Dreamily he put his comic book on the bed as he pulled himself to the edge and got off, walking slowly towards the window. Standing transfixed his hand slowly felt the lump of pennies that were in his pocket. Quickly, a barefoot Devin ran from his room, down the stairs barely touching them and went out the front door. He ran around the house and towards the back yard quickly being joined by his faithful friend Muffet both disappearing into the living wall of green that separated their home from the forest.

8

The smell of Shepard's pie filled the house as the little family sat at the dinner table.

"What's bothering you, Jeffery?" asked a concerned Geraldine as she watched her oldest son picking at his plate. This was odd behaviour considering this was his absolute favourite thing his mother made. The only other thing that came close to beating this was Skipper Jack's Pizza on Second Avenue.

"Devin... the kids at school were making fun of him again."

"It's not your fault," said Linus as he put his glass of milk down.

"It makes me mad. They threw money on the floor near the lockers and made fun of him while he picked it up," said Jeffery as he sat back, his head down clearly upset.

"Its ok son, look at him. He's happy and this stuff never bothers him," his mother said trying to make Jeffery feel better while looking at Devin. He sat at the table mashing his supper up with a large spoon putting a huge gob into his small mouth and chewing happily.

"Last day of school tomorrow," added Linus in an attempt to cheer everybody up.

"Only half a day," added Jeffery with a slight smile as he picked up his fork scooping up a mouthful.

Linus chuckled and bowed his head down. He shook his head as his shoulders jiggled with laughter. Geraldine turned to see Devin holding his large white plate to his face moving it around. The boy peered over the plate at his mother who was also now laughing at her son as he licked his plate clean.

"I guess you boys deserve a little apple pie for dessert," she said getting up from the table.

"Can you make some coffee too, hun? Please?" said Linus

"Sure, dear."

Devin put his plate down and his smile vanished as he turned suddenly looking outside the dining room window. He had a new blank expression that had replaced the grin he had moments ago. Linus picked up the now empty plates and carried them over to the kitchen placing them loudly on the counter almost dropping a few. A sudden loud crack of the screen door startled them both as they saw Devin and Muffet run into the brush at the edge of the back yard.

"I didn't tell him he could go play yet," his frustrated mother said as she took out the small plates and forks for the pie. "Go get your bother," she said harshly before realizing her tone was not very kind. She turned to the older boy and added a smile.

"Please?" she said.

The boy smiled at his mother and quickly put his shoes on and ran out the door making a loud clacking noise echo through the house yet again.

Jeffery ran slower than Devin and had no idea which way his younger brother had gone. He was just about to shout his brother's name when he heard a rustle and a bark not far away. He sprinted through the thick overgrown brush at what was obviously a happy Muffet. He knew where the dog was, Devin would be too.

Stopping for a brief moment to listen intently he heard a bark just ahead. Jeffrey burst through the brush. "Mom told me to come and get-"

The sentence cut short as the boy froze in his tracks at the edge of a small clearing of full-grown trees. Before him, Devin stood with his back to him and Muffet was chasing his tail on the opposite side of the clearing. He barked twice and ran into the woods at a fast pace as if chasing something.

But Jeffery didn't pay much heed to Muffet as right in front of Devin stood something he had never seen before. A creature out of a science fiction movie with a light blue translucent flesh that stood about five feet tall. Devin stood right before it as if unafraid. A sudden panic rose in the nine-year-old as he could think of nothing else but running to get his parents. Yet for some reason he felt stunned and unable to move. The creature slowly looked up from his younger sibling and clearly saw him. It turned its bulbous head with its clear blue eyes that held what would look like not one, but two pupils. The creature extended a long three-fingered hand towards him and locked eyes with the boy who now felt powerless to move his legs. In a panicked daze he opened his mouth to scream but nothing came out.

Devin turned and looked at him blankly and then turned to the creature again. He held out both hands palm up and extended them before the creature gesturing for him to take what was in them. The creature took its gaze off his older brother and looked into the boy's hands with an expression that one could almost call a smile. With a single finger he gently poked into the palm of the child's hand and held up his own hand looking at what had stuck to his fingertip.

While frozen in place and unable to move Jeffery watched as the translucent creature held his finger in front of his eyes and looked at a single penny stuck to his fingertip. He opened a gapping mouth and placed the copper looking coin on his transparent yellow fleshy tongue and paused as he pulled his hand away and closed his eyes.

Somehow the coin, which contained the closest mixture of metals it required seamed to melt into a puddle of copper and silver metals while sitting in the creature's mouth. Slowly it closed its mouth and for a moment its skin turned a solid copper hue as it lost its transparency. It repeated this process three more times and each time its skin would take on this copper hue. The new skin color would not last long though, and the new color would fade away revealing the same transparency as before.

Holding out its hands under Devin's, the young boy dropped the remainder of the pennies into the alien's palms. Slowly the creature inserted the remainder of the coins into what looked to be a sort of pouch in the front of its belly. For a brief moment the coins could be seen through the flesh of its belly, but they faded as if they were never there to begin with.

Devin turned to walk towards his older brother. A terrified Jeffery wanted nothing more but to turn tail and run back the safety of his home and parents. His mind wanted to but his legs wouldn't move. He felt as if he had lost control of his body and was helpless. The creature began walking on short stubby legs and oddly shaped feet when Devin stopped and looked up at the creature, extending his hand like he would to his parents. Taking the boy's hand in its, the creature and the boy walked slowly until they stood before the terrified child. Devin smiled at his brother and then looked up at the creature who slowly reached out its hands placing them on each side of Jeffery's head. He could feel the cold mushy flesh on his cheeks as the fingers coiled around to the back of his skull where they must have laced together. Jeffery's eyes rolled back into his head showing the whites only. He twitched hard twice as if in pain. For a brief moment all was clear to the boy. He could see what his brother had been doing. The creature was weak and needed help to find food and his food was copper. The easiest to come by were pennies, even though there was so little copper in them, and Devin gathered them wherever he could and so he had fed the creature for a long time.

Upon releasing the boy, Jeffery staggered as if he was light-headed and dazed. It took a few seconds for his mind to clear but before it did, he had a vision in his mind's eye of a peaceful place where many others like the one who stood before him lived. It was a strange place where the earth was grey, and the sky was pink. This image faded from his mind as he opened his eyes and felt his fear fade away as he looked up at the creature. Devin held out his hand and Jeffery took hold of it without a second thought.

The being turned to Devin and smiled at the small boy and gently touched his forehead with what looked like a long thumb and spoke a word in a language no one else here understood.

The translucent being turned and walked away as the boys watched it go back into the brush. It entered a thick part of the forest at the base of a large maple tree and vanished from sight. The boys looked at each other and then smiled and ran towards the house. Devin beat his slower brother to the house yet again. Muffet appeared out of nowhere only to scoot past the boys on their way into the house. He barked twice as each boy sat at their place at the table and began devouring the apple pie before them.

"For a minute there I thought you boys didn't want any pie." Geraldine spoke as she sipped her coffee in front of an empty plate where her piece of pie had been a while ago. Their father got up and began clearing the table as he glanced at the boys who would look up at each other while gobbling down the pie. Bedtime would come soon, and Geraldine would find each boy sound asleep comic book in hand and light still on.

"I haven't seen them that tired since Christmas," said Geraldine as she climbed into bed next to her husband. He took off his reading glassed and set his copy of "Dark Tales for Dark Nights" next to his brightly lit lamp. She snuggled herself into the crook of his arm and lay her head on his chest as he wrapped his arm around his wife. He reached out and gave the touch lamp a light tap and the room was plunged into complete darkness for a brief moment. Soon getting accustomed to the light of the moon, Linus planted a kiss on the forehead of his wife.

"I love you," he whispered.

She smiled and kissed him on the lips

"I'm a very lucky woman," she said laying her head on his chest as they held each other tight.

9

"Hey retard," said Garner Boucher as Devin was closing up his locker after getting his things. His brother Jeffery stood idly-by watching him as he did so.

"Say something," added Peter Willet as they all poked each other smiling as if they had said the cleverest things.

Devin turned and looked at Garner and then Peter and spoke.

"Like what? I doubt either of you have the intellect to comprehend anything I might have to say anyway. Neither of you are intelligent enough to come up with anything new and are always using the same old taunts that never worked in the first place. Not very bright if I do say so myself."

The loud sound of books hitting the floor made Peter jump as a stunned Raylene McPhee stood nearby with her arms now empty, her books scattered at her feet. Garner stood with his mouth gapping and speechless at the fact that Devin had spoken to him and in such an intelligent manner.

"Come on, Jeffery," he said as he held out his hand to his older brother who just smiled and took his hand. As they began walking away, Jeffery stopped and crouched as he picked up a couple of pennies that were on the hallway tiles. He stood looking at them in the palm of his hand and then tucked them into his pocket while smiling.

10

As their parent's car pulled up to the school early, a waiting Miss McPhee and Principal Sullivan were waiting for them.

"Are you sure he spoke?" asked Geraldine as she got out of the vehicle.

"Yes! I couldn't believe my ears," said Raylene.

Devin and his bother walked out of the building and towards their parents as if nothing unusual had happened. As if all was normal for them, but the waiting parents both got on their knees on the hard concrete before the boy not saying a word themselves.

"Hey, Mommy," said Devin. "Can we get pizza at Skippers tonight?"

Both parents wrapped their arms around the boy and cried while Devin watched his brother Jeffery walk past them, stop to pick up a penny from the ground and put it in his pocket and then proceed to get in the car to wait for the others.

11

Sitting in a booth in front of a nearly empty very large pizza box, Linus had his arm around his wife as they watched their sons devour the last of the pizza. Linus smiled at his wife and almost crushed her as her pulled her close to him in a sideways hug. Geraldine grunted and wiped away tears of joy with a napkin as she watched them.

"Can we have money for a gumball?" asked a smiling Devin

An overjoyed Linus pulled out a pocket full of coins as both boys scooted out of the booth. Devin picked a pair of quarters out of his father's hand while Jeffrey picked out all the pennies.

Devin smiled at his brother. "Come on."

The younger boy put the first quarter into the machine and pulled out a shiny red gum ball which he handed to his brother. Jeffrey, busy feeling the coins in his pocket didn't notice at first. Devin poked him. "Here," as he handed his brother the shiny red treat before getting a shiny green one of his own.

As the family got into the Ford, Devin turned to his brother and said. "It won't be for too long, he's almost ready to go home."

"What?" questioned their Mother.

"Nothing, Mom," said Devin as he looked at his brother who simply looked back at him and smiled as he felt the pennies through the pocket of his pants.

As a smiling father put his vehicle into drive and proceeded to pull out into traffic, his wife turned to look at her older son Jeffrey as he sat happily looking out the window.

Nothing Ever Happens in Carlton

1

On an otherwise quiet Sunday afternoon near the center of the small town of Carlton, plain-clothed Officer Libby was bent over holding onto the police cruiser; her blood-streaked blond ponytail dangling as she vomited for the second time. Her back felt like it was covered by a cold layer of molasses making her simple v-neck blouse stick to her back. The thought of all the blood on her caused her stomach to go into spasms and rock her body making tears flow down her cheeks. Her last meal now pooled in messy blotches on the asphalt before her. Never had she seen such carnage and gore. The gruesome scene from a few moments ago would be forever burned in her memory. More blood than she had ever seen before she thought as she gagged yet again when she noticed blood dripping from the tip of her ponytail.

2

Three days earlier.

A little more than a few weeks into the school year, the local kids were set in their routines already. The streets of Carlton were deserted after nine o'clock on weeknights and this evening would be no exception. After midnight, as most small towns of this stature, things got extremely quiet. So quiet in fact that few police officers were on call, all excepting one. Dwayne Adams was at his post at the station on Main Street. At least he was at his post in body to say the least. In the early parts of his

149

shift he was always bright-eyed, fully caffeinated and ready for anything. But by the early hours in the morning he was leaning back in his chair, legs crossed with his feet up on the desk. His head slumped forward a little and just below his chin sat a spot of drool as he snored ever so slightly. His left hand wrapped loosely around his belt while his right dangled towards the floor just above his well-worn hardcover copy of *Needful Things* by Stephen King. Three empty cans of Red Bull sat on his otherwise neatly organized desk.

Police Chief Clovis McPhee knew exactly what he would find on such a quiet night, which is why he opened the front door of the Carlton Police Station as quietly as he possibly could. Clutching his large stainless-steel ring of keys in his hand to stifle any noise they might make he held the door open as Officer Libby Terwilliger silently made her way past him carrying a tray of coffee and muffins. Giving Libby a knowing glance he watched her nudge her way past the wooden patrician gate that divided the public area from the bullpen of the station. Gently she set the tray from the local Santorene coffee shop down on her desk as Clovis followed quietly. As Chief Clovis walked past Dwayne's desk, he held the large ring of keys up high, dropping the large clump of metal on the wooden desk with a loud clatter. When the keys struck the desk, Officer Adams jerked from his slumber as his chair kicked over sending him sprawling on the floor. Neither Clovis nor Libby even cracked a smile as a prone Dwayne quickly scrambled to his feet. The sight of Dwayne struggling to gain his composure was rather hysterically funny, but they didn't even crack a smile. The first time this happened they had laughed so hard, they both had sore stomach muscles the following day. And many times, they had laughed at a sleeping Dwayne's expense. But the joke had gotten quite old now and nobody was laughing today.

"All's quiet I assume?" inquired Chief Clovis.

"Yes, Sir," answered Dwayne as he straightened himself up, tucking his shirt in a little and wiping the drool off his chin.

"As usual in this sleepy little town," added Clovis. "Just the way I like it." Clovis hung his jacket before fetching his coffee and muffin from Libby's desk.

"How's the book?" asked Libby as she half-pointed with a hand that held a blueberry bran muffin. Dwayne followed her pointing to the floor next to his chair where he saw his book. He blushed as he scooped up the book, placing it on his desk.

"Awesome. It's my second time reading it."

From inside his office, Clovis spoke. "Go home, Dwayne. Maureen must be home by now."

"Yes, Sir," replied Dwayne as he scooped up his jacket from a coat hook on the wall behind him. "Oh, actually I did get an email last night; from the Stonevalley Police Department."

"And?" asked Chief Clovis as he sat behind his desk and pushed the power button on his computer.

Dwayne perched himself on the doorframe of the Chief's office as he peaked inside. "They're advising all nearby communities to be on the lookout for an escaped mental patient from Brayton." Dwayne was referring to the Brayton Psychiatric Hospital. "And this one is dangerous too." Dwayne glanced behind him towards Libby and grimaced as he added. "And you would know this if you had that Blackberry I suggested you get. Instead of that antique cell you carry."

Libby clued in about his concern for Chief Clovis's reaction. Both of them were thinking about Clovis's daughter in University in Stonevalley. Libby piped up from behind her coffee cup which she cradled in both hands as she sat at her desk. "Why would they be telling us this? Did they say he's coming this way?"

"Crazy Crandall!" exclaimed Chief Clovis confidently.

"How'd you know that?" asked Dwayne.

"I heard it on the radio on the way to the station," replied Clovis. "You know. Those things they put in cars. They've been around longer than Blackberries or the interweb." Clovis smiled at his own lame joke. Just the word interweb alone would piss off Dwayne.

"You know he butchered thirteen people before getting caught. Think we should print posters or something?" asked Dwayne. "Spread them around town?"

"No need. It's all over the local news already." Clovis turned off his caps-lock and typed in his password for a third time as he logged into his computer.

"If you say so, Chief," replied Dwayne as he turned to grab his police issue baseball cap.

"This isn't Castle Rock," replied Chief Clovis who often teased Dwayne about his infatuation with stories set in small towns. "This ain't one of your Stephen King novels. Nothing ever happens in Carlton."

"Funny! Real funny!" said Dwayne as he quietly slipped a folded piece of paper into Libby's hand.

Clovis sipped his coffee before adding. "Besides, I got the perfect person to do that for us and it won't come out of our budget."

"Say hello to Maureen for me will you," said Libby as she watched Dwayne walk away. Quietly opening the note, she could barely make out the scribbling. It read.

Maureen. Burnett's place tonight at 8.

As Dwayne opened the door, he shot a backwards glance, looking for a reaction from Libby who peaked over her shoulder towards the Chief's office. She gave Dwayne a quick thumbs-up.

"Later!" said Dwayne as he left the building.

Libby sipped coffee as she listened intently from her desk as she heard Clovis speak. She knew full well he was already on the phone calling Bonnie Campbell at the Carlton Gazette.

"Bonnie? It's Clovis. Listen; are you ready to go to print yet with this week's edition?"

The Carlton Gazette was the local weekly newspaper. Most residents referred to it as "a slice of fog" due to its thinning pages. It was quite small compared to other more prominent newspapers. Holding it felt more like clutching at a wisp of air.

Libby walked over and leaned against the door frame of Clovis's office, sipping her coffee. Clovis spoke confidently. "Anna, she's fine. I spoke to her this morning." The rest of Clovis's side of the conversation was brief from there on. "Yup! Right. Perfect. Thanks, Bonnie!"

A smiling Libby spoke. "She was already on it, wasn't she?"

"Yup. She heard all about it on the news late last night. She made some calls and stayed up making the changes to be ready for print this morning." Clovis drank the rest of his coffee, dropping the empty Santorene coffee shop paper cup into his waste basket. "Good thing too, otherwise I would have called too late."

"Nothing gets past Bonnie Campbell," replied Libby.

Chief Clovis knew The Carlton Gazette would be in stores later that day. Home delivered (with flyers) on Friday morning like always. This week's edition would not be just about the town's business, politics and local sports with ads. The front page would have a large picture and a feature article with a headline reading "Lester Crandall, a.k.a. Crazy Crandall on the loose." The attached article would recap how the man, mostly known as Crandall was convicted of gruesomely killing thirteen people. All within a span of six days while on a rampage in a town not so far away. The same Crandall who had lost it back then, now had escaped from the Brayton Psychiatric Hospital.

"Has Robert called in yet?" asked Clovis as he walked out of his office startling Libby in the process.

Libby, who was typing a message, minimized her screen when she saw Clovis stop by her desk. She quickly scooped up the note from Dwayne and crumpled it up, stuffing it through the lid of her now empty Santorene coffee cup.

"No, not yet," replied Libby. She had not heard anything form Officer Robert but that was not unusual.

"Ok well, I'm gonna head out and cruise through town. See

if anything is going on," Clovis stated as he walked through the gate and towards the door.

"You want me to call Robert and see why he hasn't called in yet?"

"Naw, that's ok," said Clovis as he opened the door. "He's probably already parked at one of his favourite speed traps for the morning commuters and just forgot to call in again. I'll swing by and surprise him."

Clovis closed the door behind him.

Grabbing the phone, Libby quickly dialled and put the receiver to her ear.

"Bonnie? It's me, Libby. You didn't say anything to Clovis about tonight did you?" A worried Libby listened as Bonnie spoke.

Libby spoke while watching the door, as if expecting Clovis to walk in and catch her. "Good. I don't think he suspects anything yet. But we gotta be careful or he's liable to figure out what's going on." Opening her desk drawer, she pulled out a note pad with a long list of names and checked off Bonnie Campbell.

"Ok, Bonnie. I'll let you get back to work. But can you do me a favour. Please call Raylene for me?" She listened for a moment before speaking again. "Ok, thanks. Bye-bye."

Libby went back to her list and checked off Raylene McPhee and two more names before picking up the phone again. She ran her finger down her list and dialled.

"Winston? It's Libby."

3

The Santorene diner and coffee shop had been retrofitted to look more like it did in the fifties. One could feel a sense of nostalgia just walking into the place. All the chrome rimmed stools with red patent leather cushions lining the counter perfectly matching the benches in the booths along the outer walls full of large windows.

Everything had been restored by the new owner not so long

ago. Even the old jukebox was back to its former glory and still only cost a nickel to operate. Something the new owner insisted on even though it would cost money every time someone played it. The place was full of memories for most of the town's folk and had been the birthplace of many young romances. And even though they had the best coffee for miles, the line-up for coffee at Santorene was never extremely long at this hour in the morning. At ten thirty in the A.M. in such a small town, most everyone is at work. Either at the Sheppard's Frozen Foods plant or at some other obscure small-town job. Some are snuggled in their beds, sleeping off a graveyard shift from the Sleepy Meadows Rest Home. Only a few patrons sat at tables while the line-up currently consisted of four people.

Molly Miller was the only full-time waitress at Burnett's Place. The only real bar left in town and the only thing keeping that place in business was the gambling machines in the back. That and curvy red headed Molly's love of flirting, which kept the men coming back.

Lincoln Tingley was groundskeeper at the church. Part of his duties also included the two local cemeteries. His job was pretty secure since he also took care of all the equipment himself, which saved the parish a lot of money. This made Father Finnigan very content.

Clovis McPhee, the salt and pepper haired Chief of police for the last ten years who is originally from the sleepy little town of Carlton. The town's unofficial motto is "Nothing ever happens in Carlton" and for good reason, according to a large amount of the townsfolk. A fact that Clovis loved to remind people of every chance he got.

Jack Ledger was the previous owner of The Carlton Gazette and now Mayor of the so-called sleepy little town. Jack was a man who acted as if he owned the town, a fact which resonated throughout the entire town as a partial truth since he did own half of it. Many knew him as their landlord since he owned nearly all the apartments in town.

"Clovis," said Jack. "I heard Crazy Crandall escaped from the Brayton Psych Hospital. You think he might be heading this way?"

"Nah," replied the Chief of police. "There's no reason for him to come to Carlton. You can't hide in such a small sleepy little town."

Scruffy looking Lincoln, in his dirty coveralls spoke up. "I was thinkun, Clovis. Crandall might come here to hide because of that. I don't think he's as crazy as he makes himself out to be."

Molly, who had been elbow deep in her purse digging for money piped up and joined the conversation. "You never know, really. That would be the perfect reason for him to come this way." Molly smirked as she closed and clutched her purse to her waist in front of her. "Nobody, other than Lincoln anyway, thinks he will." Molly stepped up to the register and placed her order quickly before turning back to the conversation behind her.

Lincoln spoke. "I was thinkun, he never really was crazy you know. Just pretending so he could get away wit-it."

"Oh, he's crazy all right," said Chief Clovis. "Nobody does the sorta-things he did to people if they're sane."

Molly shuddered at the mere thought of it all, grabbed her coffee and left.

"I wouldn't be so sure," said Lincoln as he paid for his coffee with change from his pocket, which included bits of grass and lint. "Most people who call themselves crazy aren't crazy at all but just want you to think that." Lincoln shot a glance at Clovis as he walked past him and out the door.

Jack watched Lincoln walking towards his truck as he poured a little of the black coffee on the asphalt, making room for his own additive.

"Good old Thinking-Lincoln's got it all figured out, huh Clovis," Jack said with a chuckle.

"Never underestimate Lincoln's intelligence, Mr Mayor," said Clovis with a tone of seriousness.

"Yeah? Thinking-Lincoln, the high school dropout goes to spike his coffee and rake leaves in the cemetery, and you think he's a genius," replied the Mayor as he chuckled at his own sarcasm.

"He uses a leaf blower," replied Clovis with a smirk of his own.

Jack rolled his eyes and then in a serious tone, he asked. "How's Anna?"

"Fine. I spoke to her this morning," replied Clovis.

"You coming to play darts at Pinewood Lodge tonight?" asked Jack.

Pinewood Lodge was on the outskirts of town where the dart league met every Thursday night.

"Yup," replied Clovis. "Can't see why not," he said as he grabbed his coffee and left, leaving Mr Mayor standing alone at the counter.

Jack pulled out his cell phone. Squinting while holding it out at arm's length in an attempt to focus on the screen to see what he was doing. Putting the phone to his ear, he paused.

"Libby? It's Jack Ledger."

4

It was four o'clock when Molly walked into Burnett's Place to start her shift. She had been wearing her long curly red hair down for the last week after Officer Robert told her it looked really good that way. Especially with those strategically placed curls on her forehead that gave it that careless look. What Robert hadn't said was what half the men in town thought. That even though she didn't have one of those stick-thin bodies that models have, she was one of the hottest women in town. The tight jeans she always wore showed her curvaceous hips and her naturally thin waistline, which accentuated her voluptuous bosom. Between these features and her bubbly flirtatious personality, she helped the place stay in business. Floyd knew this, which is why he kept her around all these years. Even if she never took shit from him or he had to break up the occasional drunken brawl. Fights usually caused by her flirting with multiple customers in the same evening. She was a flirt but not a slut after all, which is what Floyd really liked about her.

Floyd would never admit to his bar staying afloat because he kept Molly on as eye candy to draw in the men. Or that the gambling machines in the back of the place helped with this as well. He was rather proud of his bar. He had built the bar to resemble the one in his favourite television show, Cheers. The place had the same style wood and brass mouldings all over. And here, at Burnett's Place in a small town like Carlton, everybody really did know your name. And if you were new in town, it wouldn't take long before they would.

"Molly, did you hear anything about folks who might be coming by the bar tonight?" asked Floyd as he carried cases of beer from the back and placed them behind the bar for Molly to put away.

"Floyd. It's a bar. People come in here all the time," replied a sarcastic Molly.

Floyd shot her a stern look, which Molly completely ignored. "I meant people that don't normally come in to gamble or stare at your ass."

Molly smiled. "I think so. I hear Libby called my aunt Bonnie." She cracked open one of the cases Floyd gave her. Floyd stood watching her as she put the beers away while talking. "But I think it's supposed to be hush-hush. Not sure what they're up to yet."

Floyd grabbed his universal remote and turned on the T.V. near him. The first thing he saw was a news break showing the upcoming stories to be featured on the six-o'clock news. Plastered on the screen was a picture of the Brayton Psychiatric Hospital. This was followed by a quick clip of Lester Crandall in leg and arm shackles being brought into a police station on the day of his arrest. The same clip most often used to portray the man later convicted of thirteen counts of murder. He was being pulled along by a few officers through the crowd while he shouted at the members of the press.

A reporter shouted a question in the chaos. "Why did you kill all those people?"

To which Crandall shouted in reply. "There's method to my madness. But there's also madness to my methods." Laughing hysterically as he was being pulled through the doors of the station as the press was held back.

"Crazy fuck!" said Floyd as he was emptying the glasses from the dishwasher, nearly dropping one as the phone rang. "Burnett's Place!" he was saying even before the cordless phone was to his ear. Floyd extended the phone towards Molly and said "It's for you. I think it's your Aunt Bonnie."

With an almost empty case clutched against her body while standing behind the door of a cooler, Molly tucked the phone to her ear and pinned it in place with her shoulder.

"Hello, Sweetie," she said over the clinking of bottles. "What can I do for you?"

On the other end of the phone line, she heard a familiar voice speak.

"Molly? It's Aunt Bonnie."

5

While neither of them would say it, the house had that too big feeling that often happens after the kids grow up and leave. Standing in the kitchen of their spacious house, Clovis dried the dishes while his wife Raylene washed.

"You think we should call Anna again?" asked Raylene.

"You just spoke to her two hours ago," replied Clovis. "You raised a smart girl. She'll be fine."

"We!" replied Raylene. "We raised a very smart girl."

"You mind if I go play darts at the lodge tonight?" asked Clovis.

"You ask me that every week," replied his wife as she busied herself scrubbing the pan that had contained the meatloaf which had been supper. "You know I don't mind you playing in the dart league."

"Did I tell you? Dwayne joined the league this year."

"No, but Maureen told me," replied Raylene.

Clovis dried and put away the large plates they got on their wedding day.

"You know it's good that you joined the dart league. It gives you a chance to socialize more with the locals as Clovis McPhee and not just their Police Chief."

"I know, Dear. But don't forget that I did grow up here," replied Clovis as he took the pan out of his wife's hands. "I know most of these people on a personal level from way before I was ever a cop."

Raylene laughed. "Oh, I know that. Trust me!" she said, pulling the plug from the sink and letting the water drain. Raylene spoke over the slurping sound of the water rushing down the drain. "The looks I used to get when we moved back here ten years ago. The women didn't like that an outsider had taken one of their handsome men."

Laughing, Clovis hung the damp dish cloth on the oven handle. "I highly doubt that."

Raylene stood rinsing out the sink as she spoke. "Do you think we need to worry about Crazy Crandall coming to Carlton?"

Clovis turned to face his wife. "Crandall will be heading to a big city where he can disappear in the crowds." This was a statement he made with confidence in an attempt to relieve his wife of any worries she may have. But at the same time, he also really believed this to be true. In a small town like Carlton, everybody knew everybody and so a stranger would stand out like a sore thumb. And with his picture all over the news, that would make it even harder to hide in such a small place.

Raylene grabbed her husband by the waist of his plain old-fashioned blue jeans and pulled him close, with her neck arched to reach him, kissing him on the lips. "You better get going or you're gonna be late."

He walked to the door and took his jacket off the hook and

slipped it on. "Any plans tonight?" he asked his wife.

Raylene thought this to be odd as he never asked her what her plans were. She always told him, so he never had to ask. She picked up her cordless phone from the kitchen counter. "Maureen and I are supposed to have coffee and swap recipes. She wants to try my meatloaf that apparently you told Dwayne about." Raylene smiled. "Now get out of here before you go and get a speeding ticket on the way to the lodge."

Smiling, Clovis picked up his keys form the kitchen counter and walked out the back door. Raylene watched him walk past his cruiser and climb into his truck. As he pulled out of the driveway, she was already dialling the phone. Placing it to her ear, paused a moment and then spoke.

"Maureen? It's Raylene."

6

One major difference that Burnett's Place had to the bar he idolized in the 80's hit sitcom Cheers were the flat screen televisions adorning the walls and above the bar. Back in those days, big screen televisions were not a common thing in bars. But these days, you were required to have at least three, if not more. A big screen mounted on the back wall, which was almost always kept on the sports channel. Plus a few smaller screens at various locations throughout the bar giving the option to those not wanting to watch sports. Burnett's place had four in total. The set above the bar and one in a corner were tuned onto a local channel for the news. At the end of the bar sat on-duty Officer Robert drinking coffee and checking Molly out every chance he got. A few seats down the bar sat Lincoln Tingley who was already nursing his third beer even if it was only eight o'clock. A corner table in the back had four local boys playing a friendly game of cards and drinking beer.

The ones that stood out like a black cat in a field of fresh white snow were all sitting at the table in the centre of the place. A group of four women, the likes of which Floyd had hardly ever seen before inside Burnett's Place. He knew them all but he was not accustomed to seeing them in his establishment.

At this table sat Raylene, the wife of Police Chief Clovis McPhee. She was the only one in the bar who was an outsider, not originally from the little town of Carlton. She sat next to her friend Maureen who was in her stark white work uniform, making her stand out even more. Maureen was from Carlton but was married to another outsider, Officer Dwayne Adams. Across from her sat the colourful scarf-wearing, silver-haired, bespectacled Bonnie Campbell sipping on a gin and tonic with a pad and pen on the table at the ready. Next to her sat plain clothed, off duty Officer Libby with cell phone in one hand and a near empty light beer in the other.

Walking to the bar, Molly gave her order of drinks to Floyd for the foursome of ladies. Floyd made the drinks. Lincoln, seeing both Molly and Floyd were within ear shot spoke up.

"I was thinking. You should put peanuts on the bar like they did in Cheers. Free ones."

Floyd handed a drink to Molly as he replied. "I can't afford to feed you, Thinkun."

Lincoln replied, gesturing towards the two machines by the door, one for salted peanuts and the other for barbeque. "But we gotta buy the peanuts from the vending machines."

"Yeah, so?" said Floyd as he handed Molly the second drink.

Lincoln dug out a twenty and smacked it down on the bar. "Gimme another beer and a shot-o Jack. And gimme some quarters with the change so I can buy my own damn peanuts, you cheap bastard."

A clearly annoyed Floyd set Lincoln's drinks on the bar, followed by his change and then watched him mutter curses while going to the vending machine to get a paper cup full of peanuts.

Meanwhile at their table not far away, the group of women were forging plans.

Libby sipped beer and glanced at her cell phone before speaking. "I called Winston to reserve the Lodge for Saturday night, but Jack Ledger beat me to it. Winston said Jack paid for it too. In cash."

Bonnie laughed. "Only because his buddy Winston will give him a sweet deal."

A smiling Raylene spoke as she sipped her beer. "It's only normal for him to want to since they all went to school together. A gift I suppose."

Maureen took on a serious look as she spoke. "I think Clovis suspect's something. At least that's what Dwayne told me this morning."

Libby directed a question at Raylene. "His fiftieth birthday is only a week and half away. You don't think he's suspects anything?"

"I don't think so," replied Raylene. "Although; he was abnormally curious about what I was doing tonight." Raylene lowered her voice and shot a glance at Floyd behind the bar. "We've been planning on going away for a few days the following weekend like we always do for his birthday. I made the usual plans with him to keep him from suspecting anything."

Libby glanced at her cell phone again, more out of habit than any other reason as she spoke. "What about your daughter Anna? Will she be coming down for his party?"

"She better if she knows what's good for her," said Raylene.

Bonnie gently sipped her gin and smiled. "Winston told me today that he thinks half the town will be there." She gestured to Molly for another drink as she continued speaking. "He was worried Pinewood Lodge might not be big enough."

Maureen replied. "The Lodge will be plenty big enough. I just hope Dwayne doesn't slip and say the wrong thing." She sipped her Diet Pepsi as she added, half laughing. "At least he isn't drinking since he has to work tonight."

Bonnie smiled and touched Maureen's hand. "They'll be fine. Mayor Jack Ledger's there and if anyone is a master at changing the subject, it's him."

Raylene smiled. "I can't thank you all enough for your help."

"It's our pleasure," said Libby.

Maureen spoke as she clutched her Diet Pepsi in front of her. "I'll update the event on Facebook in the morning after my shift and finish confirming all the invites."

"Good!" Bonnie added. "I wouldn't know where to start with that Facebook stuff."

"That's ok, Bonnie. There are lots of calls you can make," Raylene said with a smile.

Meanwhile, while sitting on a stool, Lincoln reached over the bar and found the remote. He turned up the volume of the TV above the bar as the station went to a news break.

The busty blonde newscaster spoke with a serious tone. "Escaped mental patient Lester Crandall was believed to have been seen hitchhiking near the University of Stonevalley. We're asking people to be on the lookout for this man." The newswoman paused. "Please note the following clip may be disturbing to some viewers."

The news footage showed Crandall wearing prison orange and being escorted out of the courtroom in shackles. As he walked by the cluster of reporters, he laughed and taunted them.

"You know what goes in one ear, comes out the other and still stays in the middle?" he asked the reporters and before anyone could reply he shouted. "A pickaxe!" Laughing, he was dragged through a doorway as he struggled against the straining officers.

"Sick Fuck!" said Floyd as he snatched the remote from Thinking-Lincoln's hand.

"Stonevalley?" said Lincoln. "You know that's only fifty-nine miles from here."

Floyd shot him a dirty look, "Shut up, Thinkun!"

7

Across town a person with a very sharp ear in the stillness of the early evening, standing close enough to the building could occasionally hear the thud of a dart hitting a dartboard. Twenty-two local men had gathered at their weekly spot inside the Pinewood Lodge. The log building sat on a gentle hillside on the outskirts of Carlton and was nestled in a thick forest rich with wildlife. A section of forest that was void of any neighbouring cottages or cabins. The only neighbour it had was the Sheppard's Frozen Foods factory. The only thing separating the factory from the lodge was a section of trees barely thick enough to conceal one from the other. The deciduous trees hid them from each other but were slowly beginning to turn as fall approached. The colourful trees were attracting many would-be photographers. Fall in full bloom would be when the trails around Pinewood Lodge would come alive with nature lovers and digital cameras.

The Lodge itself was built on the exact same spot the old log cabin train station once sat. It bore a slight resemblance to the previous building but on a larger scale. A logging operation once sat at this very spot, which had inspired the train station's location. Gravity had helped the men logging the forest as it made dragging the logs down the gentle slope much easier. The logs were loaded on the train to be brought to the mill on the other side of the small village, which flourished into the town now known as Carlton. The town still held onto the memories of its history. Much of which was on display in this very log cabin in the form of pictures and newspaper clippings framed and mounted on the walls. Sepia toned photographs of rugged men in suspenders standing next to horses that wore harnesses tied to large felled trees. More photos showed horses tied to wooden wheeled wagons loaded with large logs. Black and white pictures of men standing next to the steam engine train carrying huge logs. Antique axes and eight-foot-long saw blades were mounted high up on the walls. Other various memorabilia were strewn about including the old railroad spikes that were used to hold up the dart boards which the men played on this very night.

Mayor Jack Ledger, beer in hand, broke Dwayne's concentration when he spoke up abruptly. "So Clovis, how's your daughter Anna doing?"

Dwayne's dart flew askew and glanced off a wire on the board and sank into the roughed-up hardwood floor. Everyone knew Jack had asked because she was attending Stonevalley University. The same place that now had a serial killer on the loose.

Clovis sighed. "Good, I guess. She's dating some kid from her classes. Some kid with tattoos and piercings."

Jack, in the process of taking a drink, almost spewed beer all over himself as he stifled a laugh. "What does Raylene think of this?" he said as he wiped a little beer from his chin.

Clovis stepped up to take his turn at the board. "She says he's a nice kid. But I don't trust her judgement."

Jack chuckled as he replied. "I wouldn't either. She married you, didn't she?" His sarcasm getting laughs from many.

Dwayne asked. "Has Cotton met his little sister's boyfriend yet?"

Clovis smiled while calculating for Ernie who was supposed to be the official score keeper. "Cotton is off doing his basic training for the army."

"That's right. I forgot about that," replied Dwayne.

Ernie Woodman, manager of the local grocery store and the supposed score keeper piped into the conversion. "Clovis. Did you read today's Gazette?"

"About Crandall?" asked Clovis.

"Crazy Crandall!" said Ernie. "You think he's coming here?"

The room grew a little quiet as most of the men wanted to hear what their Chief of Police might have to say. But before he could speak, Winston spoke loudly from across the room. "He'd be foolish to come to a small hole of a town like Carlton."

Mayor Ledger shot Winston a dirty look for calling his town a hole, even if it was partially true.

Clovis poured himself a glass of water from the pitcher on a nearby table as he spoke. "He would have to be foolish to come here, yes. Downright crazy, which we all know he is. But I doubt he will. He wouldn't be able to hide in a small town." He sipped his water before adding. "He'd stick out like Mayor Ledger at the Church picnic."

The room roared with laughter at the Mayor's expense. Clovis smiled at Jack and gave him a wink. A frustrated Jack scooped up his darts and walked over to take his turn at the board before saying. "Are we gonna jibber-jabber all night or play some damn darts."

Dwayne slapped Clovis on the back while trying to stifle his amusement at the Mayor's embarrassment.

8

Back at Burnett's Place, the group of laughing ladies were wrapping up the plans for the birthday bash.

Raylene spoke as she tucked her cell phone into her purse. "Please don't tell Clovis I called Anna again."

Libby only smiled in reply knowing full well Clovis most likely was doing the same as his wife.

The most mature of the ladies at the table, Bonnie Campbell fluffed her scarf a little as she set her empty gin glass down. Leaning forward, placing a gentle hand on Raylene's arm as she spoke. "Remind me again why we didn't start planning this a month ago?"

Raylene opened her mouth to speak but before she could utter a single word, Libby replied for her. "Because he would have figured it out, that's why."

Maureen stood up and began to walk away as she spoke. "I gotta pee some fierce. Oh, and Dwayne said he's pretty sure that Clovis knows something is going on but doesn't know what yet."

"That reminds me, I had better get home soon," said Raylene as she pushed her chair back and got up. "I can't get home after Clovis if I want to avoid him asking too many questions about tonight."

As Molly noticed the women beginning their departure, she made her way over to their table to bid them adieu. And as she did so Bonnie dug out a few crumpled bills from her purse and pushed them into the palm of Molly's hand. Smiling she said to Molly. "We were never here, right?"

A smiling Molly quickly hugged her Aunt. "Sure thing, Aunt Bonnie."

Bonnie looked over her thin framed glasses at Floyd and added sternly. "Right, Floyd?"

"Gotcha!" said a smiling Floyd as he winked and wiped up the counter. "Nobody's seen you-all. Right, Lincoln?" Floyd glanced at Thinkun-Lincoln and back to the ladies. "Ah, he's too drunk and stupid to remember anyway."

Lincoln turned in his stool and looked at Raylene who was closest to him now. "You know, Raylene. I was thinkun, man is the only creature on this planet that chooses to be a vegan or a meat eater." Lincoln spun in his stool again and faced the bar as he continued. "No other creature gets to make that choice. Did you know that?" He drank the rest of the beer before him and gestured to Floyd for another.

"That's it, Lincoln," Floyd said as he grabbed the empty bottle from in front of Thinking-Lincoln. "I know you're past your limit when you start talking like that." Floyd put the empty behind the bar. "You're cut off tonight. You've had enough booze for one night."

"Fuck you, Floyd. Gimme another GODDAMN beer," said an angry Lincoln as he slapped his palm down loudly on the bar making most of the patrons twitch and grow quiet as a result. "You're only trying to impress the Chief's wife, you fuck. I'm a fuckin' paying customer. Gimme a beer!"

Libby deliberately dragged her feet as she walked up to Thinking-Lincoln. She did this so that he would hear her coming and not be startled. His face now flush and his lower lip trembling in anger, he slowly turned to face Libby. She placed a hand gently on his shoulder and spoke calmly. "Come-on, Lincoln. Let me give you a ride home. Ok?"

Lincoln knew it was in his best interest to do as Libby requested. Not only was the Chief's wife watching, Libby herself was a police officer. As a result, he slowly, submissively slid off his barstool as he gave Floyd a scowl of resentment. As they approached the door, he spoke loudly. "Any news about Crazy Crandall?"

"Nothing yet," replied Libby as she pushed the door open. Libby escorted Lincoln all the way into the passenger seat of her Jeep. She looked behind her to see the small procession of ladies exiting Burnett's place. Each woman was heading home from their secret rendezvous.

"I don't know how she does it," said Raylene clearly commenting on Libby being a police officer. "Having to deal with drunks and troublemakers."

Maureen laughed. "Libby said the same thing about you yesterday. She said; 'I don't know how Raylene puts up with a room full of rambunctious kids all day.'"

Bonnie laughed and staggered slightly, trying not to let it show that she might have had too many drinks this evening. "I think I'd rather be a cop than a teacher," she said aloud as she scooted into her car. "At least cops get to carry a gun," she said as she shut her car door on the hem of her jacket. Bonnie was oblivious to the tip that protruded slightly from under the door as she drove away.

9

On a typical Friday morning, Clovis and Libby would have found Dwayne in his usual position. With his chair leaning precariously back, his feet perched on the desk and a book strewn about somewhere. They both assumed so because this is how they found him most weekday mornings. He should have been asleep at his desk with spots of drool on his shirt. Chief Clovis gently opened the door of the Carlton Police Station not wanting to startle the sleeping beauty. He found instead that

Dwayne was sitting bolt upright at his desk. He was bright eyed, awake and waiting for them to arrive.

"Lot's happened last night," he said loudly before Libby was even completely inside the building.

"Really?" asked Libby.

"Yes, it did," replied a smirking Clovis. "But not in Carlton though."

Libby approached the bullpen giving Dwayne a knowing look as she smiled. Both she and Dwayne spoke in unison. "Nothing ever happens in Carlton."

Chief Clovis laughed aloud. Dwayne piped up and said. "Sleepy little towns aren't always so sleepy you know."

"Ok, give?" said Libby as she noticed Dwayne's desk was no longer tidy and neat. Something had definitely happened, and the evidence was the scattered newspaper, note pads and unfolded maps. "What's got you so riled up this morning?"

"Something *really interesting* must have happened," said Clovis with a smile as he pointed to the book on Dwayne's desk. The book was partially hidden by one of the maps laid out on the well-worn wooden surface. "His bookmark looks to be in the same place it was yesterday morning."

Dwayne ignored the Chief's sarcastic comment. Meanwhile Libby had a smile that stretched from ear to ear. Libby sat at her desk attentively with her Santorene coffee cup cradled in both hands. Clovis picked his up, cracked it open and perched himself on the edge of Libby's desk. Dwayne shoved over the maps and pulled his keyboard into place as the screensaver of his wife's photography dissipated and revealed a full inbox. With a few clicks of his mouse, Dwayne pulled up an email as he spoke.

"Nowlan told me they got hundreds of tips ever since the news of Crazy Crandall's escape."

"Who's Nowlan?" asked Clovis speaking from behind his coffee cup which he held before his mouth.

"Officer Nowlan at the Stonevalley P.D.," said Dwayne as he opened an email and from it, opened up an attachment as he continued. "He called me early last night about a tip he got that concerned us." The picture on the screen was a map covered in red dots. Most of the dots were in and around Stonevalley. They covered some of the outskirts of the area and after swift work of the mouse; the map now showed a single dot which was very near Carlton. Dwayne pointed to it as he spoke. "He sent me a map he made of the locations from the calls claiming to have seen Crandall. Some they dismissed with quickly for various reasons. Some they checked out much more intensely and many had not been followed up on yet." Dwayne paused and looked at Clovis. "They found an older man dead on the side of the highway just outside of Stonevalley. They still haven't identified him." Dwayne was pointing to a dot on the north side of Stonevalley. "His wallet is missing, and they believe the killer stole his vehicle."

Clovis raised his hand with index finger pointing upwards, as if shushing Dwayne before he asked a question. "Back up here. Why do you say they didn't follow up on some tips yet? Is it a lack of manpower?"

"Timing," replied Dwayne. "They found the old man not long after he had died. Nowlan says there is no way he could have been at some of those other sightings. Oh, and a lack of manpower too, I suppose." Fact was Dwayne didn't really know and that was obvious to Clovis as he sipped his coffee analyzing all the information at hand.

"But they don't know for sure Crandall is the one who stole the old man's truck do they? How was he killed?" asked Libby.

"They're waiting on an autopsy. It had to be him," replied Dwayne.

Clovis spoke. "If Crazy Crandall had killed that old man and stole his truck, you wouldn't need an autopsy to know the cause of death."

"I never thought of it that way," replied Dwayne.

"The dot near Carlton," Clovis began asking as he pointed a finger from the hand which still clutched a half empty coffee cup towards the monitor. "That one near Carlton is right outside the old Brooks farm isn't it?"

"Yup," replied Dwayne. "Old man Charlie Brooks himself called in and said he saw a hitchhiker near his place. Said it looked like Crandall."

Libby nearly choked on her coffee in surprise at Dwayne's comment. "Charlie Brooks is half blind and probably shouldn't be driving as it is."

Dwayne pivoted his chair facing Libby. "Nowlan said old man Brooks was pretty persistent. And he could hear his wife hollering at him in the background."

"Yeah, well... half blind or not, Mr. Brooks is still driving that old 58 Chevy Apache truck of his," said Clovis. "I'll go for a drive out there this morning. His wife must be worried sick." Clovis walked into his office and threw his now empty coffee cup in the open waste basket making a hollow thumping sound and sat behind his desk.

"Good idea, Chief," said Libby. "Go home, Dwayne. Maureen should be home by now."

"I'm way too wired to sleep," replied Dwayne as he put on his cap. "Call me if anything happens. Off duty or not."

Clovis spoke loudly from inside his office. "Go home, Dwayne, I'm sure you'll have your radio on to make sure you don't miss a thing anyway."

Dwayne could hear the sarcasm in Clovis's voice.

10

A few moments after Dwayne closed the door behind him, Clovis exited suddenly from his office. "Well I'm gonna go for a spin to see old man Brooks about a hitchhiker."

Libby, startled, spilled coffee on herself. "Bat shit!" she exclaimed harshly. "You did that on purpose, didn't you?"

Clovis smiled and adjusted his cap. "Don't forget to log off Facebook," said Clovis as he pushed through the gate of the bullpen.

Dabbing at her coffee stained breast with a crumpled up dirty napkin, Libby spoke. "Facebook is where the people in this town do the most gossiping these days and it can't hurt to see what they're saying about Crandall." Libby tossed the napkin away and took tissues from the box on her desk and dabbed at the stain some more. "You go see Mr. Brooks and make sure that crotchety old geezer doesn't beat you to death with his wooden leg."

"I've known Mr. Brooks since I was knee high. You just gotta know how to handle him," replied Clovis as he slipped on his baseball cap. "No discussing politics. And if you get him to tell you a joke or two, you'll learn that there ain't nothing crotchety about that old man." Clovis smiled and glanced at Libby as he closed the door behind him. Libby was pulling at the wet spot on her uniform shirt to keep it from clinging.

She shot a glance at the door as it shut, clicked on the Facebook event. Once opened, she typed up a message to the invited guests.

"Hey everybody. Just a reminder as everything is still on for Saturday night at 8PM. Please be careful around Clovis as he doesn't suspect a thing and we would really like to keep it that way.
Thanks.
Libby"

Hitting send, she sipped the rest of her coffee as she already started getting replies to her Facebook message.

"I'll be there with bells on," replied Ernie Woodman who would undoubtedly be wearing his custom-made T-shirt that had the word "BELLS" written on it.

Libby rolled her eyes but smiled just the same.

11

A fresh shirt on, Libby felt a quick surge of panic as she patted her pockets feeling for her house key as she stood on the stoop of her small bungalow. Relief washed over her as she felt the key ring in her pants pocket. She normally kept the single key on the SeaWorld keychain in her breast pocket. The idea of it sitting in the bottom of the nearly empty hamper, still in the coffee stained shirt pocket had only hit her once she had shut the door. She pulled the key out, smiling as she tucked it into her breast pocket. Her mind was so preoccupied with Clovis's surprise party that she had no memory of placing the key in her pants pocket. Stepping off the stoop, she heard the radio in the car but couldn't comprehend anything that was said. Hurrying to her squad car, she cracked open the door and reached in for the CB's mike. She waited for a moment until she heard a voice come over the radio.

"Libby, are you mobile? Over," she heard Clovis say.

"Yes, sir. Over," she replied.

"Where are you? Over."

"Home. Changing my shirt. Over," replied Libby knowing full well Clovis would think that was really funny. After a few seconds she spoke again. "Did you talk to Mr. Brooks yet? Over."

"Yup. The description does sound a bit like Crandall, but I don't think it was him. His wife made him call. Over"

Libby climbed into her car and replied. "Ok, I'll let Stonevalley P.D. know when I get back to the station. Over."

"Hey-uh, is there something going on at The Lodge this weekend? Over."

"Not that I know of," replied Libby. "Why do you ask? Over."

"I saw a beer truck going that way earlier and Pinewood Lodge never gets deliveries on Fridays. Not unless he's catering. Over."

"Fuck!" Libby said to herself. Thinking quickly, she replied. "Didn't the dart league start again recently? Maybe you guys drink more than you'll admit. Over."

A brief pause with nothing coming back but dead air made Libby worry that her attempt at deception had not sounded convincing enough. Clovis replied. "Maybe so. Hey, what's this I hear about you driving Thinking Lincoln home last night? Over."

"Fuck! Fuckin' small fuckin' towns!" exclaimed Libby to herself in frustration. She knew a few gossip hungry people had seen her driving with Thinking-Lincoln in her Jeep. Someone said something and somehow it got to Clovis of all people.

"Saw him staggering badly when I drove by. More than usual so I gave him a lift." Libby grimaced wondering how bad that lie sounded. "I was afraid he'd get run over or something. Over."

"He must have been talking a lot. Over."

"Enough," replied Libby. "He said that the only reason man evolved, and other creatures didn't is because of their imagination. All creatures can learn but man can imagine. Made me think so much I couldn't sleep. Over."

The radio crackled before the reply came. "Yeah, he was plastered alright.

"Do me a favour, Libby. When you get back to the station, find out if they've gotten any other tips about Crazy Crandall in our neck of the woods? Over."

"Will do," replied Libby. "I gotta quick stop I wanna make, grab a coffee and then I'm going back. Over."

"Ok then. I should see you in an hour or so. Over and out!" replied Clovis.

Libby racked the CB mike and pulled out her cell phone. In a brief instant she had already sent a text to Raylene. "Call me," was all the text said. Libby knew Raylene would be in class at that hour but knew she should speak with her before Clovis could. So their stories would mesh at all the right places not to arouse any more suspicion. Fooling someone who is paid to be suspicious was getting tiring and Libby couldn't wait for it to be all over.

12

Chief Clovis couldn't stop thinking about why Libby lied about driving Lincoln home on the previous evening. Thinking-Lincoln always walked home from Burnett's Place. This was the only reason he still had a driver's license. He was smart enough to walk when he was drunk and that was often enough. But Lincoln was also stubborn when he drank unless he thought it would get him into trouble. He had a temper but knew well and good not to blow up around cops. Clovis knew Libby had lied about it but why would she? What was she covering up? While on his way back to the station, he decided to take a detour by the cemetery and see if Thinking-Lincoln would be there.

As the police cruiser pulled up alongside the curb, Clovis could see Lincoln sitting in the second row of graves in the cemetery with his Weed Wacker nearby. He was leaning against one of the large very old granite tombstones with his stainless-steel thermos sitting on the ground next to him. A half-eaten sandwich in his dirty hand as he watched Clovis drive up. This thought Clovis, was a strange place for a man to take his lunch break but not for Thinking-Lincoln. The cruiser stopped with the window already rolled down. Clovis didn't want to just come out and ask what he had come here to ask as that would make Thinking-Lincoln think. Maybe he too would lie. Clovis had no way of knowing if he would or not.

"I see Father Finnigan is keeping you out of trouble by keeping you busy," said Clovis.

Lincoln smiled just enough to show that he found that statement somewhat amusing. "Two cemeteries and a Church do keep me pretty busy I suppose."

"Not to mention the leaves. They will be keeping you very busy soon," replied Clovis as he shot a glance towards the near-dozen large maple trees in the cemetery. He was clearly stalling and not getting to the point and he figured Lincoln knew this.

Lincoln looked at his sandwich and back at Clovis. "What's this I hear about old man Brooks seeing Crazy Crandall near his farm?"

Fucking small towns Clovis thought to himself. "Whoever he

saw, it wasn't Crandall. That much I can tell you." Clovis frowned knowing he was about to say something he shouldn't but did anyway. "I'm not even sure the man he saw was hitchhiking for that matter."

Lincoln picked up his thermos and took a drink, paused and spoke. "How come you're so convinced Crandall won't come this way anyway."

"You of all people should know that, Lincoln." Clovis chuckled slightly. "Nothing ever happens in Carlton. That's why we all talked of leaving back when we were in school."

Lincoln smiled. "And that's why you came back. Because nothing ever happens, right?"

Both men laughed a little. Lincoln took another swig of his thermos. "You know some people say that atheists are evil? Have you ever heard of an atheist strapping a bomb to his chest in the name of nothing?"

At that moment, Clovis noticed the pint shaped bulge in the pocket of Lincoln's overalls. "Nope, can't say I have," he replied.

"I don't think I ever hear of the atheist crusades?" Lincoln smiled. "Worship nothing or I'll kill you!" he added.

Drunk at noon, thought Clovis. His drinking is getting worse. All this talking in circles was getting Clovis nowhere he thought, so might as well just ask. "What's this I hear about Libby giving you a ride home last night?"

Lincoln paused and looked at his half-eaten sandwich. Clovis knew whatever Thinking would say next would be a lie. He could feel it in his bones. "Fuckin' Floyd was being a prick. He must have called her or something because she was outside when I left."

A lie and Clovis was sure of it. His gut told him so, but why?

Lincoln wasn't sure why he lied. Perhaps he did so because he knew what the ladies had been planning and he didn't want to be the one to spoil it. Clovis wasn't nice to him back in their school days. But he also wasn't mean to him either. Clovis had always respected him in ways that most people from their high school years didn't. For this reason, he sort of liked Clovis although he would never admit to liking a cop.

"Good talking to ya, Lincoln," says Clovis.

Lincoln hoisted up his thermos in a toast-like gesture and smiled as he watched the squad car pull away. "Cheers!" he said and drank the rest of its contents.

13

Libby felt her belt vibrate just as she reached for the handle of the steel-framed glass door of Santorene. She pulled the phone from its holster as she made her way inside the coffee shop. The line-up only consisted of two Carlton residents, Jack Ledger and Ernie Woodman. Ernie had the latest copy of the Carlton Gazette folded and tucked under his arm. A large picture on the front page showed a scruffy looking Crandall with the headline she had seen earlier that day.

Lester Crandall, a.k.a. Crazy Crandall on the loose.

A glance at her phone made her freeze in mid-step. The caller I.D. showed *Chief Clovis.*

Why would Clovis call her on her Blackberry? She couldn't help but wonder as she picked up the call.

"You want a coffee, don't you?" she asked as she tried to sound nonchalant.

"Sure," replied Clovis. "Did you make it back to the station yet?"

"Not yet. Why?" Libby knew that Clovis wasn't going to get to the point right away. He would try and get her to put her guard down. Catch her in a lie. She couldn't help but wonder if she was just being paranoid.

"I just wanted to know if I had time to swing by the school and see Raylene." Clovis was referring to Carlton Elementary where his wife was a teacher. "That and I wanted to know if there were any updates on Crandall."

"I should be there soon. I'll call you right away if there is."

There was a pause and Clovis spoke. "Oh, and I saw your buddy just now. He's already half drunk and it's not even noon."

"Really?" replied Libby. He knows I lied thought Libby. "Did he even remember me driving him home?" This question she asked to see if they had discussed that very fact.

Jack Ledger turned to listen in to Libby's half of the conversation as he waited for his coffee.

"Yup," said Clovis.

"What'd he say?"

Clovis replied. "He went on a rant about atheists."

"Poor Thinking's gonna drink himself to death," said Libby as she watched Jack roll his eyes at what she had just said.

"Lincoln was a straight A student up until the seventh grade," said Clovis. "I know because we went to school together."

"What happened?" asked Libby.

"Well, let's just say that being smart was not cool back then and getting wasted was," replied Clovis.

"Well he never really struck me as being dumb. Just a man who made bad choices," replied Libby.

"That's exactly it," replied Clovis.

14

Jack, with coffee in hand walked outside and took an old-fashioned flip phone out of his pocket. A quick search in the call history found the number he wants and dials. Standing before the glass door as he watched Libby put her phone away and step up to place her order.

"Raylene?" said an uncertain Jack in an inquisitive tone. "It's Jack Ledger. Listen. I think Clovis is getting suspicious."

"What makes you say that?" asks Raylene.

"I overhear Libby talking to him just now."

"I'm gonna call Libby right away and see what's going on," replied Raylene. "Thanks, Jack."

Jack closed his flip phone and put it in his pocket. He cracked open the plastic lid on his coffee and turned just in time to see Libby pulling out her blackberry and placing it to her ear.

15

Putting her Blackberry to her ear as she handed her money to the young girl at the counter, Libby spoke. "Dwayne? What are you doing up? You should be sleeping."

"I just keep tossing and turning. Can't sleep," replied Dwayne. "I just got off the phone with Nowlan and he says they've gotten more calls from the Carlton area."

Coffee tray in one hand and walking out the door, Libby replied. "Really? Did you call Clovis yet?"

"Nope!" said Dwayne. "I'm at the station."

Libby stopped in her tracks. "You want me to get you a coffee too, I suppose."

"No thanks. I've already got one," replied Dwayne.

Libby's Blackberry made a bleeping sound alerting her of incoming call. "I got another call, Dwayne. I'll talk to you when I get to the station."

With that she took the second call and spoke. "Hey, Raylene. Thanks for calling."

"I got your text but that's not why I'm calling," replied Raylene. "I called because Jack just called me. He says he thinks Clovis is suspicious."

"Well, I doubt he will have much time to think about it," said Libby without wanting to give anything away. "We got lots to do."

"Good. But I still have one problem," said Raylene. "I have no idea how I'm gonna get him to the Lodge Saturday night. Not without giving it away."

"Don't worry," replied Libby. "Dwayne said he has a plan."

Raylene replied without the slightest pause. "That's a scary thought."

Both women laughed.

"Ok, Clovis is here to see me. I gotta go before I need to get back to class. Thanks again for everything, Libby."

"My pleasure. Bye now," replied Libby as she climbed into her cruiser and set the tray of coffee on the passenger seat on top of a copy of the Carlton Gazette.

16

Early Friday afternoon, three of Carlton's Police Officers and their Chief were pouring over the list of leads sent by Officer Nowlan, their liaison at the Stonevalley Police Department. All were huddled around Dwayne's desk as they discussed a plan to split up the tips called into the hotline.

Clovis spoke. "You guys do realize that there are a few citizens of Carlton that look like Crazy Crandall. They could easily have mistaken that autistic boy's father for Crandall."

"You mean Devin's dad?" asked Libby.

"Linus Butler," said Robert.

Dwayne shot Clovis a glance as he looked up from his notes. "Everybody in town knows Linus."

Clovis replied. "Yes, true. But he looks a hell of a lot like Crandall though." Clovis smirked as he added. "From a distance they could easily think he was our escaped psycho."

Dwayne added, "Well Stonevalley P.D. wants us to check out these leads even if they're pretty sure they're bogus."

"Who's the Chief here anyway?" asked Libby.

Chief Clovis laughed. "That's ok, Libby. I'm more than happy letting Dwayne take a lead role in all this." Clovis got up and walked past Dwayne, patting him on the back. "He's a natural for this stuff. Besides, my birthday's coming up and I know Raylene's got something cooking."

A look of shock froze on Libby's face as she saw Clovis disappear into his office. She gave Dwayne a dirty look and mouthed words without speaking. "What the fuck?"

Dwayne, with a confused look on his face simply shrugged.

From the Chief's office Clovis said, "You guys wouldn't happen to know anything about that now would you?"

In an attempt to change the subject, Dwayne spoke up reverting to the task at hand. "Ok. I split the list into four. We've got eleven tips with names and four more anonymous ones."

"Anonymous?" asked Robert.

Dwayne looked at his list. "Two were traced back to disposable phones, one to the old pay phone outside of Burnett's Place and the third was traced to Father Finnigan's iPhone."

"Put Father Finnigan on my list," said Clovis as he came out of his office with a copy of the Carlton Gazette. "I need to talk to him anyway."

"Already done," said Dwayne as he handed Clovis a paper with four names on it.

"Ok then, let's get to work," said Chief Clovis.

"Yes sir," said an enthusiastic Libby. Each Officer now had been given a list of names as they left the police station.

<h2 style="text-align:center">17</h2>

Libby sat in her cruiser watching as the three other officers drove off. Pulling out her Blackberry, she called Raylene.

"Your timing is perfect. I just got out of class," said Raylene as she picked up the call. "What's up?"

"It's Clovis. He knows something's up."

"I figured he would catch on eventually," replied Raylene.

"What do we do now?" asked a panicked Libby.

"I'll figure out something," said Raylene. Libby could hear screaming kids and a school bell in the background. Then she heard a door slam and the background noises became muffled. "I'll tell him I was planning on taking him to Cuba instead of Bar Harbour like we planned."

Libby paused as she looked at the list of names in her hand. "But Clovis hates the tropics."

"Oh I know that," replied Raylene. "But that should throw him off the scent. He'll think I needed help to plan his absence."

Libby laughed. "You're pretty sneaky, Raylene."

Both women had a laugh before terminating the call. Libby,

feeling a slight relief that Raylene had a plan, could now focus on the task at hand. The tips from the hotline were so random that they knew the bulk of them had to be bogus. But they would not be doing their job if they didn't follow up on the leads. And one of them might turn out to be real thought Libby. What if?

She heard the police radio crackle and then Clovis's voice came on. "Dwayne?" the voice said.

"What's up, Chief? Over!" replied Dwayne.

"You're loving this aren't you? Over," replied Clovis.

Libby grinned.

There was a pause before the reply. "Let's be professional here," replied Dwayne. "There's a killer out there. Over."

Nothing more came over the radio as Libby started her cruiser and headed for the outskirts of town for the first name on her list.

18

Clovis had already dismissed the first of the possible Crazy Crandall sightings on his list of four before heading to the church. Fully convinced that Crandall would never step foot in his sleepy little town, he had taken all the information from the first caller but most of it was inconsistent. Now he intended on checking off the second name which he wanted to do personally. He had more than one reason for asking Dwayne to put Father Finnigan's name on his list. His visit wouldn't simply be about Crandall.

In the entrance of the church, other than the doors to go in and out were two thick ornate wooden doors on each side. The one on the right was a public washroom. The one to the left was the main entrance of the basement. As soon as he walked into the doorway, he noticed the lights were already lit. Clovis knew he was right about the location of the good Father. The church basement had a unique odour which you could smell as soon as you stepped foot into the stairwell. Too many church potlucks had been held here and that smell was trapped in the wood, which was blended with the scent of varnish. Clovis knew he would be right where he always was on a Friday afternoon. He would be in the basement, setting up for Friday night bingo. The proceeds going to heat the church in the winter and anything above the cost of the heating oil would be put aside to do good within the community.

"Why don't you get Lincoln to help you?" asked Clovis as he reached the bottom of the stairs.

"I usually do," replied the Father as he turned to face this familiar voice which spoke to him. "But the leaves are beginning to fall now, and Lincoln will be busy with that for a while."

"True," replied Clovis as he set down his newspaper and grabbed the other end of a table the Father was about to pick up, helping him set it in place.

As both men made their way to fetch another table, Father Finnigan asked. "You're here about the call I made, aren't you?"

"Why didn't you leave your name?" asked Clovis as both men grabbed the opposite ends of a table and carried it towards the middle of the room.

"I intended to but forgot. I guess I got nervous."

"You said you saw him in church?" asked Clovis. "When?"

"I was in the church and saw a lone man kneeling in a pew." Both men walked over to fetch the last of the tables. "I didn't think anything of it until I remembered the picture of the front page of the Carlton Gazette. That's when I realized it was him."

Clovis, taking this as his cue, retrieved the copy of the Gazette, which he had brought with him. He already had it folded to the page he wanted and so he flashed it to Father Finnigan and asked. "Is this him? Is this the man you saw in the church this morning?"

Father Finnigan looked at the small picture quickly before replying without hesitating. "Yes, that's him alright."

Clovis unfolded the newspaper and this time he didn't hide any of it with his strategically placed hands when he showed it to him for the second time. "Take another look, Father."

Father Finnigan's facial expression said it all as he read the ad next to the picture for Butler Construction. (The newspaper ad read "The Butler did it.")

The good Father knew the picture he was looking at was Linus Butler and not Crazy Crandall after all. Could he have mistaken Linus for Crandall he thought? But he had been so certain of himself this morning.

Clovis turned the paper and looked at the picture himself. "He's been having trouble with his boys."

"How'd you know it might be Linus and not Crandall?" asked Father Finnigan.

"He's doing a job not far from here," replied Clovis. He could see from the expression on the good Father's face that he now had feelings of regret for having called the hotline.

"Let me give you a hand with the chairs," said Clovis as both men began placing chairs next to the tables. Both men were quiet as they set the rest of the chairs in place. Once done, Clovis asked. "How's Lincoln doing, Father?"

Father Finnigan paused as he gestured for them to head back upstairs. "He's taken to drinking a lot more this last year. And I fear it's gotten worse in the last few months."

"Does he talk to you much, Father? About religion or other things?" asked Clovis as they reached the top of the staircase.

"We talk, yes." Father Finnigan smiled. "But you know I can't tell you what about. Lincoln puts his trust in me, and I can't betray that. Not even for the Chief of Police. Let me walk you out," said the Father. As both men exited the church, Father Finnigan added. "What's this I hear that you and Raylene are finally going to Cuba?"

Clovis adjusted his baseball cap and did his best not to let the shock he was feeling show on his face as he spoke. "Raylene has been talking about it for years but she knows I'd rather see pine trees than palm trees." Clovis smiled. "But I'm not so sure I'm supposed to know yet so don't tell Raylene you asked me about it."

"Ah poo," replied a flustered Father Finnigan. "I hope I didn't spoil the surprise."

"Don't worry about that," said a smiling Clovis as he climbed into his cruiser. "We've got bigger things to worry about with this killer on the loose. I need to go visit Linus before he gets in trouble for looking like an escaped killer."

Father Finnigan smiled and waved him goodbye as he watched him drive off. As Clovis pulled out of the church parking, he glanced into his rear-view mirror and could see Father Finnigan put his iPhone to his ear. Clovis smiled as he drove off.

Father Finnigan watched Clovis drive away as he spoke. "Raylene? It's Father Finnigan. You know I'm a terrible liar, but I think it worked."

19

Having just slept for most of the day after working the graveyard shift at Sleepy Meadows, Maureen sat at her kitchen table still wearing her pyjamas. She sipped coffee as she caught up on her friends' Facebook posts. Not long into her scrolling she noticed a post from about an hour earlier by her co-worker Jenna Wilkins. To her amazement a quick click revealed a pair of merged pictures of a clean-cut Crazy Crandall right next to Linus Butler. The resemblance was uncanny, and the large list of shares and comments confirmed just that. One of the comments said they saw this same picture on a newsbreak for the local news. The original post came from Linus's wife herself. Geraldine had posted the pic to make people aware of the uncanny resemblance before her husband got hurt. Without hesitation, Maureen shared the picture on her Facebook wall just like half the town had already done. Her written comment was short.

"I never realized it until now, but they could be brothers if not twins."

20

Not having had a single customer after half past seven, Ernie Woodman decided he would close the grocery store early that night. At half past eight he made the announcement that he would closed up in exchange for every one of the staff promising him that they would go straight home. They all did this without a fuss. Even the two young teenage girls who worked the cash registers on Friday nights didn't argue and happily called their parents to come and get them. Ernie didn't bother with any paperwork or floats at the end of the day. He stored everything away in the office safe, vowing to do them first thing in the morning. On his way home he noticed the streets of Carlton were already deserted except for a single police cruiser that drove past him slowly, a young nervous looking officer on loan from the Stonevalley P.D. at the wheel. Even the parking lot of Burnett's Place was completely empty except for Floyd's truck. It would be a quarter past nine when Ernie would get home and lock the door behind him. Something he rarely ever did in this sleepy little town. He would sit back and watch some television eventually settling on a news special about Crazy Crandall and the murderous rampage that had made him infamous.

21

Dwayne damned near shot out of his chair when the phone rang. He knocked his half empty can of Redbull off the desk in a scramble to reach the phone. This would have looked very foolish had someone been there to see his reaction. He had only gotten a few hours sleep before coming in for his graveyard shift and wanted to make sure he didn't miss any calls. Just in case he was to doze off like he sometimes did. So to prevent from missing calls, Dwayne had gotten the bright idea of turning the phone's ringtone to its loudest. And conveniently forgot all about doing this not long after. The phone wasn't to his ear yet as he spoke a slightly slurred greeting.

"Carlton Police. Officer Dwayne Adams speaking."

He heard a voice ask. "Did I wake you?"

Half asleep, Dwayne had to look at the screen on the phone's base for him to realize who he was speaking to.

"Clovis. Chief, what's going on?" asked Dwayne in a sudden slight panic. The Chief never calls at this hour.

"Nothing," replied Clovis. "I was about to ask you the same thing. I can only assume all is quiet."

"So far, yes," replied Dwayne. "A little too quiet if you ask me."

"Don't be paranoid, Dwayne. I can't believe I'm about to say this to you," said Clovis. "Log onto Facebook. If anything happens in town, most likely you'll see it there before someone calls you about it."

Dwayne couldn't help but laugh at the Chief's suggestion. "I'll tell you a secret if you don't fire me," replied Dwayne. "I log into Facebook every night for that exact reason actually."

"Well don't bother going for a cruise around town," said Clovis. "I couldn't sleep so I just spent an hour doing just that. All is quiet tonight in our sleepy little town."

"Good-good!" replied Dwayne.

"Call me if you hear anything from Stonevalley P.D. or if anything happens."

"Will do, Chief. Get some sleep."

22

The clock read "3:27 AM" as a dishevelled Clovis sat on the edge of the bed wearing his boxers and a Bangor Maine T-shirt he'd gotten on one of their last vacations. He turned off his cordless phone and set it next to its cradle on the nightstand. He turned and for a moment, watched his wife as she slept soundly as if nothing was wrong in her world.

"I wish I could sleep as soundly as you," said Clovis in a hushed voice. He leaned in and kissed his wife on the cheek before getting up from the groove on his side of the well-worn mattress.

"Cuba," he muttered to himself, half smiling as he went to their son's old room to get dressed. Not wanting to wake his wife whenever he had to get up in the middle of the night, he kept all his clothes plus cop stuff in the room across the hall.

23

Raylene woke to find the other half of the bed empty. She laid her hand on her husband's side of the bed and felt it cold to the touch. She half hoped it would still be warm and that her husband would be in the bathroom or making coffee. Lifting her head from her pillow she saw her cell phone resting on his nightstand. This meant she would have a text from her missing husband. He would have sent it for her to find when she woke. She smiled as she reached for the phone thinking about how he only learned to text once his daughter left for university.

The text read. "Gone to get Anna. Be back soon. Love you."

Raylene smiled and she rested her head thinking it would just be for a moment as she drifted off to sleep again.

24

The sun was still rising as Clovis sat in his truck outside a campus building in Stonevalley. The three-story brick building where his daughter Anna resided. He watched feeling slightly comforted by the sight of the campus security vehicle as it approached, the driver peering at him through his windshield leaning forward in his seat. The vehicle slowed to a crawl as it pulled up next to Clovis's truck. Clovis already had his window rolled down, his arm resting on the door as he watched as the campus security officer put his window down. Clovis couldn't help but think if he had been dangerous, I could have shot him before he even had time to put his window down. But the security guard looked quite young. So young in fact he could be a student himself.

Half full of arrogance the young security guard spoke. "Awfully early to be hanging out on campus isn't it, Mister."

"Picking up my daughter," said Clovis.

"She live in this building?" asked the guard.

What a stupid question, thought Clovis. "Yup, in 3B."

At that moment the front door burst open and the young Anna struggled through it pulling a medium sized pink suitcase behind her. Backpack and purse slung on her shoulder. At the sight of Anna, the young security officer struggled to open his car door and stood behind it.

"A-Anna," he half stammered. "You need a hand with that?" he asked, clearly enamoured with sight of the young woman.

"No thanks, Jaffer," she replied.

"Is this your dad?" the young security officer asked. "Is he... The Chief of Police in Carlton?"

Clovis smiled. He liked the idea that the campus kids knew he was a cop. He liked that he knew the girl he was lusting after had a father who carried a gun. This amused Clovis as he saw the look of arrogance had vanished on the kid in the security guard uniform.

Stepping out from behind the door of his campus security cruiser, security guard Jaffer spoke. "We've beefed up security on campus," he made this statement as he glanced around. "With that psycho on the loose, we're not taking chances."

Clovis knew he was looking for approval now that he knew who he was talking to. His air of arrogance had all but vanished now as he stepped up to the truck. Anna tossed her bag in the back of the truck and climbed in.

Clovis never took his eyes of the kid as he spoke. "Has anything out of the ordinary happened on campus?"

"Not so far. But we're not taking any chances," replied Jaffer.

"Heard on the radio that calls on sightings called into the hotline are down to almost none," said Clovis.

"Yeah, I heard that too," answered Jaffer hooking his thumb into the waistband of his uniform. Clovis noticed that the young security guard wore a Taser on his belt where cops wore their gun.

"That's good, kid," replied Clovis. "Remember to report anything unusual."

Jaffer leaned in and pointed at Anna. "See you Monday?"

"I don't have classes Monday," replied Anna. "Maybe Tuesday."

Clovis looked at his daughter in an attempt to read her. He wanted to know if she liked this young man who stood before him. Not sure what to think at the moment, he spoke to the young man as he drove away. "Be careful, kid."

Clovis watched the kid dwindle away in his rear-view mirror as he drove. Standing in the middle of the road scratching his head as he stepped towards his car only to stop and watch them drive off some more. Clovis's gut told him this kid had a thing for his young daughter. He hadn't decided how he felt about that just yet, but he liked that he was doing his best to keep his daughter and the other students safe.

"I hear you've got a boyfriend?" asked Clovis.

"Not anymore," replied Anna. "He was an idiot. One of those... too cool for school types."

Clovis laughed at his daughter's comment knowing full well she always wanted to be the cool girl even though she wasn't the type. Anna jerked in her seat suddenly and pulled her iPhone from her pocket. She smiled as she looked at it nonchalantly.

"So! I hear mom is finally gonna take you to Cuba."

They both burst out laughing as they turned off campus and into the parking lot of the first Jabba-da-Java Coffee Hut they saw.

25

Luckily for her, she had the country road to herself as Raylene's car swerved slightly when the cell phone in her crotch vibrated. The feeling spooked her since she had already forgotten she set it there mere moments ago as she left Pinewood Lodge. She had been so preoccupied with checking up on Winston to make sure all was in order. A quick glance showed her a text from Libby.

"Where's Clovis?" was all the text read.

Raylene drove on for a moment before giving into the urge to pull over.

"Home sleeping," was Raylene's first reply. She followed it up with a short question simply stating. "Why?"

"Can you talk?" replied Libby.

"Yes!" Raylene texted in reply a mere moment before her phone received an incoming call from Libby.

"Hey, Libby," answered Raylene. "What's up?"

"Nothing really, but Dwayne and I were getting nervous since we hadn't heard from Clovis all day."

"He's home sleeping," replied Raylene. "He hasn't slept much since this all started. He's been worried about Anna ever since those senseless murders happened in Stonevalley six months back. But now that Anna is home he's sleeping like a baby."

"Well that's good," replied Libby. "Dwayne and I figured we'd pop into the station and take care of anything Crandall related but there's nothing. Not a peep. Almost makes me nervous." There was a pause and Libby added. "Dwayne just got off the phone with Officer Nowlan."

"You want Clovis to call you when he gets up?" asked Raylene while she secretly hoped that Libby would say no. Weeks of planning a birthday party could be wasted with one phone call thought Raylene. All it would take would be the one call reporting a sighting of Crandall in the Carlton area and all her hard work would have been for nothing. Lousy timing, she thought that this escaped psychopathic serial killer would still be on the loose the same night of her husband's surprise birthday party. Raylene started to get nervous as Libby seemed to pause on the other end of the call. Her reply delayed.

"Raylene," replied Libby. "Dwayne wants to talk to you. Hang on for a sec."

"Raylene. It's me, Dwayne. Listen. I have a plan for tonight," said Dwayne as Raylene felt her heart sink at the thought of Dwayne having a plan.

26

Raylene glanced at the time as she pulled into the driveway of her country home on the outskirts of Carlton. Nearly six o'clock already she thought. At that moment she looked up and her mind went completely blank. She shut off her engine and marvelled at the empty driveway. It took her a moment before processing what must have happened. Clovis couldn't drive two vehicles at once and so he would have let Anna take the truck. And he then would have had to take his police cruiser into town. She hurried to get in the house knowing she would most likely find a note on the kitchen counter. The note sat in the same place it always did when the kids lived at home. This was the way they left messages before the days when Clovis learned to text. It sat on the cutting board with a now empty milk glass as a paperweight. Written in Clovis's familiar scribbling.

"Thanks for the meatloaf. We saved you some. It's in the fridge. Gone to the office to check on things. Be back soon. Love you."

Raylene took her cell phone from her purse and after a few swift motions, put the phone to her ear.

"Dwayne?" Raylene asked. "Is Clovis with you?"

"Libby just texted me," replied Dwayne. "He just got to the station."

"What should I do?" asked Raylene with panic apparent in her voice.

Dwayne let out a quick guffaw before speaking as if nothing was wrong. "Don't worry. I'll take care of it."

Still standing at the kitchen counter with the note in hand, Raylene disconnected the call and quickly made another.

"Libby? It's Raylene. Listen, is Clovis with you?"

"Yes-Yes, Bonnie. You know I can't share police information," said Libby.

"Libby? Is he right there with you? Can you talk?"

"Not now, Bonnie. But don't worry. It's all under control."

"Call me when you can," said a panicked Raylene before ending the call. Taking a deep breath through her nose and exhaling through her mouth, she braced herself against the kitchen counter and tried hard to calm herself.

"Not gonna panic. Not gonna panic," she repeated aloud. More deep breathing exercises although they had little affected on her state of mind. Just then her cell phone vibrated. The display screen read the name Jack Ledger.

"Jack?" she said even before the phone was at her ear.

"Raylene. What's this I hear about Clovis being at the station?"

"How'd you hear that?" asked Raylene.

"Maureen says it's all over Facebook."

"Tell Maureen to stick to the plan," said a frustrated Raylene in a harsh tone. "Her husband is supposed to take care of it."

"Ok-sheesh. Relax, Raylene," replied Jack in meek tone.

"Sorry, Jack. Call me if anything important comes up."

Raylene disconnects the call, crumpled the note and tossed it on the counter. Setting her cell phone down, she opened the fridge door, paused for a moment and then returned to the counter to pick up her cell phone again and dialled one of the many programmed numbers.

"Anna?" asks Raylene. "Where are you? Did you tell your dad about the party?"

27

Libby sat at her desk in her jeans and white blouse instead of her usual police uniform. Her blond hair down instead of tied up neatly. She glanced behind her towards Chief Clovis's office door just to be sure it was safe before pulling up her Facebook again. A quick post on the event wall she noted. "All is a go as planned. Will let you know when we arrive." And before she could lower the internet browser, she already had seven 'likes' to her post, most likely from mobile devices. A slight smile of satisfaction spread on her face as she heard something emanating from Clovis's office. She tilted her head in attempt to hear better, but she could only make out a muffled voice. She shut down her computer, scooped up her cell phone and walked over to Clovis's office doorway. She peered in and saw him sitting behind his desk as she caught the tail end of a conversation as he hung up the phone.

"Who was that?" she inquired with an obvious display of curiosity.

"Officer Nowlan," replied Clovis. "Just making sure my sleepy little town is still sleeping is all."

Libby asked. "What'd he say?"

"Not much, but I suppose no news is good news," said Clovis.

"I never got that expression," replied Libby.

"It means it's better to not have heard anything about Crandall than to have heard of him leaving a trail of bodies like his last rampage."

"Oh!!" replied Libby. "Gotcha!"

"Big plans tonight?" asked Clovis. "You've got the country girl fancies on."

"Blue jeans and a white blouse qualify as dressed up to you?"

With a wide smile, Clovis replied. "On a Saturday night in Carlton, yes it does."

"Might have a beer at Burnett's later," replied Libby.

Clovis, in his own jeans and Saturday night special chequered shirt got up from behind his desk. Libby hadn't noticed until now that he wore his police gun belt.

"Expecting trouble?" she asked pointing to the gun belt.

"You can't be too careful. Things have gotten too quiet for my liking with this Crandall business," said Clovis as his smile disappeared. "But don't tell Dwayne."

Libby knew the real reason was that Anna was in town now, but she kept that to herself.

28

Floyd peaked over his Carlton Gazette newspaper and watched in astonishment as off-duty Officer Robert walked into his otherwise desolate bar. Floyd folded the paper and laid it on top of the bar while smiling.

"Well now," said Floyd. "I thought tonight was going to be a complete waste of money. You are gonna have a beer now aren't you?" Floyd picked up a mug and held it under the tap with his hand on the handle, waiting for Robert to say yes before he poured.

"Just the one but make it the usual," replied Robert. Reluctantly he had driven his cruiser just in case he would get a call about Crandall. None of the officers had liked the idea but Dwayne was pretty persistent about them being ready, just in case something actually did happen. Chief Clovis had been more than happy to remind the entire police force that nothing ever happened in Carlton. But everyone was shocked when without a fuss; he had agreed with Dwayne that they should be ready. Just in case.

"Is Molly off tonight?"

"She's in the can," replied Floyd. "Why aren't you at the Chief's birthday bash?" Floyd already knew the answer to the question of why Robert wasn't at Pinewood Lodge. He had come by to see Molly.

"I'm gonna go a little later," replied Robert.

Floyd set the foamy draft beer in front of Robert as he spoke. "I didn't think I'd see a single soul tonight." Floyd paused as the door to the bar opened and in walked an already unsteady Thinking-Lincoln. "Except maybe for Thinkun-Lincoln. I figured he'd show up sooner or later."

Both Robert and Floyd watched as Lincoln tried hard to steady himself, but still he staggered slightly as he walked over to the bar. He knew that if Floyd knew how much he had already had today that he wouldn't sell him anything. But Lincoln had gotten very good at hiding his drinking from people in a physical sense. But the ever so quiet and reserved man known to the residents of Carlton as Thinking-Lincoln wasn't quite so quiet when he was intoxicated. Lincoln pulled himself onto a barstool at the opposite end of the bar, away from Robert.

Molly startled Floyd as she walked up behind him and took a beer from the cooler behind the bar and plopped it in front of Lincoln who already had a folded twenty under his hand which rested on the bar. He slid it forward so Molly could take it.

"It's gonna be pretty quiet in here tonight," said a smiling Molly as she winked at Lincoln putting his change on the bar before him.

"Maybe Floyd shuts down early so you can come to the lodge with me," said Robert before taking a sip of beer.

Lincoln gave Robert a scowl of a glance before reaching behind the bar for the remote and changing the channel on the set above the bar.

29

Having washed her dishes and now impatiently waiting in the kitchen, Raylene noticed a glare in her window as she fiddled with her cell phone. The sun had begun to set making the headlights more noticeable in the shadows cast by the trees on the edge of their red and orange leaf sprinkled lawn. Setting down her cell phone, perched on the balls of her feet she looked out her window as she saw Clovis pull up in his cruiser and park next to her car. She stood motionless, watching, waiting for him to get out of his car. Instead he sat looking down and then suddenly put his cell phone to his ear. She watched him for a few moments and then glanced at the metal sunflower shaped clock which hung on her kitchen wall. Panic rose inside her as thoughts of all her plans falling apart with one simple call about Crandall. She knew the safety of the people in Carlton was Clovis's first priority. His selflessness was one of the qualities she loved about the man she proudly called her husband. She watched as he lowered the phone away from his ear. His head down, he was still looking at his phone. A moment later he leaned forward slightly, and she heard the cruiser's engine come alive. Clovis wrapped his arm around the passenger seat and looked behind him as he began backing out of their driveway. The buzzing vibration of her cell phone on the kitchen counter spooked Raylene. She quickly scooped up her cell phone as she watched Clovis drive off as he disappeared behind the colourful trees on the side of their property line.

Curse words were rare for the schoolteacher but one came out without her ever realising she said it.

"Fuck!" said Raylene as she impatiently looked at her cell phone to find a text from Clovis.

The message read. "Dwayne called. It's about Crandall. Sorry but I have to go."

"If this is your big plan," Raylene said aloud. "Clovis is going to kill you. Right after I do that is." A few more curse words would be uttered before she would try her deep breathing exercises to calm herself down as she looked for her keys.

30

Floyd gave Lincoln a dirty look as he spoke. "Not too loud!" Lincoln had turned up the volume on the flat screen above the bar. A reporter in a suit was on the screen standing on an empty street in Stonevalley with a Channel 9 mike in hand. Lincoln only caught the last half of his report.

"Sources say there haven't been any tips coming into the hotline in the last twenty-four hours. Police seem to be baffled as to whereabouts of Crandall and if they have any leads, they're not sharing them with the media. This is Mike Reicker for Channel Nine News."

Molly took the remote from Lincoln and turned down the volume slightly and set the remote down on the bar. She turned, took a beer from the cooler, replaced Lincoln's empty bottle with a full one and took money from Lincoln's change that had stayed on the bar and paid for the beer.

Lincoln looked at Molly, sipped his beer and spoke. "I was thinking. The glass is half full if it was never filled to begin with. But if it was filled and then you consumed the first half, then that makes it half empty."

"Whatever you say, Thinkun-Lincoln." Molly turned and looked to see if Floyd had heard any of what Lincoln had just said. She was happy that he looked oblivious to Lincoln as he chatted with Robert. The last thing she wanted tonight was for Floyd to get angry at poor old Lincoln.

31

Darkness approached as Clovis sat in his police cruiser in the empty parking lot of Pinewood Lodge, radio mike in hand. The sun was almost completely set, hidden behind the thick red leaves of the forest casting everything into the shadows. The lights on and surrounding Pinewood Lodge were hindering his vision more than helping with the fading daylight.

"Dwayne, are you there? Over," said Clovis into the mike for the second time.

"Almost there," replied Dwayne. "Did you see anything? Over."

Clovis smiled as he spoke into his radio mike. "You mean any-one. Did I see anyone? And no I didn't. Over."

Clovis heard nothing for a moment and then the silence broke. "It has to be the same hitchhiker that Mr. Brooks saw. The call said he was on this road near Pinewood Lodge. Over."

"Well I drove up and down Short Fir Road and didn't see any-one. Not even you. Over."

Clovis sat waiting for a reply but nothing came. A glare of headlights suddenly appeared behind his cruiser. He quickly recognized the car and knew it was Dwayne's own police cruis-er as he watched him park in an awkward angle right next to his own car. Both men simultaneously got out of their police cruisers.

Clovis smiled.

Dwayne walked over to where Clovis stood. "What are you grinning about?" asked Dwayne.

"Why are you in uniform?" asked Clovis.

"I-I..." Dwayne was looking down at himself as he began to

answer Clovis's question before he stopped abruptly when a loud crack caught both men's attention. Dwayne spun around facing the forest with one hand on his gun holster and the other already holding his police issue flashlight, aiming it into the trees.

"Who's there?" shouted Dwayne as he felt the tiny hairs on the back of his neck rise to the occasion.

Amidst the trees, both officers saw a faint glow of what had to be a weak flashlight. They heard crackling that could only be twigs and branches snapping under the weight of the bearer of said flashlight. Dwayne drew his gun but kept it pointed at the ground as he pointed the flashlight towards the trees.

Clovis heard a familiar voice mumbling as he saw the shadow of a man emerge from the trees behind a dull yellow cone of light.

Dwayne took a step forward and spoke again. "This is Officer Dwayne Adams. Who's there? Identify yourself."

Clovis saw Dwayne's gun arm twitch slightly and noticed Dwayne didn't have a finger on the trigger. With a swift motion Clovis drew the Taser from his gun belt and fired it hitting Dwayne square in the back. Dwayne convulsed violently for a moment before dropping to his knees and falling forward.

The sound of crunching gravel underfoot accompanied by a loud shout came from the edge of the tree line as the man stepped into view. "Holy Jesus!" exclaimed Ernie Woodman in his BELLS T-shirt. "What the hell, Clovis?"

Clovis took a step forward looking down at Dwayne twitching slightly as he lay in the gravel parking lot.

"He could have shot me!" said Ernie.

"The safety is still on," said Clovis as he pointed to the gun on the ground.

The Lodge door burst open and a flood of people came pouring out. The crowd being led by Libby and Father Finnigan also included Clovis's kids, Anna and Cotton. In a mere moment there were forty some people gathering in the parking lot of

Pinewood Lodge and more were jamming in the doorway trying to get out.

32

Molly leaned against the bar across from Robert, her ample bosom perched on the bar. He tried to hide it, but Robert's gaze kept wandering up and down Molly and she knew it. She liked his attention more than any of the other patrons who flirted with her. Floyd was in his office and out of ear shot while she spoke to Robert.

"Lincoln's plastered," said Molly.

"He was already staggering when he came in," replied Robert. "And it takes a lot to unsteady that guy."

"I didn't expect to see him here tonight. He must have run out of booze at home." Molly leaned in closer and touched Robert's arm. "You know why they call him Thinking-Lincoln, right? The shit he says when he's drunk."

Robert, still nursing the same beer he ordered hours ago while Lincoln was now on his seventh. "Floyd would have probably kicked him out again if he wasn't his only paying customer."

Molly jumped when Lincoln set down his clearly empty beer bottle hard making a loud crack that echoed in the place. Molly smiled at Robert.

"Lincoln told me he thought the talking snake in the Garden of Eden was a metaphor for Adams dick." She let out a giggle. "How fucken crazy is that?" said Molly as she walked over to serve her only real customer of the evening.

33

Maureen pushed her way through the throng of people and ran to her husband who still lay on the ground. Dwayne, already stirring, looked up at Clovis who still had the Taser in his hand.

"What the hell!" Maureen screamed at Clovis as she dropped to her knees.

Ernie Woodman still stood near the tree line, flashlight in a quivering hand. "I almost shit myself!" he exclaimed.

"You knew it was Ernie didn't you?" asked a frazzled Dwayne as he sat up.

Clovis holstered the Taser. "I recognized his voice."

Libby stepped forward in her country girl fancies. "It was Dwayne's idea we all park at Sheppard Foods and cut through the patch of woods."

Bonnie Campbell raised her drink and yelled. "Surprise!"

Everyone burst out laughing.

Standing next to her mother Anna spoke with very little zeal in her voice. "Happy birthday, Dad."

Bonnie Campbell took a step past a stunned Linus and Charlie Brooks. She emerged out of the crowd and snapped her digital camera twice, making sure to capture the Chief of Police standing over his own officer whom he Tasered a few moments ago.

34

Lincoln staggered back to the bar with his paper cup full of peanuts and made his way back to his stool. He struggled slightly when he climbed onto it knocking over his empty beer bottle in the process. Floyd shot him a dirty look and turned towards Robert shaking his head in dismay.

With slurred speech, Lincoln spoke loudly. "The problem with today's society is we put way too much energy in trying to prove were right and the other guy is wrong." He snatched up the empty beer bottle as it rolled slowly towards the back of the bar. He set it down half on the coaster causing it to tilt slightly.

Molly looked at Floyd as she walked over to Lincoln. "You know I think you've had too many already, Lincoln."

Lincoln slapped down his money onto the bar and opened his mouth to speak but Molly cut him off before he could utter a single word.

"Ok, one more. If you behave that is," she said with a smile as she took another bottle from the cooler, cracked it open and replaced the empty bottle in front of Lincoln with the full one.

Robert spoke up. "Floyd can handle Lincoln. Come to Pinewood Lodge with me."

"Careful now, Robert," said Molly as she smiled wide. "One of these days I'm gonna say yes and then what'll you do?"

Robert sat at the bar with his empty beer mug in hand. He opened his mouth to speak but couldn't find the words.

35

Raylene stood next to Clovis by the bar, her arm around his waist. Ernie Woodman patted him on the back.

"Happy Birthday, Clovis. Thanks for not shooting me."

Clovis pretended to reach for his gun. The same gun that now sat in the trunk of his cruiser. Dwayne's gun belt sat in the driver's seat of his.

Raylene looked up at her husband. "You knew, didn't you?"

Clovis smiled leaning in so no one else could hear him. "Of course I did. You don't think anything happens in this sleepy little town without my knowing it do you?"

Raylene jabbed her tiny fist into her husband's side in frustration even though she was smiling from ear to ear.

Jack Ledger handed Raylene and Clovis beers. He then hoisted a glass of his own. "A toast! To the second most important man in this town," said Mayor Jack Ledger jokingly. Everyone knew he really meant what he said. And that the most important man in this town, according to Jack Ledger was himself.

36

Robert set his empty mug down, got up and walked into the men's room.

Lincoln waited until he saw the door close behind him before he spoke. "Atheists are not evil. They know in their minds that we only have one life and so let's live it to our best. Not in jail."

Molly, sitting on a bar stool nursing a glass of lemon water, replied. "What makes you say that?"

To which Lincoln replied. "You know religious people scare me more then atheists."

Floyd spoke with a tone bordering on anger. "That's a stupid thing to say."

Molly ignored Floyd and turned to Lincoln. "How?"

Floyd crossed his arms and leaned back against the bottle rack behind the bar as he spoke. "Atheist believe there are no consequence to their actions. They're the ones you should fear."

Lincoln drank the rest of his beer and set down an empty bottle. "Not true actually. Atheist believe this life is it and so they want to live it well. Religious people believe they can sin and then pray for forgiveness and then all will be well."

"That's messed up, Lincoln," said Molly. "Are you a religious man, Floyd?"

"Yes," replied Floyd. "I believe in God."

Lincoln stared blankly at his bottle and hesitated before asking a question. "Does that mean you could kill then pray for forgiveness and think all is well?"

Floyd replied harshly as he walked over to Lincoln and took his empty bottle from him. "Hell no! I never said that. But sadly, some would. What I mean is your religious beliefs don't make you a killer or not." Floyd looked at Molly to make sure she heard him as well. "That's enough of that crazy talk. Anymore and I'm gonna throw you out on your ass."

Lincoln smiled. "Sorry if I make you think, Floyd."

"That's it!" said Floyd. "I'm not selling you no more damned liquor. You're already plastered enough." Floyd leaned forward bracing himself with both hands on the bar and looked Lincoln dead in the eyes. "GO HOME!"

Lincoln's smile vanished as his voice quivered when he spoke. "One more and then I'll go home."

"Ok, Lincoln but-" Molly had started to reply but Floyd cut her off.

"GO HOME NOW!" shouted an angered Floyd. "One more fuckin' word and I'm barring you from the place." Floyd leaned forward and pointed a shaky finger at Lincoln. "You got that you son of a bitch!"

Lincoln, clearly beaten cast his gaze downwards and struggled to get off his barstool, almost losing his balance in the process. Tears began to flow as he stammered. "But-but... I ain't got no more-"

"I don't fucking care!" said a red-faced Floyd. "Get out!"

Shoulders slumped in defeat, Lincoln walked to the door. He stopped in his tracks while standing at the door. Molly saw Lincoln wipe his eyes with the heels of his hands. Reaching towards his left side, he grabbed the top of the peanut machines and yanked them forward smashing them to the floor. Salted and barbeque peanuts plus broken glass scattered and skidded all over the wooden floor. Lincoln muttered a curse while proceeding to pushed through the glass door so hard it cracked on impact.

"YOU RAT-FACED SON OF A BITCH!" shouted Floyd. "That's it! I've had just about enough of that old fuck!" Floyd bent down behind the bar and came back up holding a shotgun.

"Oh my God!" exclaimed Molly as she clasped her fists over her mouth in shock. Molly had been oblivious to the fact that Floyd kept a shotgun behind the bar until this very moment. She wanted to scream as she watched him climb over the bar and head towards the door, shotgun in hand. In her confusion she completely forgot about Robert being in the men's room. Shaking, she got up from the barstool and took a few steps towards the door as she watched Floyd push his way through the cracked door.

Molly stood frozen in her tracks until she heard a bang from behind her. Startled by the slamming of the bathroom door, she turned to see Robert had emerged with his shirt half tucked in.

"What was that noise?" asked a befuddled Robert.

Molly's mouth opened in an attempt to reply but was interrupted by a crack that could only be a gun shot. In that moment, Robert's eyes widened in wonderment as he looked to Molly for some sort of explanation of what he had just heard. A second shot and Robert's cop reflexes kicked in as he squatted slightly reaching for his gun on his hip. The same gun that sat in the passenger seat, neatly tucked in its holster.

"Fuck!" he exclaimed as he heard the door open.

37

An hour after the Taser incident, almost everybody in Pinewood Lodge had a drink in their hand, even Dwayne. Many of them were already too drunk to drive. But there were many designated drivers with non-alcoholic drinks as well. The party was after all, for their Chief of Police himself. The man of the hour was one of their own, born and raised in Carlton.

Bonnie Campbell, drink in one hand and camera held high in the other, looked at Clovis as she spoke with a slight slur of inebriation. "You know these pictures are gonna make the Gazette, right?" Half the room who heard her comment burst into laughter. Just like a smiling Bonnie had intended before adding. "Unless Crandall pays this town a visit tonight, they might even make the front page."

Dwayne spoke. "I'm just glad he didn't shoot me."

"You're glad?" said Ernie Woodman barking a laugh as he slapped Dwayne on the back hard enough to spill his beer.

Most of the evening would be spent teasing Clovis about his greying hair, growing kids and approaching old age. That or Dwayne for his brilliant plan of getting Clovis to his birthday party without letting on to what was really about to happen. The same plan that got him Tasered and that luckily for him Clovis knew and so had the zapper set low.

The clock would toll midnight before the inebriated crowd would start to thin out, leaving only a small band behind. Clovis had spent the first hour arguing with people as they handed him drinks. About how he couldn't drink because he would have to drive his police cruiser home that night. Same goes for Dwayne he'd say. And almost every time he would argue that fact, Jack Ledger would remind him that nothing ever happened in Carlton. Raylene would make a deal with him that she would not drink if he let loose and had fun. And with enough coaxing, he reluctantly eventually agreed.

Libby would be the last to drive home. Sober.

38

At a little past two in the morning, Dwayne and Maureen sat on opposite sides of the kitchen table sipping coffee while they both surfed Facebook on laptops. A bloop sound echoed as Dwayne got a message from Libby.

"You still awake?" was what it said.

"I work graveyard shift five days a week. Of course, I'm still awake," he replied sarcastically adding a winking emoticon instead of punctuation.

"I drove past Burnett's on the way home," replied Libby.

"So?" asked Dwayne.

"Robert's cruiser was there," wrote Libby in her reply.

"Molly must have finally given him a reason to stick around," wrote Dwayne as he grinned causing him to have to explain his amusement to his curious wife who sat across from him at the table.

"lol," was Libby's only reply.

39

The sun's rays were shining through the small slits on the sides of the layered dark curtains covering their bedroom window casting a soft glow about the room. It was close to ten thirty on Sunday morning when Dwayne's telephone rang, waking Maureen and not Dwayne. Reaching over her husband Maureen picked up the cordless phone from the nightstand and glanced at the display screen before poking her husband with it a few times while it rang. Dwayne stirred, opened one eye and looked at his wife holding a cordless phone in a hand aimed towards him.

"It's Libby," said Maureen sounding half asleep. "Ask her if she forgot we work graveyard."

Dwayne propped himself up on one elbow, took the phone

and put it to his ear. "Hello," he said as it rang again. Focusing he pushed the talk button and said hello for the second time.

Maureen had already rolled over and was struggling with her pillow in an attempt to get comfortable.

"Did you hear from Robert this morning?" asked Libby sounding slightly irritated.

"No, why? You jealous?" asked a smirking Dwayne.

Ignoring his comments, Libby replied. "His cruiser is still in the lot at Burnett's. I saw it when I went to get coffee at Santorene's this morning." Libby paused before adding. "Clovis is gonna kill him if he finds out he left his cruiser there overnight."

"You woke me for that?" asked Dwayne unsuccessfully trying to suppress a yawn.

"He's not answering his phone either, Dwayne,"

"Like I told you last night. He's been chasing after Molly since he moved back here. He's probably at her place. Now I only went to bed at six, Libby. Call me if someone dies or something. Ok?" Dwayne hung up, cradled the phone and plopped backwards into his pillow.

40

Libby sipped coffee from a Santorene paper cup with the white plastic lid as she drove up Short Fir Road. With nothing to do early on a Sunday afternoon she was on her way to the hiking trails near and around Pinewood Lodge. A thought raced through her mind and she quickly pulled her Jeep over to the shoulder and came to a grinding halt sending a cloud of beige dust billowing up only to be whisked away by the slight breeze.

If Robert left his police cruiser at Burnett's because he went to Molly's place. Then why would Molly's tiny blue car still be in the same parking lot too?

Libby was certain that she had seen it that morning. But she had been too wrapped up with the idea of Robert's cruiser still being in the parking lot of the local drinking hole to have realised it. And a sudden urge to satisfy her burning curiosity made her pull a u-turn and head towards town.

41

Libby parked her Jeep next to Robert's police cruiser in front of Burnett's Place. Her own reflection caught her eye as she pulled the handbrake. The sun's glare on the large tinted window turned it into a giant mirror reflecting everything before it. The only part not a reflection was the large red lettering spelling the words BURNETT'S PLACE.

Clovis had insisted that most of his off-duty officers drive their cruisers this weekend. Little news about Crandall meant that he could indeed show up in Carlton. And Clovis wouldn't admit it but now that his daughter Anna was in town, he wanted his officers on high alert. He had also insisted they keep their gun belts in the trunk just in case. A quick glance at Robert's cruiser made Libby's heart sink. She not only saw the cruiser in the parking lot but the gun belt neatly folded in the passenger seat. She knew he was careless enough to leave it in the seat but not overnight.

Molly's car was on the opposite end of the parking lot past the end of the building. Same place she always parked, underneath the last of the large spotlights. She always backed in so the driver's door would be towards her when she walked to it late at night. Libby pulled out her cell phone and dialled Robert's number only to end the call before it could even ring once.

Clovis is gonna fire him, she thought.

With Floyd's truck nowhere in sight, Libby wondered if he had finally let someone else come in to open up the place. Floyd was such a control freak which would make this so damned hard to believe.

But the gun belt in plain sight. Why?

Libby quickly hatched a plan to save Robert's hide. She would go to the station, get the spare keys to the cruiser. Put the gun belt in the trunk and park the cruiser at the station. Libby started her Jeep and drove off, station bound on this sunny Sunday afternoon.

42

Upon her return from the station, Libby had parked at the very same spot she had a short while before. Focused on her task, she climbed out of her Jeep making her long ponytail bob in her enthusiasm. Her haste combined with not taking the time to figure out which set was which, Libby had taken the large set of keys and shoved it into her small purse that now bulged and swayed heavily at her side. She walked at a brisk pace around her Jeep, the sound of some loose gravel atop the faded asphalt crunching under her feet echoed against the building. She pulled the large set of keys from her purse intending on going through the tags to select the right one. Before she had the chance, something caught her downward glance.

At her feet sat what looked like an imperfect circular shadow. At first the large dark spot about the size of a manhole cover had looked like a shadow but she saw now that it looked wet. The tips of her feet were just over the edge of it when it caught her eye. Without much thought she casually took a step back. Libby knew it hadn't rained at all in the last few days and so the dark stain was out of place. Plus it had a look as if it trailed off a little, thought Libby. It was as if it pointed towards the door. As if in a trance Libby took a few steps forward and could see the sunlight glinting on a spider web in the darkness of the sunken doorway. At least at first it looked to her like it was a spider's web until she got closer and noticed the glass on the front door had been shattered causing the glass to crack in web-like patterns. The safety laminated glass held in its place. The dark blotch-like puddle had led her to the door with broken glass. On the bottom sill of the door was what could only be dried blood. A small part of her assumed it was blood all along, but she couldn't bring herself to accept it. A puddle of blood that size clearly indicated something horrible and the fact that whoever had bled there had either dragged themselves or perhaps been dragged away. Either one was a terrifying thought.

Libby's police officer instincts kicked in, being careful where she stepped while backtracking to the passenger side of Robert's cruiser. She unlocked and opened the door. Libby unsnapped the holster and drew the Glock 9mm and left the gun belt lying in the passenger seat. There was no point in taking the time to try and fit into Robert's belt. Glock in hand with the safety off, Libby pushed through the doorway slowly, daylight glinting on the broken glass. She was careful not to step on the blood as she stepped into the darkness.

The contrast of the bright sunny day against the purposefully gloomy inside of Burnett's made Libby strain to see. Her eyes took a moment to adjust to the lack of light in the bar. Her gun clutched in her cop double handed grip and angled slightly downwards, she patted her side for the flashlight that should have been there had she been on duty.

"Floyd?" said Libby calling out. "Molly?"

She walked forward squinting as her eyes were getting accustomed to the lack of light when she felt her foot hit something making her stumble slightly. She glanced around the room to make sure nothing would catch her off guard before she looked down at her feet. Before she could see what was there, her other foot stepped in something slick and she was lying prone before she even realized it. Her ponytail saving her from being knocked unconscious as the back of her head hit the floor hard. Her gun hand twitched on impact and a shot went off. They would later figure out that her bullet lodged itself in a wide varnished wooden moulding, inches from one of the many flat screen television sets mounted on the wall.

Outside, in the parking lot of Burnett's, a pair of crows who had been eating the dead cooked worms from the hot asphalt flew away, scarred off by the muffled gun shot that had come from inside.

A dazed Libby opened her eyes to see a foot lying right next to her prone self. Her eyes travelled up the leg as she propped herself up on her elbows on the slick flooring. Shock filled her as she saw the legs led to a waist but stopped there. The upper body was missing. She raised an arm, gun still in hand and looked at it, realizing she lay in a pool of blood. The blood had seeped out from the severed waist and had congealed on the hardwood flooring.

Her eyes had taken time to get adjusted to the sombre inside of the bar but now she saw everything pretty clearly but was no longer sure she wanted to see what was there to be seen. She struggled to her feet while staring at the half body next to her. Turning her gaze, she saw Robert staring at her with his mouth open. Only it wasn't Robert but just his head sitting askew on the bar in a puddle of gore. Behind it was Floyd who looked like he was standing at first. But she saw his outstretched hands had been pinned to the rack of glasses above the bar given him the looked of being crucified. His head slumped forward as much as it could. That's when Libby realized the legs on the floor next to her were Floyd's.

What madness thought Libby. She felt her stomach churn and nausea washing over herself. The feeling got stronger and Libby ran for the door. She pushed through it hard hearing snapping sounds as more of the glass cracked in the process.

I can't throw up on a crime scene, thought Libby as she stopped to vomit next to Robert's police cruiser. Her knees almost buckled beneath her and her head spun as she braced herself on the car.

43

All of Carlton was oblivious to Libby's findings as she was vomiting next to Robert's cruiser in the parking lot of Burnett's Place. Most of the town's folk were spending the afternoon as they always did on Sundays.

Accustomed to a life of graveyard shifts, Dwayne and Maureen were sleeping in.

Bonnie Campbell had her short silver hair in large curlers

while she sat at her desk at the headquarters of the Carlton Gazette starting to plan her next edition. Her stainless steel Santorene coffee cup sat next to her giving off a slight aroma of coffee accentuated by a generous dose of Baileys Irish Cream.

Ernie Woodman was at home on Sunday's like he always was. While his wife was out playing the weekly bridge game with her lady friends; he was playing dress up in his wife's closet.

Linus and his wife Geraldine sat in their old dark blue Ford Escape. This time both their boys visited with Doctor Evee Melanson.

Father Finnigan was visiting the residents of Sleepy Meadows like he always did on Sunday afternoons.

Jack Ledger wore the brightest combination of yellow golf shirt, chequered shorts and Irish tweed hat of all the others on the golf course. Of course by this hour his blood pressure was rising as his game got worse and worse.

The motley crew still played the traditional Sunday game even if it was never quite the same after the mysterious disappearance of their golf buddy, local shipping tycoon Gary Chapmen.

Clovis and his wife Raylene were in the process of cleaning up after having barbequed with their visiting children. Now that the kids were grown, they didn't come home at the same time very often, so they had spent the morning as a family. They had intended on making a day of it but Raylene knew that would change when the phone rang.

"Dad, it's for you," said Anna, handing him the phone.

44

Looking through her kitchen window, Raylene watched her husband Clovis speed away in his cruiser, the roof lights flashing.

"Where's Dad going?" asked Cotton.

"What happened?" added Anna.

Raylene looked at her kids. "I don't know but I've never seen your father so pale, ever."

"He told me to stay home with you guys," replied Cotton.

Anna looked at her mother. "Seriously, what's going on? Where's he going?"

"It must be bad because he wouldn't tell me," replied Raylene. "But he went white as a ghost when I asked if it had to do with Crandall."

45

Clovis flicked on the siren and gripped the steering wheel so hard his knuckles were white as he sped up. His mind going back to the call he had just gotten from Libby.

"You know how we always say that nothing ever happens in Carlton?" Libby had said in a crackling voice. He could tell she was emotional. And for Libby to get emotional that meant someone she knew was involved.

"Yeah, why?" he had asked in reply.

"Crandall's in town. You better get over to Burnett's and fast." Libby had said.

46

Dwayne sat on the edge of the bed with his back to his wife as he spoke on the phone. He set the cordless phone back in the cradle and turned to see if his wife was going back to sleep. Maureen wasn't asleep as she lay there, wide awake and curious as hell.

"What's going on?" she asked. "It has to be important for Clovis to call you on a Sunday afternoon."

"He asked me not to tell anyone," said Dwayne as he got up off the bed. "Even you!" Dwayne could see his wife was not pleased by that comment.

Maureen knew it must be serious. It must be extremely serious for Clovis to insist that Dwayne not tell his wife about it. She would try to get him to tell her something before he was able to get dressed and leave but he refused. She got the impression that Clovis hadn't told him everything either which only strengthened her theory that it had to be something serious.

47

Maureen kissed her husband as he left. She watched Dwayne hurry and drive away in his cruiser with the lights on as soon as he pulled out their driveway. She could still hear his engine roar as he vanished from sight. That sound was soon replaced by his siren and that faded away as well as he drove towards the center of town.

She flicked off her coffee maker, pouring a cup and sat at the kitchen table before her laptop. A few moments later she was logged into Facebook and looking at pictures someone had posted on their wall. Clovis in one picture as he hung police tape surrounding the parking lot of Burnett's Place, a few cruisers could be seen. Rumours were already spreading on the website. This was expected, especially in such a small town. A few people messaged Maureen to ask what was going on, but she ignored the messages but stayed glued to the screen waiting for updates.

48

Word spread quickly about the police being at Burnett's Place. Social media only fanned the flames as rumours of Crazy Crandall spread like fire in tall dry grass on a windy day. Word reached Bonnie Campbell through her usual source. Her police scanner set atop the beige metal filling cabinet alerted her early on. She dropped everything and got to the scene as Clovis strung up the police line tape.

Bonnie, now curler free but still smelling like hair products was visibly shaken when she spoke.

"Is-is Molly in there?" She knew full well she was as Clovis didn't make eye contact. This told her Molly was inside and she was most likely dead. The ambulance sat just outside the police tape with one of its paramedics standing by, pale as ghost. A still shaken Libby wrapped in a blanket while sitting in the back of the ambulance with the other paramedic as she breathed into an oxygen mask.

Jack Ledger stepped past a few stunned onlookers as he placed a comforting hand on Bonnie Campbell's shoulder.

"I guess Lincoln was right after all, huh Clovis?" remarked Jack.

"I can't comment," said Clovis as he tied the end of the caution tape and snapped off the roll. "You know that."

Not long after, all of Carlton was crawling with Stonevalley Police. Crime scene investigators had taken over the scene at Burnett's leaving Chief Clovis and his officers wondering if their sleepy little town would ever truly sleep again. It had been a long time since the town has seen something even remotely like this. The town would need time to mourn long after this day had passed.

"They don't seem to be locking down the town like I expected," said Dwayne to Clovis.

"I know," replied Clovis. "They seem entirely too calm about everything for my liking."

"What're you thinking, Chief?" asked Dwayne.

"I'm thinking I wish I wasn't so popular right now."

A clearly befuddled Dwayne replied. "What's that supposed to mean?"

Clovis scratched his salt and pepper covered scalp as he spoke. His voice lowered as he glanced at the Stonevalley Officers milling about. "I mean half the town was at my birthday party. If it wasn't for that, Robert might still be alive." He sighed and added. "Molly and Floyd too."

"You're seriously not blaming yourself for a serial killer killing are you?" asked Dwayne.

"No. But had the usual Saturday crowd been at Burnett's I don't think this would have happened." Clovis stopped talking while a Stonevalley officer walked past him. "Because of my party there are no witnesses either. Don't tell Raylene I said that. This is police business, right?"

"Yeah, of course," replied Dwayne. "But there's always Thinking-Lincoln. He wasn't at your party so he must have been at Burnett's getting drunk like always."

"True. He has been drinking more than ever these days. He could have been at Burnett's and might have seen something that might help us understand how this could happen." Clovis looked around assessing the situation. "I think they don't need us here right this minute." He clapped Dwayne on the shoulder. "Let's go for a drive and pay a visit to my old school buddy Lincoln."

49

"I sure don't like the look of this," said Dwayne from the passenger seat of Chief Clovis's cruiser.

"Me either," replied Clovis.

They were parked on the roadside looking at Floyd's truck, which sat askew in Lincoln's gravel driveway. It had a large dried blood smear on the driver's door. Upon closer inspection they would see the interior completely smeared in blood as well. Clovis didn't have to say anything to Dwayne as the look on his face said it all. Something was terribly wrong here. Both men drew their guns as they approached Lincoln's small dilapidated house. Clovis smelled the vodka before stepping on the broken glass on the porch. A shattered bottle no doubt full at the time still lay where it had broken. Clovis glanced behind him to see Dwayne stopped in his tracks at the bottom of the stairs as he fiddled with his pocket and pulled out his Blackberry. With a confused look he put it to his ear and spoke.

"Hello!"

Clovis knew their element of surprise had just been blown. If anyone was inside, they would've heard Dwayne. They probably would have thought he was speaking to them. The door was ajar and now the smell of death assaulted Clovis as he took a step closer. The gun in his right hand was pointed towards the floor as he gently pushed the door open. Daylight streamed through the thin curtains of the double wide living room window. A quick glance behind him showed Dwayne talking on his Blackberry, scratching his head with the barrel of his gun, which was pointed skyward. Luckily his finger wasn't on the trigger thought Clovis. He also felt a little relieved that Dwayne's gun wasn't pointed in his direction as he stepped through the doorway.

The strong stench of death for the second time that day made him gag slightly as he covered his mouth with the back of his hand. Bloody footprints in no discernable pattern covered the already littered floor. On the recliner, which had its back towards him, he could see feet propped up and an arm outstretched limply. The reflection in the blank television screen confirmed it to be Lincoln before he even stepped in to have a closer look.

Clovis stood next to the recliner when Dwayne walked through the open doorway. He still had his gun casually in his right hand as he extended his left holding up his Blackberry.

"It's for you," he said grimacing from the smell as he gave the phone to Clovis. "It's Nowlan."

Clovis took the phone from Dwayne. "Hey, Nowlan," he said as he put the phone to his ear.

He heard Nowlan speaking to someone on the other end as he did so. "Clovis. It wasn't Crandall who killed those people at Brunette's."

"That's Burnett's," replied Clovis. "And how do you know that?"

"We had a couple places under surveillance for days now. Crandall finally came out from hiding and so he couldn't have been in Carlton last night."

"You caught him?" asked Clovis.

"About a half hour ago," replied Nowlan. "And the way the victims were found at Burnett's, I think we have a copycat on our hands."

"I'm thinking something went terribly wrong and all of it was a cover up," replied Clovis as he stood before Lincoln's body.

"What makes you say that?" asked Nowlan.

"Let's just say I'm pretty sure I've found my killer."

Clovis asked Nowlan to send a team of CSI to Lincoln's address as he looked about the room. On the coffee table was a blood-smeared cardboard box full of liquor bottles. On the floor beneath Lincoln's outstretched arm lay an empty bottle of spiced rum. Lincoln's lifeless body, covered in blood, was slumped in the recliner. The smell indicated that he had died in the night. Clovis assumed he died most likely from alcohol poisoning or a stroke or something. On the floor next to the empty rum bottle lay a very large blood-caked kitchen knife. Also on the floor next to the knife was a blood-smeared copy of the Carlton Gazette with the headline reading.

Lester Crandall, a.k.a. Crazy Crandall on the loose.

Dwayne stood with a hand over his nose as he spoke. "Why would Lincoln do such a horrible thing?"

"I guess we'll never really know," replied Clovis. "But my guess would be that he killed Floyd in self-defense." Clovis gagged on the smell and wiped a tear away as he continued. "Then panicked and tried to cover it up and make it look like Crandall. But that's just a guess."

Author's Note

First I want to use this note to explain the fact that the title of *Sleepless Nights* wasn't intended to mean the contents of this collection of short stories would be so horrific that they would keep you up at night. Instead I hoped they would peak your curiosity so much that you couldn't stop reading and so you, the reader would spend many a sleepless night lost in my weaves. Every would-be writer dreams of hearing the words, *I couldn't put it down*. Why should I be any different?

All of the tales from this book are not drawn from some giant source of inspiration but rather from my imagination only. *Nothing Ever Happens in Carlton* for example was written after I read two books of stories set in small towns with many characters. One of those books was *Needful Things* which crept in as sort of a nod to the book and its author.

Penny For Your Thoughts was a concept born from a sit down in a coffee shop with my sometimes collaborative partner, Angella Jacob. She is one of those people who shares in my passion for stories. Be they movie, television series or book. We chatted about story ideas coming from anywhere. Like the rows of pennies which fit perfectly into a slot in the moulding around the very booth we sat in. The bronze color trim inserted by the patrons went around the coffee shop. This became one of my examples.

"Penny for your thoughts," I said as I proceeding to blurt out the idea of the character of Delroy and his gift / curse.

Bill and Frank and *The Statues of Pine Glen Forest* were not originally intended for publication, but I liked them enough to want to share them.

I love all aspect of story creation but the best part of it for me is imagining the characters and places. I get great pleasure

221

from dreaming these up as they would have never existed if my imagination had never given them birth. Stonevalley which is the setting for *Subliminal* was originally created because I needed a small city that was large enough to have a university. So, I loosely based the idea of it on the community of Moncton, NB which is where I currently live. A city that has a small-town appeal if you want it to. But one that also feels like a bigger city of one hundred and twenty or so thousand total strangers.

(I should also mention that *pierre* means stone in French.)

Stonevalley is a short hour-long drive along a winding country road away from a small town I named Carlton. This town I created as a fictional version of my hometown of Rogersville, NB. Said town was once known as Carleton before being renamed by a religious figure for whatever reason they had back then. I dropped the 'e' and pretended the renaming had never happened in my fictional version of this tiny town of twelve hundred people. I also revived an old dinner and coffee shop named Santorene which was owned and operated for a time by two of my many uncles. This was the very same place where my father first laid eyes on a woman who would become his wife and my mother. Mind you the town of Carlton was inspired by my hometown it was not meant to be that town at all. The town is completely fictional, and its characters and places will most likely reappear in some future stories as I feel a there are many more to tell.

On another note, the cover picture is a house nestled in my hometown. In my younger days I spent many a night perched on its porch, hanging out with friends and I felt it would be a great fit for the cover. It would be especially fitting with the idea born from the previously mentioned book title. I took the picture myself while standing on the sidewalk in front of the home in broad daylight. What you see on the cover is a combination of photography, photo editing and creative inspiration.

With all that said, if you're anything like me and so read this book from start to finish then this would be the last of the book which you're about to close. I do sincerely hope that you enjoyed this book enough to want to read more from me, whether in collaboration or not as I do have many more stories to tell.

Regards,
Pierre C Arseneault